M.J. Arlidge has worked in television for the last twenty years, specialising in high-end drama production, including prime-time crime serials *Silent Witness*, *Torn*, *The Little House* and, most recently, the hit ITV show *Innocent*.

Andy Maslen writes thrillers across a number of genres: police procedurals, vigilante, psychological, suspense and horror. He spent thirty years in business before turning to writing full time. He is the creator of bestselling series featuring Gabriel Wolfe, Stella Cole and Inspector Ford, plus standalone novels and short stories. He lives in Wiltshire.

T0349979

YOUR CHILD NEXT

M.J. ARLIDGE

ANDY MASLEN

ORION

An Orion Paperback

First published in Great Britain in 2025 by Orion Fiction,
an imprint of The Orion Publishing Group Ltd.
Carmelite House, 50 Victoria Embankment
London EC4Y 0DZ

An Hachette UK Company

The authorised representative in the EEA is Hachette Ireland,
8 Castlecourt Centre, Dublin 15, D15 XTP3,
Ireland (email: info@hbgi.ie)

1 3 5 7 9 10 8 6 4 2

A CIP catalogue record for this book is
available from the British Library.

ISBN (Mass Market Paperback) 9781 3987 1663 6
ISBN (Ebook) 9781 3987 1662 9
ISBN (Audio) 9781 3987 1661 2

Typeset at The Spartan Press Ltd,
Lymington, Hants

Printed and bound in Great Britain by Clays Ltd,
Elcograf S.p.A.

www.orionbooks.co.uk

For my family

Andy Maslen

Day One

Chapter 1

Annie's stomach lurched as her daughter's funeral began.

She was weeping uncontrollably. Face blotched and red. Tears streaming from her eyes, leaching her make-up down in parallel black rivers over her cheeks. Grief distorted her mouth, the cords of her neck standing out like wires. The hem of her black dress snapped at her legs in the sharp breeze.

Distraught, she stared at the hearse. A long-faced man in tail coat, top hat and grey-striped trousers stood beside it, head bowed. A floral tribute leaned against the side of the simple pine coffin. White carnations, roses and lilies:

ISLA

She was so close to the flowers, she could almost smell their cloying scent through the glass.

Annie's best friend looked stricken as she hugged her tight. Other friends, too. All black-clad. Clutching each other, weeping, pushing crumpled tissues against their eyes, noses, mouths. It was windy, and their hair blew around their faces, lashing their cheeks, flicking into their eyes. She leaned into her friend's embrace and wept again, her shoulders jerking spasmodically.

A crow swooped low over the mourners. Then stopped in mid-air.

A tear hung suspended halfway between Annie's left eye and the ground.

The pallbearers froze in the act of lifting Isla's coffin onto their shoulders.

Heart pounding, Annie released her grip on her mouse, having just paused the video. On the screen in front of her, an impossible funeral. In the real world, a world that had suddenly slewed off its axis as if hit by a meteorite, she shoved the laptop across the kitchen table, her heart hammering against her ribs.

She'd been working late on the next quarter's marketing plan, struggling to focus, eyelids drooping, when the alarm bell alert for an incoming email had jerked her fully awake. As she took in the brief but horrible subject line, her stomach churned and cold fear uncoiled in the pit of her belly. With a trembling finger, she opened the email. How could she not when it mentioned her daughter?

Condolences on Isla's passing

There'd been no meme. No text. No 'haha' payoff. Just a link. A string of random letters, numbers and symbols. A link leading to this disgusting, terrifying video.

Shaken, Annie stared at the screen, desperate but unable to look away. Sweat had broken out on her face, her neck, her back. She felt cold and clammy. Nauseous. Who had done this to her? Who? And why?

Seized with irrational terror, she shoved her chair back, hard enough to send it clattering to the stone-flagged kitchen floor, and ran upstairs.

Chapter 2

Outside Isla's door, Annie paused with her knuckles raised, for maybe half a second.

The rule was clear. Not written down, but understood by both parties as if drafted by a lawyer. You knocked. You waited. No answer, no admittance. You went downstairs and maybe you fumed, but you absolutely, definitely, one hundred per cent, did *not* just go in uninvited.

Annie burst in.

Isla was wearing a pair of baggy white trousers and an old grey Hello Kitty T-shirt. She was leaning back, fists clenched, kicking out with her right foot.

She whirled round, off-balance, and stumbled against the bed.

'Mum! What the hell? I'm doing my taekwondo practice.'

Annie grabbed her fifteen-year-old daughter in a fierce hug.

'Oh, thank God. You're OK.'

Isla wriggled free and pushed Annie back.

'Of course I'm OK! Jesus, what is *wrong* with you?'

'Sorry, lovey. Sorry, I...'

The sentence died, unfinished, in her throat.

Isla's face had paled, red spots on her cheeks, a reliable sign of an impending storm.

'This is literally the only place in the world where I get any privacy, and you just barge in here acting all weird. Can you go, please? I need to finish my pattern.'

Free now of the irrational fear that something had actually happened to Isla, Annie retreated.

'Yes, of course. I'm ... I'm sorry. I was just ... I just wanted to check you were OK.'

She closed the door quietly behind her, desperately wishing there was a way she could reach Isla. Lockdown had pushed her once-happy daughter into constant low-level anxiety. And when she and Grant had told her they were separating, her condition had worsened and she'd started having panic attacks. Once again, Annie felt a sickening sense of guilt wash over her. Isla's anxiety was all her fault.

The doctor had prescribed mild tranquillisers. They'd made Isla's skin break out and given her nightmares. Annie returned them to the pharmacist. Then there had been that dreadful day when she'd found Isla watching a video about suicide on TikTok.

Isla had assured her it didn't mean anything, but Annie had been terrified. First thing the following morning, she'd taken Isla to the Oaks, a private clinic in Harborne specialising in mental health in teenagers and young adults, and arranged for her to see a psychologist. Ekaterini managed to form an instant connection with her, and Isla appeared happier over the next few weeks. But Annie still found sleep elusive, waking at 3 a.m., her heart pounding, stealing along the hallway and peeping through a crack in Isla's door to check she was still alive.

Back in the kitchen, she poured herself a large glass of Merlot from an open bottle on the kitchen counter and gulped down half. It did nothing to calm the jangling nerves that were making her feel lightheaded and scared.

In a sudden panic that Isla might somehow see the video and spiral into another anxiety attack, she spun her laptop round and stabbed a couple of keys to delete the email and the hateful video along with it. She emptied the trash, too, and reset her cache for good measure. Her glass was shaking so much she needed both hands to steady it enough to take another mouthful of the wine.

Was this someone's idea of a sick joke? Because Annie wasn't laughing. Who could have done such a thing? A bully from Isla's school? Surely not. A friend pranking her? Unlikely. Then the answer came to her. The man Isla was always so quick to defend.

Grant.

After the divorce had been finalised, in Merlot-and-sympathy sessions with girlfriends, Annie had referred to her and Grant's post-separation relationship as 'toxic'. But only because she couldn't find a stronger word. Think box jellyfish crossed with a funnel-web spider then gene-spliced into a black mamba and you'd be about halfway there.

Never mind the financial settlement. The real source of enmity between them had been the terms Annie had insisted on relating to Isla. Grant had wanted joint custody, with Isla living with him half the week. Annie had instructed her lawyer to resist that at all costs. Reason one, Grant's nomadic lifestyle. Reason two, his general unreliability and fecklessness. Reason three, and why she was prepared to fight him until her funds were exhausted, his infidelity.

Grant's cheating had started in the third trimester of her pregnancy, when she'd been laid up with extreme morning sickness. His ultimate betrayal was a brief but apparently passionate affair with another school mum. Until that point, Annie had thought of Vicky Hill as a friend. When she found out, the news left her shaking, so overwhelmed she dropped the mug of coffee she was holding. It exploded on the polished stone floor, scattering dozens of razor-sharp pieces.

According to one of Annie's real friends, Vicky had been the instigator of the affair. Her masterstroke, if you could call it that, was tucking a piece of paper in Grant's pocket she said she'd seen him drop. It turned out to bear her number. Plus a message most women would dismiss as obvious and cheap, but which Grant apparently found seductive and irresistible.

Dismayingly, the school-run posse had picked sides, not all siding with Annie. One particularly vicious bit of gossip, shared at a volume she couldn't possibly ignore, revealed that Vicky had demanded she and Grant 'christen' his marital bed. 'More than once, apparently,' the woman added, giving Annie the side-eye.

Humiliated, devastated and angry, Annie had stripped the bed that evening and burned the sheets in the garden, coughing in the smoke until she broke down in tears. When she'd confronted Grant about it, his reasoning was so petty it left her speechless.

'You were working late again and I had to go to the parents' evening instead of working on my new burrito recipe. She was there and she looked a little lost, like me. So I said hello and things, you know, snowballed.'

Vicky Hill had been the last of many straws. You could have thatched a roof with them. It hadn't lasted, of course. A friend had told her Grant had recently taken up with a woman half his age. Melissa.

And now he was taking some kind of twisted revenge because Annie hadn't given in to his demands for joint custody. Well, he'd gone too far. Way too far.

Feeling that crushing humiliation all over again as if it had happened that very evening, she grabbed her keys and headed out into the night.

She was going to make him pay.

Chapter 3

His grief had flayed him. Every nerve ending was exposed, raw.

It didn't take much to set him off. The mention of her name. A glimpse of her face in a photo. Her perfume lingering on a sweater she'd borrowed. The dark waters of his grief would close over his head again, drowning him.

Michael drained the tumbler of scotch by his elbow and sloshed more in, spilling some on the bank statement beneath the glass. Another long, dark night mired in Lucy's accounts, both business and personal, trying to untangle her finances.

In life, before she got ill, she'd run a small but very successful chain of hair salons. She'd called it Locks. A play on the hair she and her team cut, coloured and styled, and the locks that divided up the city's canals.

She had shops in Harborne, in Edgbaston and in Birmingham city centre. Her clients had loved her. They confided their secrets, their traumas, their infidelities, even. Lucy had never shared so much as a single detail with him.

'I'm a walking safety deposit box of other people's secrets,' she'd said once, an unusually poetic phrase he'd never forgotten.

As well as running his own business making bespoke wooden kitchens and bedrooms, Michael was now trying – well, struggling would be a better word – to keep Locks afloat.

He rubbed at his eyes, which felt gritty with fatigue. Took a slug of the whisky, which burned on the way down.

He swallowed, hard, against a lump in his throat, and leafed back through the bank statements. The doorbell pealed, startling him. He looked up and around. What the hell? The ceiling and walls were strobing with blue light. Fear kicked in hard. An ambulance? A fire? The police? Aaron! Oh God, was he OK? Had he been in an accident?

He raced downstairs, careful even in his panic not to look at the black and white photos of him, Lucy and Aaron in happier days. He didn't have the courage to take them down. Or to face them head-on. Maybe he was in denial after all. If he didn't look at her, he wouldn't have to admit she was really gone.

He opened the front door, and frowned.

A burly six-foot police officer was standing a couple of feet back from the door. Then Aaron stepped out of the shadows. Eyes downcast, arms folded. Behind them, a marked police car, lights flashing, engine idling. In the driver's seat, a female officer, the deep red of her hijab glowing in the light from the street lamp overhead. She offered what might have been a sympathetic smile.

'Michael Taylor?' the burly cop asked, though clearly he knew the answer. The police didn't make a habit of returning surly teenagers to the wrong house.

'Yes. Is everything all right? Aaron, mate, what happened? Were you attacked?'

'Your son was observed vandalising a bus stop on Hagley Road,' the cop said, laying a hand the size of a baseball catcher's mitt on Aaron's skinny shoulder. It sagged slightly under the weight. 'No permanent damage, but obviously still a crime.'

Michael's temper flared before he had a chance to control it.

'For God's sake! Aaron, is this true? What the hell were you doing?'

Aaron looked up at him from under the mop of loose curls he'd been growing out since the funeral. The school had emailed Michael about it. They'd explained, in a mealy-mouthed way, that while they could make a temporary allowance in view of Aaron's 'difficult personal circumstances', the dress code was there for a reason – *esprit de corps*, school values and image, etc. etc. – and he needed to get it cut. He'd ignored them.

'We were just kicking the window. It's not even glass! Just plastic,' Aaron protested. 'God, talk about an overreaction.'

'He was with three other lads,' the cop said. 'Faster on their feet than Aaron here. Look, we're not charging him, or even giving him a caution, so there's no record, nothing like that to worry about. But I have offered him some words of advice. Maybe you'd have a talk with him, too? He told me about his mum, and obviously that's sad. But we can't have him taking out his feelings on public property.'

Michael was shaking his head as the policeman concluded his speech. Thank Christ they didn't have to worry about a bloody court case on top of everything else.

'No . . . yes . . . I mean, of course, Officer. Thank you. I'll speak to him.' He turned to the eighteen-year-old package of resentment, anger and grief standing in the giant cop's shadow. 'Inside. Now.'

On the far side of the street, curtains were twitching. Great. Michael gave it two minutes more before the local WhatsApp group lit up with speculation about 'that mixed-race boy'.

Giving them a hard stare, and an imaginary middle finger, he went back inside. With a sinking feeling, he mounted the stairs.

He knocked. 'Aaron?'

Silence.

On a normal day, if any day they spent together counted as normal any more, he'd have left it at that. But this wasn't a normal day, was it? He'd finally found the headspace to try and tackle Lucy's personal affairs, only to be interrupted in the middle of it by the police.

He knocked again, louder this time.

'Aaron!'

'What?' came the answering bellow.

Michael took that as permission to enter. Aaron's room reeked of teenaged hormones, Davidoff Cool Water and, beneath it all, a sweetish aroma Michael told himself was just incense. Hoodies, T-shirts and jeans were scattered across the room, even on vertical surfaces. How did he do that? Some kind of adolescent Jedi mind-trick?

Aaron lay back on the bed, headphones clamped over his ears, scowling like he'd won Olympic gold for it.

Again, not going to wash.

Michael gestured at his own ears. 'Off.'

With a sullen glare, Aaron pulled the headphones free and held them in his fist.

'What?'

'What do you think? The police, Aaron? Seriously? I've got enough on my plate without you being arrested for criminal damage.'

'OK, well, one, they didn't arrest me. Two, it wasn't criminal damage. What were they going to charge me with? Doing rubbish karate?'

Michael stared at his son in disbelief.

'You're grounded. For a week.'

Aaron shrugged. 'Whatever.'

Michael's pulse was clanging in his ears. He'd wanted to be mature. Considered. The adult in the room.

'Two weeks!'

Aaron glared at him, those deep brown eyes boring into him.

'You love this, don't you? Acting like you're my father. Jesus, it's pathetic.'

'I *am* your father, Aaron.'

'Adoptive, Michael. Don't forget the key word. A-dop-tive.'

Christ, why was this so hard? Even before Lucy had died, Michael had been walking on eggshells around Aaron. He didn't know if he'd traced his biological dad or had just been chatting online with other adopted kids. But after his mum's death, he seemed full of rage at Michael. The GP had recommended therapy, which Michael took him to gladly. But it was slow going.

'Yeah, well, your adoptive dad is grounding you for the rest of the month. Enjoy.'

He left the room, congratulating himself for not slamming the door. Behind him, silence. In his own youth, which had been punctuated by spells of bad behaviour, mainly fighting at school, Michael would have retaliated by playing a heavy rock album at full belt. Nothing like Metallica turned up to eleven to rile the parents. But the kids these days lived in their heads. Headphones on and let the world go to hell.

Sighing, he paused midway along the hallway and half turned, wishing he could find the words to reconnect with Aaron, to help him deal with his anger. But he knew it was too late for tonight. Maybe he could try in the morning.

Michael had been to see a grief counsellor himself in the early days. They'd given him a leaflet at the hospital. He'd sat opposite her in her cramped consulting room, which smelled faintly of cats, while she told him about the five stages of mourning. Anger was one. Denial was another, apparently. Bargaining? Maybe. He couldn't remember the others. But he felt, on mature reflection, that the counsellor had missed out the big one. Paperwork.

Shaking his head, he returned to the office. However grief made you feel – angry, sad, anguished, baffled, resentful, depressed – nothing stood in the way of the grim logistics of death.

Two hours later, he turned over another sheet in the thick pile of bank statements. Just one more, then he'd call it a night. His eye caught on a debit halfway down the page. A thousand pounds to a bank in the Caymans. By standing order, too. What on earth for?

Shocked at the amount, and the destination, he flipped back and found another. And another. Ten minutes later, he had twenty-three statements all showing the same amount sent to the Caymans.

He read and reread the statements, desperate to make sense of something so completely baffling. His wife, who he'd thought of as his soulmate, had been keeping secrets. And not just the guilty kind – loving seventies disco or binge-watching *Love Island* – the real kind. *The dirty little kind*, a nasty, sly-sounding voice whispered in his ear.

He stood suddenly and had to grip the edge of his desk as the world wobbled and stars sparked inside his eyes.

How was this possible? What had Lucy been *involved* in?

Had he really known his wife at all?

Chapter 4

Wiping his damp palms on the stained fabric of his army surplus jacket, John Varney crouched behind a dustbin, watching the two children through the window of the front room.

They looked so happy. Bouncing on the sofa cushions like usual. Wearing those beautiful innocent smiles you only saw on the faces of children before the pain of the world settled over them like a shroud.

The faces of other children – screaming, blood-spattered – flashed in front of him. He shook his head, blinked them away.

She was there, of course. Laughing like she didn't have a care in the world. Dolled up in a dress. She never used to wear dresses. And then *he* came into view. Oh, and wasn't he enjoying himself? Playing the big man with a ready-made family.

Vanessa hadn't even had the decency to wait a couple of years before moving her boyfriend in. John out, Alex in. Standard operating procedure, apparently.

Rain started. Big fat drops out of nowhere. Ice-cold shrapnel whacking the top of his head and trickling down inside his collar, making him shiver. Anxiety lanced through him, but he fought it down. His face was still sore from the fight over a can of extra-strength cider with one of his so-called mates the previous night. The bruise over his left eye had spread down to his cheekbone. He sucked his lower lip, split now and swollen. Tasted the coppery tang of blood. Not for the first time.

Inside, Ruby was holding her arms up. And that smug bastard lifted her and whirled her around. Benji didn't want to be left out of the fun either. Benji! His son. *His!* Clinging on to Alex's legs.

How was this fair? When Sergeant John Varney had been

watching his mates get blown to pieces by the Taliban, what had Alex been doing? Selling saunas and hot tubs, for Christ's sake! Hot? Nothing got hotter than Helmand on a nice sunny August afternoon. Bullets whining like the world's angriest hornets, all intent on giving you the biggest bloody sting of your life.

Filled with rage so fierce it felt like the sides of his skull were melting, John marched up to the front door and stuck a blunt fingertip against the bellpush. Held it there. He heard footsteps on the hard wooden hall floor and readied himself.

The door swung inwards.

'Daddy!'

He looked down and smiled.

'Benji!'

He crouched and accepted his son's fierce hug. This was how it was meant to be.

'Have you missed me, buddy?'

'I want you to come home, Daddy.'

'I want to as well, buddy.'

A shadow threw them both into darkness.

'Benji. Go back to the game. Alex and Ruby are waiting. Now!'

John looked up, into his ex-wife's contemptuous stare. She folded her arms across her chest and glowered at him. He stood, took a step forward, but she barred the way. Keeping him out in the rain.

She wrinkled her nose, like she'd caught a whiff of something rotten.

'What the hell happened to your face?'

'Nothing. I came to see Ruby. And Benji. It's his birthday in a couple of days.'

'It was his birthday yesterday,' she said in a flat voice. 'You missed it. Again.'

'Then let me come in and see them.'

She shook her head. 'Not going to happen. You need to go.'

'They're my kids, too, Ness,' he said, feeling desperate and hating himself for it. Then her. 'You can't stop me.'

'I could take out a restraining order if you like. How about that? Would that stop you?'

'Let me in, Ness,' he said, dropping his voice, feeling the bones in his hands cracking as he tightened his fists.

'No.'

Alex appeared behind her.

'Everything OK, love? Oh. Hello, John.'

John ignored him. Stayed focused on Vanessa, trying to speak without baring his mangled teeth. 'I want to see my kids.'

Alex squared his shoulders. Basic move.

'Yeah, not going to happen. You heard Vanessa. Just piss off before we call the police.'

That was it. The trigger. John's brain fizzled with pre-combat adrenaline. Nobody talked to him like that. He picked his target: the soft spot in the throat. Prepared to strike.

And then the words of the prosecuting officer at the court martial floated back to him.

'... *evidence he failed to control his men, or himself ... unnecessary civilian casualties ...*'

It was all lies. The army had cooked up the whole thing to protect itself. Ops went wrong all the time. Nobody had meant to kill those people. Fog of war. But they'd binned him anyway: dishonourable discharge. No pension, no self-respect, no prospects in civvy street. Just PTSD, and his addictions to keep his demons at bay.

Ness despised him. Alex, too, obviously. They all did. But he still had some shreds of honour left. Of self-control. He turned away. Thrust his hands into the sagging pockets of the camouflage jacket.

'Get some help, John,' Vanessa called after him. Then the door slammed shut.

Lightning flashed. So bright it turned the world white. Thunder crashed overhead. His heart pounding, he clenched his fists, wanting to scream his defiance at the bruise-coloured sky.

The anger had never been far from the surface, ever since he'd held Corporal Heather Jones in his arms as she died. Nobody understood. Nobody knew the powerlessness and despair he'd felt as she begged him to help her, racking coughs spraying a mist of her blood into his eyes. Especially not Ness and that smarmy git Alex. It wasn't fair. How come he was the only one suffering? No money, no hope. Not even a place to live.

Vanessa's parting shot about getting help came back to him. He shook his head. Like he could afford that.

He marched away, kicking up water from the river now running down the gutter, fists bunched. For once he didn't try to tamp down the anger lighting up his mind like tracer fire. He let it have its head, threatening to erupt at any moment.

Chapter 5

Boiling with rage, Annie hammered on the door of Grant's flat. The flat the judge had ruled *she* should pay for.

How was this fair? Grant had always blown his own money on boys' toys. DJ decks. An electric guitar he'd never learned to play. Even a motorbike. His glib justification: 'You make enough for both of us, babes.'

When he wasn't shagging other school mums, he had spent their marriage disappearing off in his camper van to one festival or another, leaving her to juggle a demanding career and the child they'd both wanted so desperately. Only now, she was seeing more clearly. Grant had loved the *idea* of fatherhood. It was just the reality he found hard to cope with.

And now he'd sent her that terrible video. Well, that was a massive line he'd just crossed, and no amount of cajoling, excuses or winning smiles was going to smooth this one over. She was going to make him own it.

'Come on, Grant,' she yelled through the door. 'I know you're in.'

The latch clacked and the door swung inwards. Grant stood before her in a pair of tartan pyjama bottoms. He scratched at his beard, audibly, a habit she'd always hated.

'Keep your hair on, we were in bed,' he said, stepping aside and beckoning her in with a sweep of his hand.

Oh God. She'd interrupted him and Melissa mid-shag. She blanked the image hazily forming in her mind's eye. No. Not going there.

'What the hell were you thinking, Grant?' Her heart was

pounding and she was struggling to breathe. 'Sending that revolting video. Are you insane?'

He blinked. 'What video?'

'Oh, come on. Please don't give me your "Who me?" face. I know all your moves, remember? The video you made of me at Isla's funeral. Jesus, I know you think I screwed you over in the settlement, but really? You didn't get the custody arrangement you wanted, so you brood and brood and this is your response? I should report you to the police.'

'What do you mean, Isla's funeral?'

'You know full well what I mean! Jesus, Grant, even in your *wildest* revenge fantasies, how could you think it was OK to create something so vile?'

Grant held his hands out wide.

'Annie, please. You have to believe me. I didn't send you any video. But you've got me worried. Look, please calm down. You're right, I *was* pissed off about the custody deal. Still am, to be honest. But I have *literally* no idea what you're talking about.' He scratched his beard again. 'What exactly was in this video?'

The fury that had propelled her through the rain-soaked streets of Harborne had curdled into a sour emotion that left her queasy, her stomach cramping.

'Never mind. Just promise me it wasn't you,' she said, her pulse beginning to settle.

He sat down on the sofa, facing her.

'I swear on Isla's life. Where's your phone? Show me, I want to see.'

She shook her head.

'It's on my laptop.' She bit her lip. 'Was. I deleted it.'

His eyes narrowed. 'You deleted it? Wasn't that – I don't know – careless? If it's as bad as that, you should have taken it to the police.'

'I was terrified, OK? I just wanted it gone.'

'And it was anonymous? You just *assumed* it was me?'

20

'Yes.'

'Then how come it got through your spam filters? You're in the IT department.'

'It's the School of Computer Science, actually, as you well know. And how should I know? It just did.'

Grant reached for a half-finished bottle of lager on the coffee table, took a long pull, then dangled it from its neck.

'It's kind of convenient, though, isn't it? You know, an anonymous email arrives, slips past your security software. It's got some fake video attached that freaks you out. And then you naturally assume your ex-husband is, what, some kind of psycho? But you can't show me the video because you deleted it? Why don't you get it out of the trash?'

Annie swallowed her anger. 'I deleted that, too. And I resent your insinuation that I cooked up some story just so I could spend my evening having this conversation with you. I've got better things to do with my time.'

He smiled. Not the roguish one he used on anything identifying as female. This was slyer.

'Let me guess. You were checking work emails at the kitchen table. Nice big glass of Merlot for company.' The grin widened into a smirk. 'I can see the attraction.'

'Can you, Grant? *Can* you see the attraction of hard work? Because as far as I can tell, the only thing you've ever found attractive was girls half your age.'

He took another pull on the beer.

'Lovely to see you, too, Annie. You can find your own way out, yes?'

As Annie turned away, a young woman emerged from the bedroom. Toned, tousled, wearing one of Grant's branded T-shirts – *FestLife!* – which almost reached her thighs. The famous Melissa. Annie experienced a moment's envy as she took in her child-free figure.

'What does she want, baby?' she asked Grant, sliding a hand around his waist and nuzzling his neck.

'Nothing. She was just leaving.'

Annie heard Melissa's voice again as she reached the front door. The younger woman had pitched it just right.

'Seriously? You were married to *that*?'

Grant shushed her, although not too convincingly.

'Hey, Annie. Keep me posted, yes?' he called after her. 'You know, about this alleged video. I care about her, too, you know.'

Annie pulled away from the kerb, confused and scared. And, though she hated to admit it, stung by the younger woman's parting shot, which had reignited the humiliation and feelings of inadequacy she'd worked so hard to overcome.

Her belly was tight with anxiety. If Grant hadn't sent the video, then who had?

Day Two

Chapter 6

Wrecked from a sleepless night, Annie parked outside the conference centre and clambered out of her electric Audi.

A black SUV loomed out of nowhere and hooted, startling her. Holding up a hand in apology, her nerves fizzing, she hurried inside to register for the event she'd long planned to attend. But as she surveyed the crowd of feverishly networking delegates, the horrible image of the hearse with Isla's name picked out in flowers kept intruding into her thoughts.

Who would send her something like that? Imagine if Isla had seen it. The poor child was already struggling. Seeing something so horrific could push her over the edge. Phrases she'd only heard on the news floated up into her consciousness. *Secure psychiatric unit . . . severe mental illness . . . suicide watch.* She shuddered.

Pasting on a smile she didn't feel, she gave her name to the bright young thing on the reception desk and collected her badge on a lanyard.

Come on, Annie, best foot forward. It's only half a day. You can do this.

She strode towards the throng of university business managers, all clutching their conference brochures and nodding frantically while looking over each other's shoulders.

After introducing herself to another woman on the low side of fifty, she tried to focus on the conference rather than the video. The trouble was, every time she let her mind drift, or worse, closed her eyes, it started playing.

Her new friend was a sponsorship manager at the University of Liverpool. While she chatted amiably about the pressures of finding new income streams in a stagnant economy, Annie nodded distractedly.

Sometime around 3 a.m., lying awake in the dark, she'd realised where the footage of her grieving had been shot. It was at Juliet's funeral. Her good friend had died from breast cancer seven weeks earlier.

Now that poor Juliet was dead, 'the gang' was fractured by grief and some sick individual was using Isla to mess with Annie's mind.

Had someone followed her to the funeral and secretly filmed her? She couldn't remember seeing anyone. But then she'd hardly been in a fit state to put on matching earrings, let alone notice strangers taking covert videos.

And that hearse – like a shiny black barge – with Isla's name spelled out in flowers. Was that a lucky search from a stock photo library? Or had someone whizzed it up on a computer specially for the video? And why? She could understand Grant having a motive for upsetting her. But as much as she didn't want to accept his denials, she believed him. So who, then?

Another troubling thought intruded. Whoever had committed that violation hadn't just turned up on a whim. They must have planned it weeks in advance. Finding out about Juliet having cancer, and then stalking Annie on the day of the funeral.

In front of her, the woman from Liverpool was scrolling on her phone. She offered an excuse about needing to check in with the office, then bolted. Annie didn't blame her. She'd hardly been aware she was there.

She looked around, hoping to spot a friendly face in the crowd, but everyone merged into an undifferentiated sea of bland features. They all seemed to be having a great time.

Her phone vibrated on her hip, making her jump.

Isla! She was having a panic attack. Annie scrabbled for her phone, breaking a nail as she dragged it free of her pocket. But it wasn't Isla. She didn't recognise the number. Tentatively, she pressed Accept.

'I hope you enjoyed the video, Annie,' a woman's voice said, coldly.

'Who is this? I could call the police,' Annie said, her voice shaking.

'No, you couldn't. If you want to protect your daughter, you're going to do exactly what I tell you.'

'Protect...?' Annie's stomach flipped. 'Look, I don't know what sort of sick, twisted game you're playing, but it's not funny. Now, either you tell me what's going on or I *will* call the police.'

'No, you won't. What you *will* do is set up a standing order for a thousand pounds a month to a bank in the Caymans. I've emailed you the details. If you don't pay, or if you call the police, Isla will die. No more taekwondo. No more parties with her bestie, Naomi. No more hot dogs at the fair. It might be next week. Or next month. I might wait for a year. But she *will* die. A bad pill at a party. A mugging gone wrong. A hit-and-run. I will see to it. And only you will know the truth. That you caused your own daughter's death.'

Annie felt faint. Her vision telescoped to a pinprick. She reached out a hand to steady herself on a nearby table, knocking over someone's glass of water. She barely registered their protest as she moved to a quiet corner of the room.

Her stomach rolled over. How was this possible? How did a complete stranger know every last detail about Isla's life? She was shaking so much she almost dropped her phone, fumbling a catch just as it slipped from her grasp. She clamped it back to her ear.

'I can't pay you,' she gasped out. 'I don't have that kind of money.'

'Not my problem. You've got until midnight tomorrow. That's the deal. Take it or leave it, Annie. Oh, by the way, I love your jacket. Victoria Beckham really suits you.'

Horrified, Annie spun round, desperately scanning the room

for her tormentor. But there were dozens of women here on their phones, none of them remotely interested in her. Was the caller really here? Watching her even now?

'Who are you?' she blurted out, casting around desperately.

But the line went dead, leaving her staring at the black glass reflecting her own terrified face.

Chapter 7

'I'm sorry for your loss,' the smartly dressed young man said. 'Mrs Taylor, Lucy, was a good customer. We were all shocked when we heard she'd passed.'

The bank manager seemed genuine enough. Michael found it hard to tell these days. Most people seemed to want to talk about anything other than the fact he'd lost his wife to brain cancer. He knew the young man meant well, and he had to respond with appropriate words – the dignified grieving husband – but his guts were churning at the thought that Lucy had been keeping a huge financial secret from him.

'Thank you. It's been tough. The thing is, the reason I'm here, I mean, is that…' He took a deep breath, tried to steady his nerves. 'I've been going through Lucy's financial affairs, and I discovered she'd set up a standing order for a thousand pounds a month to a bank in the Caymans. It's been going on for almost two years. Can you shed any light on that?'

The bank manager frowned.

'Well, let's have a look.' He swivelled a screen round on a canti-levered arm and tapped a few keys. 'OK, yes, I can see it here. On the seventeenth of the month. As you say, one thousand pounds.'

Michael didn't like that 'As you say'. It felt as though the smooth young man behind the desk wasn't prepared to accept anything he said without evidence from the computer.

'Where's it going? What's it for?'

'I can only tell you what's in front of me, Mr Taylor. It's a bank in the Caymans. The amount we already know. Beyond that, I'm afraid, it's a closed door.'

Was that it? Was that all he was going to give him? Michael

wanted more. *Needed* more. No way was he about to accept a bland corporate brush-off.

'But why would Lucy have been doing business with anyone in the Caymans? She ran a chain of hairdressers in Birmingham.'

'The *account* is in the Caymans. The account *holder* could be anywhere. London, Paris, New York. Even Selly Oak. All kinds of people have accounts there.' The young man paused. 'Or perhaps your wife simply felt she was paying too much tax in the UK.'

Michael fought down a sudden urge to lunge across the desk and grab him by the lapels of his immaculately tailored suit.

'Are you saying my wife was a tax dodger?' he grated.

Shaking his head, the bank manager held his hands up.

'No, no. Not at all. But there's very little I can do from here. You'd really need a court order. And even then it could take months, years even, before they'd open their books.'

Michael pulled back. The poor guy was only doing his job. But he had to know why Lucy had been sending that money overseas every month.

'It's just, she wasn't like that. Lucy wasn't a secretive woman. We told each other everything.'

Clearly not everything, a quiet voice whispered in his ear. How was this possible? Why was it that with each passing day since her death, he felt he knew his wife less well? As if the woman he'd been so happily married to had been the ghost and only now was he meeting the real Lucy?

The bank manager spread his hands. 'Is it possible that Mrs Taylor was investing in an international financial vehicle of some kind?'

'I doubt it. The business was making good money. Well, you probably know that.' The man inclined his head. 'But Lucy was brought up in a Labour-voting household. That never left her, even when she became successful. She believed in paying her taxes, supporting the NHS, being a good citizen. No way would she have tried to shelter her income from the taxman.'

The banker looked out of the window, speaking thoughtfully.

'So, if it wasn't for tax purposes, perhaps Mrs Taylor had a relative out there. Someone she was helping out financially?'

Michael shook his head. 'No. Lucy's family are all from round here. She used to boast she had Birmingham written through her like a stick of rock.'

'A charity, then. A school, perhaps. Or a children's hospital? Could it have been something like that? I know Mrs Taylor was very socially concerned.'

'Maybe. But she'd have told me. She'd have posted about it on social media. I'd have known.'

The banker looked genuinely troubled by his inability to solve the mystery. He spread his hands and sighed.

'I'm sorry, Mr Taylor, that's all I can think of.'

Breathing heavily, Michael sat back in his chair. He wiped a palm across his face. Oh God, what had Lucy been doing?

In her last months, the tumour had dug its black claws into her brain and squeezed until her personality had changed into something unrecognisable. She'd been out of her mind at the end, alternating between screaming in pain and staring through half-lidded eyes and a fog of morphine. What else had it done to her? Had it affected her before any of them knew it was there, buried deep in her brain like a poisonous seed waiting to flourish?

It was too late to find out now. But Michael was a practical man. If he couldn't find out where she'd been sending the money, at least he could choke off the supply.

'I want it cancelled.'

'The standing order?'

'Yes, I want you to stop it now. I don't want any more payments going out.'

The banker frowned.

'You're sure? Your wife may have wanted them to continue.'

'Yes, well, sadly, my wife is dead.' Michael spoke flatly, weirdly able to say that without, for once, wanting to cry. 'I have control over her affairs now, you know that, right?'

'I do, yes.'

He took a beat. Whoever had been receiving a thousand a month from Lucy's account wasn't getting another penny.

'Cancel it.'

Chapter 8

The young woman enjoyed the way her red leather biker jacket tightened across her shoulders as she typed. It was the first thing she'd ever bought for herself.

She liked tight clothes generally. The jacket, T-shirts, skinny jeans – even if all the magazines insisted they weren't fashionable. Maybe because the rags the children's homes and the foster parents gave her to wear growing up were always the wrong size. Baggy hand-me-downs that made her feel like nobody cared. That made her a *target*.

But people cared about her now. She'd *made* them care.

The bank of screens ranged in a shallow curve in front of her were her window into the marks' lives.

Social media feeds. Those were the bankers. It delighted her how willing – no, how *compelled* – people were to share intimate details of their and their children's lives with total strangers.

Like this woman here. Announcing that she was currently at the Royal Albert Hall waiting to watch her thirteen-year-old daughter, Elsie, play the violin with the National Youth Orchestra. Nothing wrong with that. But her husband was with their other child, Henry, at a hockey match in Coventry. Which meant their Victorian vicarage on Edgbaston Park Road was currently empty.

Thanks to its owner's constant online crowing, the young woman knew the place was stuffed with antiques and fine art. Had she not decided extortion was both more lucrative and more fun, she might have paid a visit and selected a few pieces for herself. Not because she needed them. Just because of the distress it would cause.

So, socials. But also banking apps. Nannycams. Doorbells. If it came with an internet connection, it could be hacked. Not all her marks used social media as a personal journal. But even those who were a little more careful were no match for her. She listened in, she watched, she duplicated their feeds, she all but moved in with them: an invisible presence in their lives, gathering information until she was ready to make her presence felt.

One of her favourites was the Samaritans call-routing software. She'd brought in outside help for that one. Russian hackers were the best. She didn't use it much for the business, but it was fun to see the pain other people were going through. And occasionally you got a little titbit that you could exploit.

Right now, though, she was focused on Snapchat. And a new friend. Grace was fourteen.

She took off her jacket and hung it over the back of her chair. Raked her fingers through her cropped hair. Closed her eyes and summoned up one of her many alter egos: Jack Thomas. Sixteen, shy, artistic, into anime and manga, non-binary, ADHD, and a really good listener. She flexed her fingers. And started typing.

hey grace u ok

hi im a bit down today actually

oh no whats up im here for u

my mums being a bitch and my dads an arsehole

what have they done now

i want to go on the pill but they say im too young
but im 14 which is way old enough

are u doing it then

34

maybe

whos the guy

hes at school in year 12
I dont want to say his name in case i jinx it

She bit her lip. A name would be useful, especially since Grace's boyfriend was seventeen. But she'd learned to pace these conversations. A flashing red light on a banking screen distracted her for a second, but she maintained focus. It was important to stay in character.

i gotta go but try to stay positive ok

do u have to go ur my only true friend

She glanced back at the flashing alert on the other screen. It showed the status of dozens of standing orders in a custom-designed spreadsheet listing monthly amounts and running totals.

Anger flashed through her. One of them had just been cancelled. Swallowing down her rage, she tapped out a final message.

sorry my dads yelling for me to come downstairs
catch u tomorrow

Grace and her statutory-rapist boyfriend would have to wait.

Slowly she rose to her feet, rolling the expensive contoured computer chair back so she could step around her desk. She inhaled deeply, filling her lungs, then let the air out in a controlled hiss. Nobody got to cancel. Not unless they wanted to find out the true meaning of pain.

She strode to the window and looked down at the street. The few people there were all aimlessly scrolling. Pathetic little sheep.

Checking their alerts and notifications just like they were told to by the social media companies. Filling in every last detail of their lives. And here she was, above them all, harvesting their emotions, their petty triumphs and tragedies, their kids' names, birthdays, schools, allergies, mental health conditions, exam dates, holiday photos. It almost wasn't fair. Almost.

But now one of them had dared to go against her wishes. And that couldn't be allowed.

She made a call, rubbing at the tattoo on her arm: a rope circlet ending in half a knot.

'What's going on, Maya?' a man asked.

She forced herself to speak calmly.

'We've got a problem.'

Chapter 9

Frowning, Isla slung her bag over her shoulder as she left the school grounds. What was up with Mum? God, she'd been acting even weirder than normal. Last night, and this morning on the drive to school. As if she was worried Isla might suddenly throw herself out of the car.

She pushed the thought down. Thinking about other people's worries only made her own worse. Like how Mum always wanted her to walk the 'safe route'. Westbourne Road, Harborne Road, Westfield Road, home. *Lots of cars. Lots of people about, Isla. It's much better.*

Isla would point out patiently that cars equal accidents, never mind the damage they do to the environment. And Mum would always say the same thing. 'That's why I drive an electric.' Then she'd pat the car's bonnet and say, 'That's right, isn't it, Sparky? Saving the planet one charge at a time.' Mum tried, and she had arranged for Isla to see Ekaterini, which was about the only thing keeping her sane, but she could still be a bit lame sometimes.

The trouble was, the things that worried Isla, she carried around inside her head. They went wherever she did. Safe route or not, they were always there.

Already bored by the thought of an afternoon of study leave at home, she left the school grounds and reached the main road. If Mum was collecting her after school because she had an appointment, they always went the same way. Out of school onto Vicarage Road. Left onto Harborne Road. Then Augustus Road, and left on Norfolk Road, where their big red-brick Victorian villa sat behind a fence and a high hedge.

But she didn't have an appointment today, so she could take

her favourite route home. Not the car way. And not the safe one, either. First cutting through the big green grounds of the Edgbaston Croquet Club and the hockey pitches. It just felt cleaner. And it had Chad Brook running through it. She'd seen a kingfisher once. And her bestie, Naomi, had claimed she'd even seen an otter the previous summer. Although to be fair, Naomi was prone to just a teensy bit of fantasising. If you challenged her, she'd just roll her perfect golden eyes and say, 'I prefer the term "world-building".'

Her anxiety hadn't been too bad today. The just-bearable, always-on, jittery feeling she called 'the buzz'. It was hard to relax, and she still hadn't managed to eat much at lunchtime, but when she was with Naomi they could have a giggle over TikTok. To top it all, Ronan, the self-proclaimed bad boy of the school, and its premier dealer, had asked her out. As if.

In the distance, a hockey match was in progress. Shouts drifted across the open grassy space. Some oldies were playing croquet. And by the way, what even was that supposed to be? Using massive hammers to bash wooden balls through hoops. Like the world's worst crazy golf.

She forced herself to smile at her own joke. Ekaterini said that if you smiled even when you were sad, you could trick your brain into thinking you were happy. It hadn't worked so far, but Isla did her best to follow what Ekaterini told her. *Something* would have to work.

Nobody else was around, though, so she could just be herself. Taylor Swift was playing in her head: 'You Belong With Me'. The lyrics made her think of Josh. She smiled at the memory of kissing him. Not just at the memory, though. At the thought of what poor Mum would do if she knew about him. She'd probably call him *unsuitable* or something. But he made her feel safe. Like he'd never leave her. When she was with him, her fears pretty much completely faded away.

She left the park behind, crossed Harborne Road and – *Sorry,*

Mum – squeezed through a gap in the fence leading to a disused railway track that ran behind the big houses on Westfield Road.

It probably only saved her about a minute, but it was another of the secret routes Isla had amassed in her four years of walking to school. Not just her either, to judge from the empty Coke cans, fag packets and used condoms.

She looked around as she hopped from sleeper to sleeper. Rusting bike frames tangled in brambles. Bits of soggy old carpet all mossy and slimy. If there *were* nonces around, this was exactly the sort of place they'd hang out. But then they'd also get a taekwondo kick in the balls from her if they tried anything.

Something flickered in the corner of her eye. She whirled round, her fear spiking. But it was just a blackbird pecking at red berries on a branch. She shook her head. Did the smile trick again. This time it worked.

As she reached the far end of the path and climbed back out into the real world, her phone rang. Mum.

'Hi, lovey, just wanted to make sure you got home from school OK.'

'Why wouldn't I?'

'So you are home then, yes?'

'Nearly.'

Isla darted across Norfolk Road, judging it perfectly so the oncoming FedEx van didn't even have to brake. Still hooted, though. Loser.

'What was that? You're not crossing the road with your AirPods in, are you?'

'Of course not. You told me not to.'

She hurried up the path and stuck her key in the lock, holding her iPhone close while she rattled it. 'I'm going in, OK? Can I go now, or do you want me to FaceTime you so you can see for yourself?'

Call ended, she dumped her bag and hung her blazer on the hooks. She popped her AirPods into their case, then went into the kitchen and grabbed snacks and a Diet Coke from the fridge. With the snacks balanced on her hand, she fished out her phone to Snapchat Naomi. Then a faint noise somewhere in the house stopped her. Her pulse sped up and she felt the familiar tightness in her chest. She listened intently for a few seconds, but the house was quiet. Just the hum from the fridge. She breathed out. *It's nothing, Isla. Relax.*

There it was again. The same noise. And this time she recognised it at once. The creaky floorboard in Mum's home office. She froze, her finger poised over the phone's screen, her heart fluttering in her chest. Someone was in the house with her.

Another creak. Cold grey panic slithered its way out of her tummy and up her spine. In her mind's eye she always saw it as a long, slimy eel. Her chest tightened again, making it hard to breathe. She spun round, heart pounding. Maybe Mum had given her key to a handyman. Yes. That could work. But then why was he being so quiet? Why hadn't he called out to reassure her? The eel was coiling around her brain now, whispering her worst fears: *It's a burglar, Isla. Or maybe worse – and we both know what kind of worse.* No! She was being paranoid. Mum was probably just working from home. But then why had she called to check if Isla was home?

She called out. 'Hello? Mum? Is that you?'

Nobody answered. Oh God. This was bad. This was really bad. Just like Mum was always saying. You had to be so careful. She crouched in the corner, half hidden by the fridge.

Someone entered the kitchen.

She tried to dial 999, but her hand was shaking too much.

'Don't touch me, I've got a knife!' she shouted.

Silence. Her heart crashed against her ribs. The worst anxiety she'd ever felt. Total terror. Another creak.

Then someone chuckled. 'Bloody hell, Isles, don't stab me. It's Dad.'

She stood, pulse still racing, and ran into his arms.

'Daddy! You scared me.'

'Sorry, baby. Just having a nose around.'

'You're not even supposed to be here. You know what the judge said.'

He winked. 'You going to tell on me, are you?'

She shook her head, but his question made her anxiety flare up again. Isla had found out about his affair with Mrs Hill before Mum had, thanks to her class group chat. She'd told Dad and he'd begged her not to tell Mum.

It's already over, Isles. Let's not worry her with it, yeah? Our secret.

Reluctantly, she'd agreed, worried that if she didn't, they might get divorced. And then a year later he was gone anyway. Living with Melissa, who was really young. He'd told her it was because Mum was emotionally unavailable. Not really present. Not sharing her truth with him. It sounded to Isla like he'd learned the phrases specially.

Now he was looking at her expectantly.

'Isles? You won't tell, will you?'

She forced herself to smile. Even though she felt a pang of guilt about keeping stuff from Mum.

'I didn't last time, did I?'

'That's my girl.' He scratched his beard. 'Listen, is everything all right with Mum? Only she came round last night and she was acting weird.'

Isla shrugged. 'Tell me about it! She literally burst into my room last night going on about me being safe. And she just rang me fussing about whether I got home OK. Like she's even more worried about me than normal.'

'Your mum was always a bit of a mystery to me.' Her dad's eyes narrowed a bit. 'Has she been doing anything else weird recently?'

'Weird like how?'

'Oh, I don't know. Going out and leaving you alone in the house? Messing around on her laptop when she should be spending quality time with you?'

Isla frowned. 'No. Nothing like that. She works hard, Dad. But we still do stuff together. *Normal* stuff. Last Saturday night, for example. We were just cuddled up on the sofa eating popcorn and watching pet videos on TikTok. That's not weird, is it?'

'No, of course not, Isles. Look, let's not waste time talking about Mum. I've got a little something for you.' He paused. Grinned. 'Well, you and Josh, really.'

Isla felt her heart swell like it might burst. He hadn't actually got them, had he?

'What kind of little something?'

He made a big deal out of fishing around inside his velvet jacket before pulling out two brightly printed slips of paper.

'Two VIP tickets to next year's Glastonbury. Keep tight hold of them. No ID photos on them, 'cause they're not assigned to individual artists, so if you lose them, anyone could use them to get in.'

Isla screamed. 'Daddy, you are literally the best. Josh is going to go crazy!'

He shrugged. 'I know Mum doesn't think much of my festival business, but your dad does have the odd high-level connection.' He tapped the side of his nose. 'In fact, best not to tell her about them. She wouldn't approve. It'll be our little secret.'

Isla threw her arms around him, breathing in his lovely warm Dad smell.

He hadn't been the best husband, but he still loved her. Of course she wouldn't tell Mum.

Chapter 10

Though confused and upset by his discovery, Michael was keeping it together. Just.

He'd barely been able to concentrate on work as he tried to figure out what lay behind Lucy's mysterious payments to the Caymans. Now he was late leaving to take Aaron to his appointment with his therapist.

He reached his office only to find Chris Tebbut, his production manager, waiting for him.

'What is it, Chris? I have to take Aaron to an appointment. I don't have time for a long discussion.'

'That's just it, isn't it, Mike? Time. Well, materials as well. I haven't got enough limed oak, and what with ash dieback disease, we're running perilously low on stocks to meet our end-month deadlines. *Perilously*,' he repeated, as if Michael might not have encountered that particular word before.

Michael felt a familiar resentment welling up inside him. Chris had been with him since the beginning. Not a friend, not exactly, but he'd worked like a dog in those early days, running the bandsaw until midnight while Michael jointed, sanded and varnished. There was loyalty there, and if Chris had turned out to be a less than stellar manager, Michael felt he had no choice but to work around him.

'I thought you told me you'd found an alternate source for the ash. And if we're running low on limed oak, why? That's literally your department.'

Chris ran a hand over his thinning hair.

'I'm doing my best, Mike. What can I say?'

'How about "Leave it to me, Mike. I'll get it sorted"? That would be a real help.'

'It's just, if you could, you know,' he offered a hopeful smile, 'work the old Mike magic?'

Michael checked his watch. He really did have to leave.

'Fine. Leave it with me. I'll make some calls.'

'You're a star. Now don't let me keep you if you've got somewhere to be.'

Shaking his head, Michael grabbed his briefcase – actually an old leather toolbag – shoved his laptop inside and headed out.

Thirty-five minutes later, and with just three minutes to spare, he was parking his Ford Ranger pickup truck outside the clinic.

'Let's go,' he said to Aaron, who was nodding along to music, lost in his own world.

He nudged his son, who grudgingly removed his headphones.

'We're here, Aaron.'

'I noticed.'

'Come on, then. We'll be late.'

Aaron heaved himself out of the truck. The depression had descended a week after the funeral. Now it dragged behind him like a load of fresh timber from the mill. An emotional load the poor kid hadn't the strength to carry alone.

Once Aaron was ushered beyond the blonde wooden door of his therapist's office, Michael settled down to catch up on emails in one of the leather armchairs grouped around a coffee table.

But his mind wouldn't settle to the slew of enquiries, notes from the accountants, reminders from suppliers, and the million and one other irritating tasks that running a business involved. Not while those payments were unexplained.

He looked over at the door through which Aaron had just passed. It felt as though his family was fracturing all over again. If only he could fix his son as easily as he could a missing load of timber. At least at work he had the power to put things right. But inside Aaron's head was a blank space to him.

The diagnosis was hardly helpful. Michael had pretty much figured it out for himself. Aaron's mum had died of a horrific illness that had left her, in her final days, raving and swearing like a devil at anyone who came near her. And then Aaron had gone off his food. Taken the normal teenage inability to get out of bed to Olympic heights. Lost interest in sport, which he used to be mad for, from football to paddleboarding on the canal.

He'd grown more sensitive about his mixed-race heritage, too. Nothing as overt as actual racial bullying happened at the college. But there were casual remarks, maybe even well-intended ones, that once he would have been able to brush off or ignore, but now left him bruised and angry.

Michael sighed deeply. The therapist would never tell him anything about what he talked to Aaron about, but he did say that they were making progress.

His thoughts drifted back to Lucy. They'd been so happy together. Theirs had only been a short marriage. Just five years and a month. But he truly believed he'd met his soulmate. When he'd asked her what she thought about his adopting Aaron, she'd hugged him tightly for the longest time, leaving a damp patch on the shoulder of his sweatshirt.

Their life together now seemed to have split into three parts.

Those wonderful, love-filled years, when each day brought a new pleasure. They discovered they shared an interest in identifying wild birds that flew down into their garden. They bickered over the correct way to pronounce 'scone'.

Then, the brief but devastating period during which her tumour had consumed her, inch by inch, until everything he'd once treasured about her lingered only as memories.

And the aftermath, when, finally able to sit with her paperwork in the home office, he'd discovered that perhaps he didn't know his wife as well as he'd thought, after all.

He knuckled his eyes, anxious not to be seen crying by the other people in the waiting room, though most were occupied with their phones.

Oh Lucy, what were you keeping from me?

Chapter 11

Stunned by the caller's hideous ultimatum, Annie fled the conference at the morning break. She drove fast through the traffic and arrived at the School of Computer Science feeling she might scream.

Despite the car's frigid air conditioning, her shirt was glued to her back and her stomach was churning. A thousand pounds a month? Where would she get that kind of money? And even if she could, it would take far longer than the deadline. Midnight tomorrow? It was impossible. Oh God, please let it be a troll or the modern equivalent of a poison-pen letter writer. Because if there was even a *shred* of a chance the threat was genuine – and Annie was working really, really, hard to convince herself it was just a nasty joke – what the hell was she going to do? She shuddered involuntarily at the thought of someone hurting Isla, the only good thing to come out of her marriage to Grant.

As she arrived in front of the building, two students were descending the short flight of steps from the main entrance, smiling and chatting. They perched on the plinth of the huge bronze sculpture of a scientist caught mid-transformation from man to machine. One leaned in towards the other and whispered something behind her hand. Then they both looked straight at Annie. Her heart somersaulted: did they *know*? She hurried inside, avoiding their gaze and telling herself it was just idle student curiosity. Slowly, as she took the lift up to her department, her chest muscles unclenched.

Alone in her office, she picked up a framed photo from her desk. Her and Isla laughing at a funfair two years back. Isla holding a teddy almost her own height. She'd give anything to see her daughter that happy again. That free. She sniffed and knuckled a tear from the corner of her eye.

A sliver of fingernail peeled back where she'd been nibbling it, making her wince. She checked her watch. Thirty-seven and a half hours until the deadline. Deadline? What the hell was happening to her? One minute she was a happily married professional with a carefree teenager and a prestigious, well-paid job. The next she was a betrayed divorcee, struggling to cope with a depressed daughter and the death of her best friend whilst being blackmailed by some unseen nemesis.

Sometimes it felt like her own emotions were a luxury she couldn't afford. She would often wake in the small hours thinking of Juliet, and instead of trying to get back to sleep, she'd go downstairs, wrap herself in a coat and sit on the garden swing, crying quietly in the darkness.

Losing her oldest friend to that insidious disease had been bad, but this was on a different level. They'd known how to behave when Juliet died. You wept, you drank together, you talked endlessly. You went to the funeral. You sang the hymns and you said the prayers and you bloody well got through it. But this? This was something so far outside Annie's experience she had no way to process it.

Could she possibly pay the blackmailer? Maybe once, but for ever? And even if she did pay, would the woman keep her word not to harm Isla? It wasn't as if Annie could control her daughter's movements. Even before all this, Isla had been drawing away from her, despite the odd lovely moment when they would share a pizza and watch some silly reality TV show. And it was hardly as if she could enlist Grant's help. He'd seize on any sign of weakness as a pretext for revisiting the custody battle.

Her stomach in knots, she struggled not to run from her office, from the campus, and race straight home to Isla. She pulled her phone out to text her – *hey lovey ru ok just checking in* – before slapping it down on her desk. The school rigidly enforced the no-phones rule, and besides, Isla would probably just roll her eyes and ignore it.

She forced herself to be calm. This couldn't be real. It had to be a hoax. A nasty hoax, but a hoax all the same. She was being paranoid. People like her didn't get blackmailed. Their children didn't get death threats made against them. She was *normal*.

She racked her brain for anyone she might have offended, hurt or angered so badly that they'd be willing to go to the trouble of creating a deepfake video and hiring an actor to pose as a vicious blackmailer. She'd had spats with colleagues, of course she had. But who hadn't? And now she came to think about it, a couple of her online dates hadn't gone so well. But were they bad enough to warrant this kind of response? No. The idea was ridiculous. Crazy!

The trouble was, this thought gave her no comfort at all. Because if her only idea was crazy, that left just one possibility. That this thing was *real*.

Chapter 12

The elation Isla had felt when Dad gave her those precious festival tickets had evaporated as soon as the front door closed behind him.

Now, as she changed out of her school uniform, that scary sensation of falling away from the world returned. Dad had left. Maybe this time he wouldn't come back. He and Melissa might move to a different city. Or even a different country. Maybe he hadn't left because of Mum at all. Maybe he just couldn't deal with having Isla to look after. Had she been too needy? Too clingy?

She shook her head. She couldn't afford to get swallowed up by her anxiety. That was what Ekaterini said. They'd agreed she should use music to take her to a better place.

She plugged her AirPods in and messaged Naomi.

She was meeting her best friend at the Bullring. A couple of hours' window shopping, maybe a quick Maccy's, find somewhere to hang out, check Snapmaps, see if anyone else was around.

hey babe u cool

yep u

im ok see u in 20 mins
luv u

luv u 2

Concentrating on the music, she slammed the front door behind her. She turned out of Norfolk Road and paused to take a quick selfie, anxious to get everything right. It was so important, unless you wanted everyone to have fun sharing it with their sarcastic little comments.

She checked the picture and frowned. The butterflies in her stomach flittered. She looked awful. She had a double chin, and her left eye looked totally weird. After three more tries, she had something she thought she could use. She added a filter, the regulation cute caption, then, swallowing the doubts down . . . posted.

Finally the music got inside her and she adjusted her stride to the beat. The buzz subsided. But it was all so hard. Get good grades, but don't be a neek. Be in the popular group – as if! Talk to him, ignore her. Look like this, but not too much, don't want to look like you're easy. Listen to this, dump on that. Buy that top, wear that eyeshadow. And, more than anything else, live your bloody best life.

God, it was exhausting.

And it wasn't as if she was the only one. They were all screwed up. No wonder, with that relentless pressure to be perfect. If it wasn't your reputation, it was how many likes, friends and followers you had. It was so unfair.

Everyone she knew had some sort of mental health issue. There were plenty of girls so sad and mixed up they'd started self-harming. Naomi even confessed once that she'd come pretty close to cutting herself before her mum found her and screamed at her for five minutes straight. At least Mum wasn't like that. She was trying so hard to be nice, even though her job was really demanding.

It was just, if only there was some magic wand you could wave and get even like five minutes of peace when the world didn't have to know what you were doing.

Her chest was tight and she had that shallow rapid breathing Ekaterini had taught her to recognise. She focused on the here and now. That was what Ekaterini had told her to do. Working on muscle memory, her feet had taken her along a little-used cycle path that ran parallel to the road, through a narrow strip of woods between two residential streets. One of her faves.

It would be getting dark soon. No way she'd come back from seeing Naomi this way, but it was safe enough for now. She timed her breathing to her steps: in for three, out for three, rinse and repeat.

Slowly she felt her ribcage easing, and the horrible cold, panicky feeling fading away. She forced herself to smile. Imagining her and Naomi larking about in the Bullring, pointing out all the clothes they'd buy if they won the lottery. Not that they even did it. Gambling was for losers.

Ahead, a bunch of pigeons flapped up into the air out of a tree.

The sudden movement startled her, and as she jerked her head up, her left AirPod popped out and fell to the cracked tarmac of the path. Bending to retrieve it, she caught movement in the corner of her eye. Probably just another bird. Like before.

She straightened as she turned. And that icy, panicky feeling came rushing back, snaking down her spine deep into the pit of her stomach.

He looked properly dodgy.

Lank, thinning hair. And a massive black eye. Jesus, his whole cheek was purple. And his lip was cut. Shabby camo jacket, horrid greasy trousers almost black with grime.

Isla turned away and doubled her pace, though she didn't want to run, because that would mean admitting to herself how scared she was. She tried to give it a bit of sass, a bit of a pimp-roll, so it would look like she was just enjoying the music that was now only coming tinnily into her right ear.

She looked down. She was clutching the other AirPod in her hand. She stuffed it into her pocket.

Not scared... not scared... not scared... she chanted in her head. Just some wino or tramp or whatever. She took out her remaining AirPod. Strained her ears to pick out the sound of shuffling steps following her. Nothing.

Thank God. She was just being paranoid. Poor old guy was probably like her, looking for somewhere quiet to be by himself. Smiling with relief now, she glanced back.

He was ten yards behind her.

How was he even doing that? She hadn't heard a single sound.

He had this totally evil expression on his face. Leering. She folded her arms across her chest.

'Get lost, OK? Stop following me!'

He kept staring at her. And then he took a sudden step forward. 'Hello, Isla.'

He bared his teeth. Isla screamed in pure fear. She spun round and ran. The worst pictures flickered behind her eyes. Memories of movie nights with Naomi when they'd binged crap slasher movies from the nineties. Killing themselves laughing as they tried to pick out the final girl, then squealing with pleasurable terror when Jason, Chucky, Michael or Freddy jumped out with a big bloody carving knife.

She snatched a deep breath and put on a burst of speed. The guy didn't look like the type to win track medals. She could just outrun him. There was a cut-through coming up that left the cycle path for the main road. She could nip through there and be in the middle of school-run traffic and people walking into the city centre. No way he'd try anything then.

Pain lanced under her ribs on the right side. A stitch. Not now, please! She slowed to a jog and told herself she was just being stupid. She twisted to look over her shoulder.

The wino was keeping pace with her. Only now he wasn't leering. He was scowling. His right hand had snaked inside his jacket. Oh God, he was going for a knife. He was going to cut her up. Or use it to force her to … to … No! She wouldn't, couldn't go there.

Stomach churning, almost crying with terror, she pulled her phone out. Crap. No data, no signal. Not even one single bar of 3G. But maybe there was one thing she could do to send him packing.

She darted left, then right, then spun round, held her phone up and took a photo.

'I see you, you freak! Just fuck off!' she yelled at him.

He stopped, blinking. Maybe he'd never had a girl fight back before. Or was it the fact that she was taking his picture? Was he scared? No time to worry about his reasons: Isla turned and ran like she'd never run before. The cut-through was coming up. She hit the metal barriers at speed, swung herself round the offset gate and streaked down the narrow alley before bursting out onto the street.

No time to look properly – she just ran out into the road, aiming for a gap in the traffic. A truck loomed out of the dusk towards her, horn blaring, tyres screeching. She ran on, glanced left at the halfway point, took a check-step as a bright yellow sports car blew by. She sprinted the rest of the way and reached the safety of the pavement on the far side.

Weeping with fear, she risked another look over her shoulder.

He was gone.

Oh thank God, he was gone.

There was a Starbucks not too far ahead. If she could just make it there, she'd be safe.

Chapter 13

Michael swallowed hard as he pushed open the front door.

A cold, heavy feeling settled over him. He hadn't got used to the smell of a Lucy-less home. She'd never worn much perfume, except if they were going on a date night. But there was just something that he'd always been able to detect, maybe just subconsciously, that said that this was a home with his soulmate's presence infused into every corner. Every floorboard, every skirting board, every door, window frame, joist and rafter.

They'd had a few good years together. Scrap that. A few bloody amazing years. Until the brief pain-filled rush towards the end and that final morning when the world emptied out of all colour.

He turned the lights on as he went down the wide hallway and into the kitchen. Aaron trailed behind him.

'What do you want for tea?' Michael asked him.

Aaron slumped onto one of the black leather and chrome barstools ranged along a sparkling grey granite counter. Flicked stray toast crumbs off the otherwise immaculate surface.

'Not hungry. I might get something in town later. I'm meeting Will and Gurvinder.'

'Come on, mate, you've got to eat something. You're a growing lad.'

Aaron's eyes flashed.

'I said I'm not hungry. Why can't you ever just accept anything I tell you?'

Michael held his hands up. They were slipping down a well-worn slope that led to the same destination every time. Just for once, he'd like to sidestep this particular trajectory and talk about something – anything – else.

'Sorry, mate. How about a coffee? I picked up some pods on the way into work. We have cappuccino, latte, flat white—'

'Christ, just leave it, will you? It's like you think you have to keep talking to fill the gaps just in case I mention Mum.'

Aaron laid his head on his arms, his curls flopping forward and obscuring his face.

Michael felt winded, as if someone – a grey-cloaked giant with an undertaker-solemn face – had just thrust gnarled fingers through his chest and around his heart and started squeezing.

'Aaron, that's not true and you know it. We can talk about Mum if you want.' He drew in a breath. '*Do* you want to? I mean, I don't know what you talk to Leo about in your sessions. Or is it your dad? Because, you know, we can talk about him, too.'

As if he'd touched a live socket, Aaron reared back and glared up at Michael.

'Don't mention my dad! Everything was fine until you came along. They were working things out. They'd have fixed their problems. But you were just...' He smashed a fist onto the countertop. 'You wouldn't stay away, would you? You started an affair with Mum and that's why Dad left us. So don't pretend you care about my mental health now, because it's all bullshit and you know it.'

Lord, he tried to be patient with Aaron. Losing his mum at seventeen, well, how could the boy be expected to keep his emotions under control?

Michael had spoken to his form tutor at Harborne College, the head of sixth form, the school counsellor. They'd all said the same thing. Basically, Aaron needed space and time to heal – and yes, carry on with the therapy.

But what about me? Michael wanted to shout. *I lost her, too. I never thought I was going to find anyone to share my life with, and then I met Lucy Reeves and I knew she was the one.*

He returned Aaron's dark, brooding gaze. He was the adult, he told himself. He had amassed the life experience. He'd developed emotional maturity. He'd assumed, willingly, the duties and responsibilities of parenthood. So he should damn well keep it together.

Should.

'Bullshit, is it?' he shot back. 'That's what you think? Is it bullshit when I drive you to therapy every week? Is it bullshit when I deal with the cops when they rock up on my doorstep because you've been vandalising bus stops? Was it bullshit when I adopted you?'

He was breathing heavily. Sparks were shooting round the edge of his vision. He knew he would never win the war of words with Aaron, but he'd lost his cool. And now it was too late.

'You're not my dad!' Aaron shouted. 'And you never will be.'

The dam burst. Just like that. No trickle turning into a stream, a flood, a torrent. The whole thing gave way in one catastrophic failure to keep the dark waters at bay.

Michael jabbed a finger towards his son.

'You know what? If I'm not your dad, your *real* dad, I'm pleased. I am really grateful. Because he is the kind of man I would never want to be. He used to hit her, Aaron, did you know that? *That's* why she left him.'

He sagged as these final words left his lips. His heart was racing so fast he could feel it in the soft places under his ears. Oh Christ, what had he done?

'Aaron ... I'm sorry. I'm sorry. I shouldn't have said that.'

Aaron slid off the stool. He closed the distance between them to eighteen inches.

'But you did, didn't you.'

The crash as he slammed the heavy oak front door set the wine glasses ringing on the kitchen shelves.

Michael slumped into a chair and cradled his head in his hands. He sat unmoving and watched the sweep second hand of the big chrome clock on the wall make five complete revolutions. He let his head roll back on his neck, which crackled like bursting bubble wrap, and stared at the ceiling with its many harsh white downlighters, at least one of which was always failing.

He levered himself out of the chair and went into the sitting room. Picked up a framed photo of the three of them on their wedding day. Stroked picture-Lucy's cheek. A tear splashed onto the glass. He wiped it away with his shirt cuff and set the picture back among its fellows.

The room was filled with memories of her. A teal suede cushion with an embroidered whippet's head she'd made for his fortieth birthday. A piano, 'because when I retire from the beauty biz, I'm going to learn to play every song Adele ever wrote'. A chaise longue in buttercup-yellow velvet he'd refused point blank to have in the house until, patiently, and with a smile playing around her lips, Lucy had persuaded him to 'give it a day'. By the end of that evening, he'd been ensconced in it, reading the news on his iPad, and had refused to yield it to her. She'd bait-and-switched him with a flash of her bra and a come-to-bed look, before darting around him when he came towards her and throwing herself down onto it with a shriek of delighted laughter.

Nobody laughed in the house any more.

He picked up the whippet cushion and drew it to his nose, inhaling deeply, searching for the merest wisp of her contained in its fabric.

How had it come to this? He'd not been able to save Lucy, and now he was failing their son, too.

Chapter 14

Stomach churning, Annie stared at the screen saver. She hadn't touched her keyboard for ten minutes, and the report that her boss, Letitia, had asked for by the end of the day wasn't even half written.

A new image faded up. Annie and Isla gurning for a double selfie, the Italianate column of Old Joe, the university clock tower, in the background. She smiled. It had been taken six months before the divorce. Her guilt over Isla's mental health problems came rushing back. Maybe if she'd tried a bit harder with Grant, she could have saved Isla all the pain of the separation and the damage it had caused.

Her chest clenched. Her daughter looked so free of worry. Yes, there had been blow-ups, of course there had. At fifteen, Isla was well into the teenage tunnel. But there had been happy times, too. Plenty of them. Like when Grant would be at a festival and Annie would organise one of their 'girls' nights'.

Hot chocolate with marshmallows, whipped cream *and* Flakes. Proper popcorn, shaken in the big cast-iron pan until the burbling explosions started and Annie made Isla shriek by threatening to take the lid off. With the air filled with the smell of hot melted butter and charred kernels, they'd snuggle up together under a thick tartan fleecy blanket and gorge themselves while watching *Gilmore Girls* reruns.

Tears pricked her eyes. They'd get through this. They would. The hoaxer would reveal themselves, and though it would be unpleasant, eventually Annie would get things back on track. Except what if it wasn't a hoaxer? What if it was one of those awful stalkers who just kept going, making their victim's life a misery from the shadows?

Suddenly, like a shaft of sunlight piercing a bank of charcoal clouds, Annie saw salvation. Hoaxer or stalker, it made no difference. She could simply go to the police. How had she not seen it? But then the grey clouds closed again, and cold rain drowned her brief moment of optimism. Yes, she *could* go to the police. And what would they ask her?

Police dealt in facts, didn't they? Who, what, where, when. Dates. Email addresses. Phone numbers. She could almost hear a sceptical detective's voice.

Can you show us this video, madam?

And when she admitted she'd deleted it, they'd give her a look like Grant had, only tinged with official displeasure for wasting police time.

Oh God, why had she trashed the video? Why? It was the only real, tangible piece of evidence she had. And if it turned out it *was* some troll, the police could use it to prosecute him. Instead she'd acted like a frightened child, as if deleting it meant it didn't exist. *I can't see you so you can't see me.* Not only that, but she'd cleared her trash, too. Out of sight, out of mind. She must have been out of *hers*.

The phone call at the conference ought to be traceable, surely? Except, no. It had come from a withheld number. Didn't they all use burner phones these days? Christ, you could buy one with five quid of credit along with a Mars bar and your favourite flavour of vape. The same went for the anonymous email address the blackmailer had sent their bank account details from. Useless from a police point of view.

And that terrifying comment about Annie's Victoria Beckham jacket. These people had planted someone at the conference. They'd filmed her at Juliet's funeral. They knew about her work routine and off-site appointments. They must have been watching her, collecting information, for *weeks*.

An even more horrifying thought elbowed its way forward. If they were this sophisticated, maybe they had people inside the police, too.

Her phone rang, making her jump. She snatched it up.

It was Isla.

At first Annie couldn't make out a word her daughter was saying. Isla was crying hard, clearly terrified. Sobbing out breaths between low, fearful moans.

'Baby, what's wrong? Where are you?'

When she did speak, her words chilled Annie's heart.

'C-come and get me, Mum. Please. I'm in Starbucks on the high street. There was a man f-following me.'

Chapter 15

John strode away from Harborne, blood pounding in his ears. First the girl had called him a freak. Then she'd got away from him. Things couldn't have gone any worse.

His phone buzzed. A text from his employer. He wanted to meet, and had even supplied a GPS reference. Scowling – things just *had* got worse – John headed down to the canal. This was the old, unloved Birmingham. Empty factories, graffiti, supermarket trolleys poking out of the greenish water like half-submerged skeletons.

He pushed through a gap in some chain-link fencing with a sign dangling from one corner – *Premises Protected by Elite Security Solutions* – and wandered a few hundred yards up the towpath.

He shook his head. Forget the girl. Ness had no right to speak to him like that. As for that waste of space Alex... He'd like to see how he coped with fighting terrorists in fifty-degree heat while your guts turned to water and your mates were screaming in agony all around you.

And if jealousy had been the only problem facing him, maybe he'd have coped. Used his last remaining cash to buy an eighth and stick it straight into his arm. Or if he didn't have enough, then a few cans of super-strength lager would do the trick for a while.

But the girl had snapped him, hadn't she? Turned round, stood her ground and taken a bloody photo on her phone. He could almost admire her for having the balls to do it.

He knew what he looked like, even without Ness's cold stare. The way she wrinkled her nose like there was a bad smell under it. He'd never been exactly good-looking. Now? Now he looked like shit. And, it grieved him to say, he could never get to the showers as much as he knew he ought to. Hostels were rank places, and the bathrooms were the rankest places inside them.

Fuck, he was in a bad way. Frightening kids for a few quid. He balled his fists. It wasn't fair.

'Hey, you! This is private land. What are you doing?'

He turned. Two men were striding towards him. Middle-aged guy in a suit and tie. Younger guy in a high-vis vest holding a clipboard. Both wearing blue hard hats.

The older guy was red in the face. From indignation or exertion John couldn't tell.

'I'll ask you again. What are you doing on private land?'

John glared at him, feeling his belly tightening. His anger rising.

'I'm walking. Got a problem with that?'

'Yes, as a matter of fact, I do. My company acquired this land for housing. You have no right—'

He took a quick stride forward, squared his still muscular shoulders. He was gratified to see the way the suit blinked and stepped back.

'I'm taking a walk. I'm not hurting anybody.' *Yet*, he wanted to add. 'So just fuck off and leave me alone, yes?'

The younger guy laid a hand on the older one's arm.

'Come on, let's go. He's not doing any harm.' He turned to John. 'Just be careful. Some parts of the towpath aren't safe.'

The two men turned back the way they'd come, leaving John alone again. The pleasure he'd felt at winning the stand-off lasted for another few seconds. He grimaced as withdrawal cramped his insides. Thrusting his hands deep into his pockets, he rubbed the biscuit crumbs he found there between his fingertips as he walked on.

Reaching an upturned packing crate, he sat down, kicking a few loose pebbles into the canal. Imagined he was lobbing mortar bombs into a Tali stronghold.

'I've got another job for you.'

He started. The voice was right behind him. So much for situational awareness. If it had been a Tali gunman, his brains would be all over the place by now. He turned.

The man facing him frightened him in a way the blustering property developer never could. He had a cold look in his eyes. One that suggested he wouldn't just be willing to use violence – he'd actively enjoy it. Some kind of dark energy came off him in waves. And yet, he looked like that film star Ruby was always gushing about. Black hair in a floppy fringe. Full lips quirking up in a smile like he knew something you didn't. The tattoo on his bicep, a rope loop ending in a half-knot, swelled as he flexed his arms.

'How've you been, John? You look like you've been in the wars.'

'It's nothing.'

'Doesn't look like nothing. Looks like you've been fighting.' The man smirked. 'And losing. Hope the kids weren't frightened to see their daddy looking like that. How are they, by the way? Ruby still enjoying ballet? Benji still desperate for a drone?'

Fear and anger curdled in John's chest. He jumped to his feet. 'Leave my kids out of it.'

The man jabbed a finger, hard, into his chest, making him stagger backwards. A predatory snarl flickered across his features and then was gone.

'Don't you *ever* give me orders. I tell *you* what to do, not the other way around.' He smiled and straightened John's camo jacket, brushing the front down. 'And if I want to talk about your kids, I will, yes?'

John couldn't maintain eye contact. He stared at the ground. It had seemed such a good idea when the guy now pushing him around had bent to help him out of the gutter – literally, since he was pissed at the time. Fifty quid to deliver a parcel to a posh house in the suburbs.

The jobs had kept coming. A bit nastier, some of them, but

the money was good. Then there'd been that awful day when the man had appeared holding a cuddly toy by one floppy ear. Ruby's favourite. Lacey, a plush pink rabbit she'd had since she was tiny.

He hadn't said much. He hadn't needed to.

Your kids are so lovely. We had such a nice chat in the park. A bit prone to running off, but that's kids for you. They'll always come home to Mummy and Daddy. In the end.

His meaning was clear enough. And the jobs had started getting darker. Making threats. Following people. Burgling homes.

They paid him. But they knew his weak spot. And they exploited it without mercy.

'Just leave them alone, OK? That's our deal.'

'Of course. Wouldn't have it any other way.'

'So what's the job? Not terrorising another schoolgirl?'

'It's a boy. Here's his picture. He goes to Harborne College.'

John scrutinised the photo. Good-looking lad. Eighteen, maybe nineteen. Mixed race. Curly hair. Sullen. And an emotion behind the eyes he needed no help translating. Sadness. Grief. His face framed by an enormous rucksack, big as an army bergen. Flag half visible in the background. Duke of Edinburgh's Award.

'How much?'

A sheaf of shiny, plasticky twenties passed from hand to hand.

'There's five hundred there. Another five when it's done.'

That was a lot more than normal. John looked up into those cold, dark eyes.

'For putting the frighteners on him?'

'For killing him.'

Chapter 16

Annie slewed the car to a halt on a double yellow line. Rushed inside the coffee shop, heart pounding.

Isla sat in the centre of the room, an untouched hot chocolate clutched between her hands. She looked so small, so frightened. Her already pale complexion whitened to translucency, her round, wide-set eyes glistening. Her lower lip trembled as she looked up at Annie's cry.

'Isla!'

Annie rushed over and crouched beside her daughter, wrapping her arms around her and squeezing tight. At this moment, anger swept fear aside. If anyone tried to hurt Isla, she'd kill them.

'Are you OK, baby? What happened?'

Isla sniffed, but no tears came. Maybe she'd cried them all out. She was clutching a soggy tissue in her right hand.

'It was awful, Mum. I was walking to meet Naomi, along the cycle path. And I know you say to take the safe route, but I didn't, OK, so just don't. And then I got this feeling, you know? Like someone was following me? I turned round and there was this really creepy-looking guy behind me.'

Annie hugged her daughter tighter.

'Oh my God, lovey, you poor thing. What did you do?'

'I was going to say something. You know, shout at him to leave me alone? Only then he said hello.' Now the tears did come. Loud sobs into Annie's chest as she hugged Isla close. 'He said my name, Mum. How did he know my name?'

Annie's heart stuttered. He'd known Isla's *name*. Was he connected to the woman on the phone? Jesus, this wasn't just a lone troll. This was organised. She shut her fears down. No way could she tell Isla any of that. It would send her anxiety skyrocketing. She had to say something, though.

'I don't know, love. Maybe he heard you on the phone or something.'

'But I wasn't on the phone.'

'Look, don't think about it now. Let's get you home.'

'OK, yes please.' Isla's eyes widened. 'I forgot. I got a photo. Look.'

She held her phone out.

The photo wasn't perfect, clearly taken on the move. But it was sharp enough to send a vicious wire of fear snaking down Annie's spine. A man in a camouflage jacket. Leering into the camera. His face disfigured with a huge purple bruise over his left eye.

She held out her own phone. 'AirDrop it to me.'

Isla complied, her fingers jerky, uncoordinated. Annie's phone vibrated with the incoming image.

'What are you going to do with it, Mum? Are you going to the police?'

Annie paused. How could she tell her there was no point?

'They'd only get us to fill out a report they'd never act on, love. You know how overstretched they are. You're safe, that's the main thing. Come on, let's get home. I'll make you another hot chocolate. That one must be stone cold.'

As she got to her feet, she noticed a lone woman at a corner table. She was watching them, Annie was sure of it. Young. Confident-looking. Sharply dressed in a punky charity-shop style: leather biker jacket and velvet scarf. Laptop open in front of her, though that could be a blind.

Fear rushed through her, wrapping cold fingers around her insides. She glanced around the café. At the counter, another woman sat on one of the leather-cushioned stools, forking cake delicately between red lips. She turned her head, meeting Annie's gaze. Was that a grin. Was she in on it, too? Were they working as a team, spying on her? Had they hacked her office phone? Followed her from the university?

No. She was being paranoid.

Except, the video. The threatening phone call. They'd happened. They were real. She felt shaky. Sparks wormed around her peripheral vision.

'Come on, Isla,' she urged. 'We need to go. Right now.'

She hustled her out to the car and pulled away, checking her rear-view mirror every few seconds, looking for any vehicle that might be following. Alternating that with anxious glances at Isla, who was already engrossed in her phone. For once, Annie let it pass without comment. If she was messaging her friends, maybe that would help her deal with the scare of being followed by that evil-looking man.

Back home, Isla retreated to her room, wrapped in a fluffy pink and white fleecy blanket she rescued from the sofa in the living room, and clutching a fresh hot chocolate Annie had made for her. With a Flake *and* whipped cream *and* mini-marshmallows.

'God help your stomach, Isla Barnes,' Annie said, faking a smile she didn't feel.

With Isla upstairs, Annie sat at the kitchen counter.

What the hell was happening?

Whoever it was, they were well organised. And well resourced, too. The *reach* they had. They'd infiltrated Juliet's funeral, though Annie couldn't remember seeing anyone she didn't know. Mind you, the state she was in, the state they were *all* in, that didn't mean anything. They'd produced that disgusting video. They'd known she'd be at the conference, even what outfit she was wearing.

Cold dread wrapped her as tight as a shroud.

Isla's fright on the cycle path wasn't a coincidence at all.

It was a warning.

Chapter 17

Tilly leaned across the table so her date could top up her glass. Made sure to squeeze her arms together a little to deepen her cleavage. His eyes glittered.

He'd offered to pick her up outside her place, but she'd declined, suggesting they meet at the restaurant instead. 'It'll be more romantic.'

Except the married people who used the Private Liaisons website weren't looking for romance, were they? The company talked a good game about meaningful encounters, but all its members wanted was no-strings sex with someone other than their spouse. Good name, though. Just subtle enough to allow its users to forget what they were really doing.

He was a dentist in Solihull. Specialising in cosmetic work. 'I'm not saving lives, but people will pay a lot of money for a nice smile.' He'd married at thirty-five, 'once the practice was doing well', become a father at thirty-seven, and again two years later.

Only thing was, wifey turned out to have the sexual imagination of a nun. Or so he claimed. Hence he'd made contact with Tilly.

Blonde, sexy, *flirtatious* Tilly, who was working it tonight as if she were sitting opposite Austin Butler rather than an average-looking dentist who she'd walk straight past on the street without a second look.

He leaned forward, laid a cool, long-fingered hand on the thick white tablecloth. Almost touching hers. He sipped his wine. Regarded her over the rim.

'If you don't mind me saying, Tilly, you don't really look old enough to be in an unhappy marriage.'

'Oh, I'm not married.'

'Then forgive me, but why do you do it? A good-looking girl like you could get boyfriends by the bucketload.'

She offered another look from her catalogue. Tugging her lower lip in between her teeth as if caught out in a lie. Frowning. Just a little.

'I'm about to confess my guilty secret.' She wished she could blush on cue. Lowered her gaze instead. 'I prefer what married men have to offer.'

He nodded. 'Experience.'

'If you like.'

Once they'd finished eating, Tilly leaving half her wagyu steak untouched, he leaned forward again.

'You know what the worst thing about being a modern father is, Tilly? I'll tell you. It's the endless bloody spectating. Football. Ballet. End-of-term plays. Sports day.'

Like she cared. Like *any* woman on a hook-up with a married man would care. She sipped her wine.

'I bet you win the dads' race, don't you?'

His self-satisfied smile slipped a little.

'I came second this year. Not bad, all things considered.'

She pouted. 'Only second? What happened. You're so fit, I'd have thought you'd ace it against the dad-bod brigade.'

The smile came back. Amazing what a bit of flattery would do.

'Would have, but you know,' he winced theatrically and patted his thigh, 'pulled something in my quad. Affected my performance.'

She lowered her false-lashed eyes for a second. Smiled up at him from beneath their spidery canopy.

'I hope it's not going to affect your performance in any other ways.'

His eyes dropped to her chest again.

'Oh, I think it's safe to say I'll be mounting the podium.' He took a mouthful of wine, the punchline so glaringly obvious she had to restrain herself from supplying it first. 'Not to mention my beautiful companion.'

She relaxed. Gave him a seductive smile a porn star would reject as too obvious.

'Well perhaps we'd better head off to the stadium, then. Wouldn't want you peaking too early, would we?'

He drove his Porsche carefully to Chamberlain Square, where he told her, unnecessarily, that he had a two-storey penthouse. The lift emerged directly into his apartment.

'Welcome,' he said, sweeping an arm towards the floor-to-ceiling window overlooking the square, the modern office blocks lit as if they had spent too long ogling Manhattan's Instagram. 'Drink?'

'Got any champagne?'

'There's a couple of bottles of Krug stuffed down behind the cornflakes. Joke. They're in the wine store. It's downstairs. Won't be a tick.' He gestured at a fatly upholstered leather sofa. 'Make yourself comfortable.'

He might as well have held up a banner. *Strip down to your lingerie.*

So she did.

He returned swinging a narrow-necked bottle, which he almost dropped as he took in her underwear-clad figure.

'Hell's teeth,' he moaned.

She crooked a finger. 'Why don't you come over here and tell me all the deviant things you're going to do to me?'

She stood facing the window, her reflection superimposed over the sporadically lit block of One Centenary Way. He grabbed her by the hips and nuzzled her neck. She kept completely still, not even a shudder.

'Well, Tilly,' he said thickly, 'first of all, I'm going to remove this *disgustingly* sensuous lingerie with my teeth.'

'Oh, really? This is Agent Provocateur, you know. It cost me a fortune.'

'I'll buy you more,' he panted, moving his hands around to grab her breasts.

'You'd better. Then what? I'm naked and...' She drew in a sharp breath as he pinched her nipples, hard.

'And what?' he murmured, right in her ear.

'...and defenceless.'

He swallowed audibly, grinding himself against her bottom.

'Then I'm going to give you the seeing-to of your life.'

Tilly jackknifed sharply, shoving him back a step. Then turned to face him.

He leered at her. 'Want to play it rough, eh? We can do that.'

Maya cocked her head to one side. Dropped the coy, girlie voice.

'Actually, I was just wondering what your wife would make of all this.'

His eyes flashed. 'What the hell's she got to do with it? You do know how Private Liaisons works, right?'

'Oh, I know. It's just, Sophie's got to be a saint to put up with you. I mean, here you are, about to give naughty little Tilly a good "seeing-to", the day before your fifth wedding anniversary. You're hardly going to be winning husband-of-the-year after she finds out, are you?'

His face was blotchy, the heat of passion quenched by a cooling mixture of disbelief, suspicion and fear.

'What the hell are you talking about? Private Liaisons is supposed to be discreet. It's all *about* discretion. My wife won't know anything.'

She eyeballed him. Time to turn the screw.

'I imagine Maisie and Immy would be a bit sad, too.'

In fact she found it impossible to imagine how his children would feel. But she knew they'd cry. The wife would shout, scream, throw things. Carnage. She fought the urge to smile.

Breathing heavily, he took a step towards her. Jabbed one of those long, cool fingers in her face.

'I don't know what game you think you're playing, you little tart,' he snarled, 'but you're leaving. Get dressed and get out before I throw you out!'

She stood her ground. Revelling in the thrill of power despite the fact she was dressed in an ounce and a bit of lace while he was fully clothed.

She pointed a finger of her own. At the light fitting in the centre of the high ceiling.

'The first camera's up there,' she said matter-of-factly, waiting for him to follow her finger and spot the tiny lens. 'There's another one in the bedroom. And one in the office. Wasn't sure where you'd want to give Tilly her seeing-to, so I had to cover the bases. Mics, too. Just so Sophie gets sound *and* vision.'

He bared his teeth.

'Let me tell you something, Tilly, or whatever the hell your actual name is. I have some very powerful friends. And a lot of influence. Your half-arsed blackmail scheme won't work.'

'Yes, it will. I think it will work just fine.'

He grabbed her round the throat, thrust his face against hers. 'Well, you won't be able to enjoy it if you're *dead*, will you? Bitch.'

She'd been waiting for this. Commanding every muscle to go limp, she dropped. He let go as her weight dragged her down to the cool marble floor.

The bathroom door shot open, banging back against the wall. Her insurance policy had just arrived, wearing that look he always got when things were about to turn nasty. She caught his eye. Tried to signal to him not to overdo it.

The dentist stuck fists on hips. His teeth still bared.

'Who the hell is this, your muscle? Looks like he's never seen the *outside* of a gym, never mind the inside.' He squared up to the younger man. 'You've got precisely three seconds to—'

Ollie's first punch caught him square in the throat. Not hard this time. Maya'd seen Ollie punch people hard. They stayed punched. This was his way of handing out a business card.

73

The dentist staggered back, face pale, clutching his bruised throat. His attacker followed him across the room until his thighs hit the sofa.

Another punch, to the gut, doubling him over.

She started to get dressed, hoping she wouldn't have to call him off.

The dentist yelped as Ollie yanked him to his feet by a fistful of hair held in a cruel, twisting grip.

'Don't hurt me, please,' he gasped.

This earned him a flurry of slaps that grew harder, and louder: percussive pops that echoed through the hard-surfaced apartment.

Ollie was grinning as he continued hitting the dentist rhythmically. His biceps were pumped with blood, making his rope tattoo writhe as he brought his arm back for another punch. The dentist screamed as his head slammed back.

Fearing what would happen if she didn't intervene, Maya shouted.

'Enough!'

Ollie looked at her, eyes hard. Hand raised.

She held his gaze for ten seconds.

'I said that's enough.'

Finally, he shrugged. Dropped the now-sobbing dentist to the floor.

'You want money, yes?' the man whimpered. 'I ... I can do that. I can pay you, yes? Whatever you want. I'm rich. I'm very rich. How much?'

'A grand,' she said, pulling one of her heels on.

He nodded rapidly. 'I can do that. I've got cash in my bedroom.'

'A month.'

'What?'

'To an account in the Caymans, I'll give you the details in a moment.'

'Twelve grand a year? Are you joking?'

She shrugged.

'I never joke. But if you don't want to, that's fine. We'll just make a nice little video for Sophie and the girls. Maybe you could watch it together.'

He looked as though he might throw up all over his expensive marble floor.

She'd seen the expression before. Utter dejection. Pain. Fear. Result.

She pulled on her other shoe. 'That's the deal. Take it or leave it.'

He took it. Of course he took it. They always did. In the end.

'Thank you,' she said. 'Now, you need to go home to Sophie. *We* need a little time to get our gear out of here.' His face fell further, if that were possible. 'Don't worry, we'll leave it exactly the way we found it.'

Their latest target staggered to the lift door and pressed the button. While he waited, casting fearful looks over his shoulder, Maya was seized with a sudden urge to drag him back and finish what Ollie had started. The way he'd laid his hands on her, pinching her like that. Rubbing himself against her. The face of her last foster father swam queasily into view. She fought the image back down.

The lift doors slid open with a discreet whisper, saving the dentist. He stepped in before turning to stare out at them, a man dazed by events far beyond his control, unaware how close he'd come to dying.

The doors slid shut, leaving her alone with Ollie. He locked eyes with her. She knew that look. He was angry.

'I don't like it when you tell me what to do, Maya,' he said quietly.

Day Three

Chapter 18

Metal drowned out his thoughts. It helped with the stress.

Eyes glued to his phone, headphones clamped over his ears, Aaron walked to school, his pace automatically syncing to the music playing loudly inside his head. Metallica. *Master of Puppets*.

All the teachers were going mental about the A levels, urging the boys on to work hard, hard ... harder. Lessons, homework, revision, past papers. On and on and bloody on.

How could he explain that every time he sat alone with his thoughts, all the history and English and geography just flickered away like little fishes dodging a shark, and in behind them, looming out of the darkness ...

It. His grief.

His therapist, Leo, told him to visualise it as an animal if it helped. He had. And it didn't. Now it came after him, swimming lazily in looping curves, dead black eyes, wide mouth ringed with millions of razor-sharp teeth. During the day, if he dared let go and daydream. And at night. When he had no protection against his nightmares. Where metal couldn't help him.

He turned up the volume. Checked Snapmaps. Gurv was on George Road, almost at school. Must have left home early. Jesus, his parents were so strict.

He rolled his eyes at Gurv's latest message:

miss chambers is going to lose it when she sees your english essay bro

miss chambers can do one

its so lame shes gonna think its chatgpt

well it isnt but soon ai gonna replace teachers so fk her

Nobody used AI to write their essays. The teachers had warned them that they were using anti-AI software to detect it. Aaron had a simpler strategy to avoid punishment for poor-quality homework handed in late. He just pleaded his mental health. If that didn't work, he'd remind whoever was giving him grief that he had the actual kind. It worked.

He felt bad about it. No, scrap that. He felt terrible about it. But the truth was, he couldn't concentrate anyway. Not since Mum died. At the end, Michael hadn't even wanted Aaron to see her. The drugs the doctors gave her for the pain turned her into a crazy lady. Swearing, shouting at them, then crying and pleading for Aaron to kill her and put her out of her misery.

Poor Mum. He'd never cried so hard. The weed helped a bit. Took the edge off. So did his weekly chats with his therapist, Leo, though he'd never tell Michael that.

He glanced up from his phone just before crossing the street. No sense in being depressed *and* getting run over.

Twenty feet to his left, at the traffic lights, a white Ford Transit van waited. The bloke driving was staring at him. Pretty impressive black eye. It covered half his face. Why was he staring, though? Aaron returned the stare with interest.

He reached the far side and carried on walking. Now checking Instagram, flicking out likes and the odd comment. Gurv messaged him.

snapmaps says u still only on harborne rd
u gonna be massive late bro

like I care about school

but u need good grades for uni

who says im going maybe im gonna travel instead

4 real

ye

my dad would kill me if I even joked about that

your loss bro

A noisy engine behind him drew Aaron's eyes up and away from his phone. He looked over his shoulder. It was white-van man again, driving really slowly. He wasn't actually following him, was he?

'Loser!' he mouthed at the driver. Gave him the middle finger, too.

Despite his bravado, though, Aaron was scared. Something about the way the black-eye guy was looking at him was really off. On an impulse, he darted left, down a narrow passageway between two big detached houses. High evergreen hedges screened the back gardens.

He emerged onto Westbourne Road, then immediately took a second detour, down a curving cul-de-sac that led to another of the pathways – or gullies, as the locals called them – that criss-crossed Harborne, linking the wide tree-lined residential streets.

He emerged onto Vicarage Road and checked both directions. No sign of the dickhead in the van. No sign of any traffic at all. Not surprising really. It was a narrow street that connected the much busier routes of Harborne Road and Westbourne Road.

Well, that was easy.

Relieved, he headed up towards the main road. One of his mates had just uploaded a video of his black Lab to TikTok. He half smiled. Life might be shit, but at least there were pets doing the samba.

He rejoined Westbourne Road and the safety of crowds.

Checked both ways – no sign of the weirdo in the Transit van – and stepped out into a gap in the traffic.

Chapter 19

John's pulse was racing. The kid had spotted him.

Had given him the finger, too. So, one point for having a pair of bollocks. But it wasn't going to save him.

He swallowed down the revulsion he felt at what he was about to do. Scaring the girl was bad enough, but at least he hadn't done any more than that. But now they wanted him to off this teenage lad. What had happened in Helmand had been a genuine error, despite what that smooth-talking Army Legal Services lawyer had insinuated. But this? This was the real deal. He shuddered, wiped his hands on his jeans. Gripped the steering wheel.

If he'd had a choice, no way would he be doing what he was about to do. But the real freak in this dirty business – the one handing over the cash and the orders – had made it pretty clear what would happen to Ruby and Benji if he stepped out of line. And they were the last thing left in this world that John valued. He flexed his hands on the wheel.

The kid had run. Not a bad move.

But he'd left Snapmaps open.

John followed the little cartoon figure on the map. He waited until it emerged from one of the gullies, back onto the tarmac. Up Vicarage Road, right onto Westbourne. The target was about to cross.

Go-time.

His mouth tasted of metal. Sparks wormed around inside his eyeballs. He tried to breathe calmly. Focus on the mission. But it was no good.

He closed his eyes for a second. Heard distant chopper blades slashing the air, Miniguns rasping like chainsaws, IEDs exploding.

Shouts in English, and Arabic. Rifle fire, grenades, screams for medics and mothers. He was back in the unreal moment when Heather trod on that IED and screamed as her legs flew away. He felt the panic rising.

This was no good. He shook his head, trying to refocus on the mission. *Not now, John, not now. You have to go through with it. Think of Rubes and Benji.*

He eased his foot down on the throttle: no sense giving his position away. Heaving in a breath, he pulled out round an SUV and mashed his foot down hard.

Now the motor did bellow. Screaming like a goat being slaughtered in a dusty market square as John raced down the outside of the traffic queue straight towards the boy.

Sunlight bounced off a car windscreen, dazzling him. And he was back. There. Driving the Humvee towards the Tali roadblock. Gunfire chattered all around him. Muzzle flashes from AK-47s blinded him. The terrorists were blowing car horns to try to distract him from the mission. No way. Sergeant John Varney did not flinch from danger. Beside him, Heather gripped the handrail, urging him on. A real fighter, that one. Didn't complain even when her legs ended in bloody rags below her knees and a bit of steel pipe was sticking out of her belly.

'Get him, Sarge. Get the bastard!' she screamed.

Jaw set, John shot towards the insurgent spinning to face him in the middle of the road and levelling his AK. Had time to see his terrified face…

One second before impact, he closed his eyes and locked his elbows. He felt the impact all the way from his wrists to his shoulders. A big, booming bang inside the Transit's cab.

He opened his eyes to see the kid's body cartwheeling through the air before bouncing off a car bonnet and landing in a tangle of arms, legs and school bag on the tarmac.

The sickening crunch jolted John back fully into himself. He stared through the windscreen. Blood was leaking from the boy's nose, forming a pool on the road surface.

People were shouting, screaming. Pulling out phones. Some taking video of the van, others focusing on the dead boy.

Shaking, refusing to look at what he'd done, he rammed the gear lever into first and tore away from the scene, tyres squealing, blue smoke billowing up to obscure the rear of the van.

He felt sick. He had to get away. Far, far away.

Chapter 20

Annie turned left into Westbourne Road and slammed her brakes on, almost rear-ending the car in front. It was stationary at the back of a long queue of traffic.

Heart pounding, she backed up a foot or so. The other driver glared at her in his mirror, then craned round, mouthing something, face contorted.

'It's not my fault,' she shouted.

She groaned. Great. Now she'd be late for work. One more small failing in Letitia's eyes.

She lifted her bottom off the seat and craned her neck to see what was causing the hold-up. Blue lights flickered. Sirens. Oh God. An accident? She hoped nobody was badly hurt. But all the same, why now?

She touched a couple of buttons on the steering wheel and switched to Radio WM from the podcast she'd been listening to. The presenter was speaking in one of those low voices they always used when something bad had happened.

'...Thanks to Steve who's on Westbourne Road on his way to work for this eyewitness report. Apparently, there's been an accident involving a pedestrian. Steve tells us there are police and ambulances on the scene. Well, we hope nobody's been seriously injured and we'll be bringing you more on this story at the top of the hour. Now, Ed Sheeran—'

Annie jabbed at the button to silence the radio.

At least she knew now why the traffic was at a standstill. Someone was going to be having an even worse week than she was.

It took another forty minutes for her to make the two-mile

journey to the university. She arrived on campus completely frazzled, the stress of the delay intensifying her worries about the anonymous woman's demands for money. Being late for work meant she could only find a space right in the far corner of the car park, leaving her with a long and windswept walk to the school.

She paused long enough to grab a cup of black coffee from a machine, then made for the sanctuary of her office, desperately needing to think. She sat at her desk and put her head in her hands.

The woman had given her until midnight, but could she even *afford* to pay? She had savings and limited investments she could draw on, but she had a big mortgage that had recently gone up. Finding that money every month would break her. It would be financial suicide.

But what choice did she have if Isla's life hung in the balance? She'd just have to find a way.

Her phone rang. The head of school and her own line manager, Letitia.

'Annie, have you got a minute?'

The line went dead. Letitia never waited for answers to rhetorical questions. Annie left her office at a half-run.

Letitia's office was grand. Which, at Birmingham University's School of Computer Science, equalled light and space, lots of it. Plus modern art. Plate glass. Stainless steel. Carbon fibre. All in all, a statement space.

As soon as Annie arrived, Letitia offered coffee. Annie refused, feeling wired enough from the vending machine Americano and the ongoing anxiety that was losing her more sleep than caffeine could put right.

'You've got your dinner with the Chinese tomorrow,' Letitia said. 'Everything set? There's a lot riding on this for us, Annie.'

Annie had always admired Letitia's talent for understatement, which had reached Olympic levels here. She'd been developing – no, cultivating – the relationship with Dan Gao, the CEO of Gao

Industries, for two years. Now he had promised to endow a chair in computer science and she was within sight of the finishing tape, which in this race would be constructed from a great many banknotes.

The thought of money sent Annie's thoughts spiralling back to her anonymous blackmailer. She was simply going to have to pay. She couldn't risk anything happening to Isla. Pay now, worry later. Like some awful loan shark company's late-night TV advert.

'It's all good,' she managed to choke out.

Letitia's lips tightened for a split second. 'That's it? It's "all good"? Can you share a little more of your strategy with me? I'm under the cosh financially, Annie, you know that. I can't stress this enough, but it's imperative everything runs smoothly.'

Annie tried to focus. To outline her plans for the dinner, from the restaurant, Barker's, to the list of topics of conversation she had lined up and the research into the CEO's background she'd completed.

It felt like she was back at uni herself, being grilled by her professor over subjects she'd barely studied. She stumbled over her words, mispronounced Dan's company name, even dropped an F-bomb, all the while trying to avoid Letitia's piercing gaze.

Her day had started badly, and it was only going to get worse.

She needed time to release funds from a couple of investments to cover the first payment to the blackmailer. And she had the standing order itself to set up. But how was she supposed to do any of this with Letitia grilling her? How was she supposed to carry on as normal, wining and dining potential donors, when someone was out to kill Isla?

Chapter 21

Maya leaned back in her chair, jacket creaking as she hugged herself in triumph.

Michael Taylor had thought he could get away with breaking the deal, and now he was finding out the true cost. Wife dead. And now his son as well. That would teach him. And he'd be racked with guilt. Because it was all his fault. All he'd had to do was keep paying. So that was on him.

He'd be there now, at the mortuary, with some female cop putting on a sympathetic face while he identified his son. Like that uniformed PC did when Mum had stuck her final load of junk into her arm. He'd led Maya by the hand out of the cellar. Dirty, scrawny, blinking in the light, traces of the Cornettos she'd found in the freezer smeared around her mouth.

The cop would have had a different expression on his face if he'd seen her after the funeral. When nobody was watching, she'd gone right up to the grave and, very carefully, squatted over the freshly turned earth and released a stream of pungent urine.

Maya had never been good with emotions. Something important had been burned out of her very early in that hellish time they called childhood. But she knew what they meant to other people. She knew all about pain. Grief. Loss. Love. They were the most effective levers you could pull to get people to do what you wanted. And through trial and error, she'd worked out that the best, the most powerful lever was the one marked 'children'.

Oh, possessions were fine, and pets were definitely better. But kids were the prize. Something her mum, Charly Kinton, had never bothered to learn. Better yet, kid *singular*. Like Taylor. Like

Barnes. Find a target with an only child and it was so much easier to twist the knife.

She smiled. Knives were more Ollie's department. Though she tried to keep him on a tight leash. They'd made a video a few years ago, back when they were operating on the south coast. Ollie at his absolute worst, holding a butcher's knife to a kid's throat. Now *that* had been a payday worth celebrating. OK, the kid was mildly traumatised, but weren't they all? That was the lesson Maya had learned. Parents fuck up their kids. There was even a poem about it, although she'd only read a couple of lines.

Yes. Parents did. Only now, Maya fucked them up right back.

'And we're going to carry on doing it,' she murmured as she watched another couple of thousand-pound payments ping up on the screen in front of her.

Her phone buzzed loudly.

'What is it, Ollie?'

'You're not going to like it.'

Heat flared inside her chest and she rubbed her hand hard over the tattoo, making the rope burn.

'Just tell me.'

'John messed up. The kid's not dead.'

'What? How? Did you see it?'

'Yeah, I saw it! I had a grandstand view. I mean, it was beautiful, Maya. John smashes into him, up he goes like a rag doll, ten, fifteen feet into the air. Slams down into the road. His leg is bent all over the place and there's blood pouring out of his nose.'

'So how do you know he's not dead.'

'Because I'm at the hospital. They brought him into A&E and, you know, saved him. He's on a ward. But there's police everywhere. I can't get near him.'

'And you shouldn't. Don't you dare even try. Leave it to me.'

There was a long pause. Maya knew what was coming. Ollie had been getting ideas recently about who was the boss. And his temper was flaring more and more: that cold way he had of making whispering seem like roaring. It worked on marks when she was being Tilly, but it didn't work on her. It just worried her. She had to control him or everything could fall apart.

'I think I said this before, Maya,' he said. 'Don't tell me what to do. I really don't like it.'

She sighed.

'Just get back here, Ollie.' Scowling, she rose to her feet. 'I'll deal with John.'

Chapter 22

Michael sighed with pleasure.

At last, a job he could really sink his teeth into.

Maybe the MD wasn't supposed to roll his sleeves up and actually design a kitchen, but he had cleared most of his paperwork and was looking forward to a morning working with wood.

He rummaged around in a box full of timber samples, enjoying the smoothness of the sanded oak, the meandering black rivers through the spalted sycamore, the soft glow of the ash. He leaned over the box and sniffed. Again, deeper this time, drawing that gorgeous smell of properly cured timber deep into his nose.

His phone rang. He answered automatically.

'Yep.'

'Mr Taylor?'

'Speaking. Who is this, please?'

'Mr Taylor, my name is PC Dawn Jaeger. Could you confirm that you're the father of Aaron Taylor? A student at Harborne College?'

He put aside the strip of ebony he was holding, trying to keep his breathing steady.

'Yes, Aaron's my son. What about him? He's not in trouble again, is he? I did speak to him after the last time, when your colleague brought him home.'

'No, nothing like that. I'm sorry to tell you Aaron was involved in a road traffic collision earlier this morning. He's quite poorly, I'm afraid. I'm currently at Queen Elizabeth's, in A&E. The doctors are with him at the moment. Can you come in? Or perhaps Mrs Taylor?'

Time slowed down to a treacly crawl. Michael felt cold. He

heard someone speaking from far away. Reading from a script in a flat, expressionless voice.

'My wife is dead. I'll be there as soon as I can.'

He stood rooted to the spot for a few more seconds. Then he swept the box of timber samples to the floor with a clatter and ran from the workshop.

Halfway to the car park, he physically bumped into Chris, who held his hands up.

'Blimey, Mike, where's the fire? Actually, I'm glad I caught you. Bit of a cock-up with the master bedroom suite for the Thwaites. I was wondering—'

'Jesus, Chris, just deal with it yourself for once, OK? Aaron's been hit by a car. I've got to go.'

Chris's face fell. 'Oh God! Of course. Go, mate, I'll hold the fort here.'

Michael climbed into the Ranger's cab and sped away from the unit in Victoria Works, tyres screeching.

The hospital was fifteen minutes away. Heart hammering, he shot down Bristol Road. The first set of lights he approached were green. He sped through, not even readying to brake. The second were on amber. He accelerated hard. They changed to red. He blasted through, causing a car approaching the crossroads from his left to flash its lights, its horn blaring. Pulse hammering, vision telescoping to the centre of the windscreen, he swerved around a queue of five cars and snaked inside a traffic island at the last moment. More horns. More headlamps flashing him.

And all the time, one insistent thought blaring louder than any enraged driver's horn: *Don't die, Aaron. Oh please, don't die, son.*

The roundabout was coming up too fast and the traffic already on it had slowed to a crawl. Michael clamped his teeth, aimed for a gap and shot out between a van and a goods lorry, hauling the wheel over to the right and looping around the wrong way. The cacophony of car and truck horns was deafening. He ignored them all and skidded off the roundabout, heading straight towards a Honda Jazz slowing carefully before the junction. He and the terrified driver exchanged looks of horror before Michael wrenched the wheel over, missing the stationary Jazz by millimetres. He yelled, 'Sorry!' before speeding away, leaning on his own horn to clear the way.

The hospital came into view as he tore around a right-angled bend on Mindelsohn Way. He hurtled towards the emergency department and swung the wheel sharply to take the access road. The Ranger careered over the edge of the kerb, its offside wheel leaving the ground and sending Michael's belly into freefall for a hair-raising split second before righting itself with a bump as he slammed the brakes on, bringing it to an untidy stop at the end of a row of parked cars.

He jumped out and sprinted towards the door, his muscles finally able to use the adrenaline that until now had been squeezing his stomach into a tight, hard knot of fear. He stabbed the bell push. Nobody came. He pushed it again and again.

'Come on, come on, for Chrissake, please!'

An angry-looking paramedic admitted him.

'There's no need for that, sir. We're all doing our best to—'

'My son was hit by a car. Aaron Taylor. Where is he?'

The paramedic lost his scowl. Nodded.

'Let's get you to reception. They'll tell you where he is.'

Trying to stay calm, and failing, Michael followed the green-uniformed paramedic down a sterile white corridor that stank of antiseptic.

Queen Elizabeth's was where he'd lost Lucy.

Was he going to lose Aaron here too?

Chapter 23

Freed from Letitia's probing questions, Annie didn't return to her own office. Instead, she sought out her star student.

Deanna Robinson was pursuing a PhD in large-language AI models. For a generous fee that Annie had willingly paid her, she had agreed to be the face of the School of Computer Science in a year-long campaign aimed at recruiting overseas students.

That she was attractive, with beaded braids framing an open, intelligent face, helped, of course. Nobody could work in higher education without being acutely aware of the need to live the values of diversity and inclusion. But it was her story – working-class girl from a poor part of the city transformed through education into a future star of the hottest technology on the planet – that gave the campaign its heft.

From the very first photo shoot, Annie had bonded with Deanna. The meat of the young woman's PhD was many, many miles above her head, as she cheerfully admitted over a drink one evening. But they shared enough interests to help their friendship blossom. The need to get more women to the top in the field of computing. True-crime podcasts. And eighties band the Human League, who, unbeknown to each other, they'd both been to see at the same gig a few years before Deanna started her PhD.

But now, Annie desperately needed Deanna's help. Even though she had no clear idea what kind of help she could offer. Annie wasn't a computer expert, no matter how many times Grant made unfunny jokes about her working in IT. But surely a doctoral student could figure out how to retrieve a deleted video? Couldn't she? Or was that only a thing on TV crime shows?

She prayed Deanna would say yes. Because otherwise, Annie

didn't know what she was going to do. Yes she could pay the blackmailer, but it wasn't a long-term option. Her funds wouldn't stretch to a thousand a month for ever. Caught between the need to protect Isla and the hard fact of her limited funds, she was at her wits' end.

She found Deanna, as she'd expected, peering through heavy-framed black glasses at a huge computer monitor. On screen, a rainbow-coloured waveform pulsed and shifted on a black background laced by a fine green hexagonal mesh, like a deep-sea jellyfish caught in a scientist's net.

Annie nodded toward the monitor. Tried to smile.

'Should I even bother asking?'

'Probably not. I barely understand it myself. My supervisor's supposed to be walking me through it, but he's in with Letitia.'

Annie's heart sank a little further. Maybe Deanna wasn't going to be able to help after all. She offered the story she'd come up with overnight, lying awake at 3.25 a.m. True enough to be believable, vague enough not to worry Deanna.

'So I got this anonymous prank email a couple of days ago. Silly thing, really, but it got me thinking about a possible way I could use it in the campaign we're featuring you in. Trouble is, I deleted it before I meant to and now I can't get it back. I'd love to discover who sent it, too. I don't suppose there's any way...'

Deanna's smiled widened. 'Oh God, I'd love to. Anything to get me away from quantum neural modelling, even for a half-hour. Have you got your laptop?'

Gratefully, Annie handed the machine over.

'How long do you think you'll need? I mean, I don't want to rush you. It's just...'

'It's fine. It won't take me long. It's harder to delete things than most people think. And as for the IP address. Yeah, there are encrypted anonymous email servers, burner accounts, IP maskers like VPNs or Tor, metadata strippers, all that...' she paused as if Annie would know what these terms meant, 'but if you know what you're doing, ninety-nine times out of a hundred you can retrieve it all. Just takes a little magic. Which, luckily for you, I can work.'

For the first time that week, Annie felt a glimmer of hope. Genuinely relieved that maybe, just maybe, she was pulling back some ground on the blackmailer.

'I owe you,' she said, as she got up to go.

Deanna smiled. 'You owe me *massively*.'

Returning to her office, another cup of coffee in her hand, Annie's mind whirled.

Was it enough, putting her faith in Deanna? What if she *did* trace the location of the person who'd sent the video? What would Annie do then? Confront them? What if they were armed? They were clearly ruthless.

But she had to at least try. Unless she did something to stop them, her money would run out and then they'd kill Isla. No, she would *never* let that happen. She'd sell the house. They could live in a flat. Anything. *And what about when* that *money runs out, Annie?* the woman's cold voice whispered between her ears. *What then? We'll come for her eventually, you know we will.*

She gripped the edge of a table for support as fear crashed over her like a tidal wave.

What if she tried to stop them and failed? What if the woman who'd phoned her found out Deanna had traced her IP address?

She shook her head. Set her jaw. No. Goddammit, no! She was not a quitter and was not going to let *anyone* hurt Isla. The strategy wasn't perfect, but it was the best she had. Pay for now. Pursue her tormentors – to the ends of the earth if necessary.

And, at all costs, protect her daughter.

Chapter 24

Fear making him lightheaded, Michael ran from the A&E reception area into a wide white corridor, heading for the lifts and stairs.

The meaty waft of hospital meals kept hot in stainless-steel trolleys assailed his nostrils. It brought back unpleasant memories of the days and nights he'd spent here with Lucy.

He jabbed the call button. All the lifts were way above him on floors beyond the fourth. No time to wait. He yanked open the door beside the furthest lift and took the stairs two and three at a time, swinging himself round each half-landing on the handrails.

At Aaron's ward, his breathing ragged, he had to ring a buzzer and wait to be admitted.

'Come on, come on,' he muttered, holding the button down.

Eventually the latch clicked and he was in. He hurried to the nurses' station and introduced himself.

A sister in a navy-blue tunic and a badge giving her name as Danni ushered him into a side room.

'Aaron's going to be fine. He's a little sleepy from the sedation the doctors gave him while he was examined. We've run all the tests, taken X-rays and given him a head CT scan. He's a lucky boy. He's broken his left leg and his collarbone and he's got a couple of cracked ribs, but other than that, it's just bumps and bruises, some nasty grazes. No internal injuries. No apparent trauma to the head, either, beyond a gash to his nose. It's a miracle, actually. It could have been a lot worse.' She smiled, briefly. 'I'll be at the desk if you need me.'

And then he was alone with his son.

Wires and transparent plastic tubes led to and from Aaron's

body. Michael knew their functions from the time with Lucy. An EKG for his heart rate. EEG for brainwaves. A driver for painkillers. An infusion to keep his fluids up. A pulse oximeter clipped to his right index finger.

He blinked back tears and fought down a sudden surge of terror. Aaron's face was a mess. Two black eyes, a cut stitched closed across the bridge of his nose. Peeping from the blue and white sheet, a dressing swathed his collarbone. The bedclothes were drawn away from his left leg, which was encased in a gleaming white cast from hip to toes.

Michael sat beside him and gently picked up his free hand, trying to stop his own from shaking.

'Hey, mate. Can you hear me? Aaron?'

Aaron's bruised eyelids fluttered open.

'What happened? Where am I?'

'You were hit by a van. You're in Queen Elizabeth's. They brought you to A&E but this is a general ward. You're going to be fine, mate.'

'I feel fantastic, actually,' Aaron said. 'I wanna go home.'

Michael smiled as relief flooded through him. Poor Aaron was high on the painkillers and sedatives they'd pumped into him.

'That's probably the drugs they've got you on. I'm afraid you'll be here for a little while yet.'

Aaron went for a shrug, then winced. Clearly the painkillers had their limits.

'You've got a couple of broken bones,' Michael said softly. 'Try to keep still, mate.'

Just then, the door opened and a uniformed female police officer came in, a notebook open in her hand. She introduced herself to Michael as PC Jaeger – 'call me Dawn' – then turned to Aaron.

'Hi, Aaron,' she said. 'Glad to see you're awake. How are you feeling?'

'OK, I guess. Bit sore. Basically fine, though.'

'So do you feel up to talking about the accident?'

Aaron's eyes flashed.

'It wasn't an accident.'

She frowned, then flipped over to a new page in her notebook.

'Can you tell me what you remember about the collision?'

'There was this bloke following me on the way to school in a white van. He had a massive black eye. He was giving me this evil look and I tried to shake him off but he was waiting for me at the lights on Westbourne Road. He tried to kill me. I heard this really loud engine roaring and I turned round. I tried to dodge out the way just before he hit me. That's probably why I'm still alive.'

PC Jaeger looked at Michael, her eyebrows raised just a fraction. As if to ask him whether Aaron was concussed. What could he say? He wasn't a medic. Who on earth would want to follow Aaron? Let alone hurt him?

'Are you sure, Aaron? I mean, that sounds like a pretty strange set-up. And you took a bump to the head, remember.'

'Yeah, but the doctor told me I wasn't concussed.' He glared at Michael, then at the cop. 'I'm not making this up, you know. You've got to listen to me. You should be putting out pictures on social media. Like I said, weird-looking bloke, huge black eye. And a camo jacket like some weekend warrior.'

Suddenly worried that Aaron was getting himself wound up, which surely couldn't be a good thing, Michael decided to shut the conversation down for now.

'Aaron, mate, nobody's doubting you. But you need to rest. Please. I promise we'll talk about this later.'

He exchanged a look with the cop, who went for a sympathetic half-smile. Maybe she had teenage kids of her own.

'I'll pop back later,' she said.

With the officer gone, he squeezed Aaron's hand tighter. Time to build a few bridges.

'Look, Aaron, I know things haven't been great between us

recently. And I said some stuff about your dad I probably shouldn't have. I hope you can forgive me.'

'It's not about that! Can't you see? Some weirdo tried to kill me. Why won't you believe me?'

Michael didn't reply straight away. He paused, looking into his son's eyes. *Was* it possible? Had the van driver *targeted* Aaron? Why would he? Aaron had no enemies. Or not on the scale that would lead to attempted murder.

'I'm trying, mate, believe me,' he said, finally. 'But you have to admit, it's pretty out there.'

'No!' Aaron said sharply, raising his head off the pillow and immediately wincing before lying back again. He inhaled deeply and spoke on the out breath. 'What's "out there" is that I just nearly got wiped out by some rando driving a Transit van.'

The effort seemed to have exhausted him. His eyes fluttered closed and he turned away from Michael, muttering angrily. Gradually his voice slowed and fell to a disconnected murmur of random words. Whatever they'd given him for the pain had just kicked in hard. Over the next minute or so, his breathing slowed and deepened. He was asleep.

Michael kept Aaron's hand in his as he looked down at his son. His mind swirled with questions. What if the boy was right? What if it wasn't just the kind of bad luck that happened every day in a city where pedestrians and cars tried to share the same space? No. It couldn't be. The poor lad was concussed, or else the shock of the accident had sent his imagination into overdrive. Since his mum had died, he'd been prone to seeing hostility everywhere he looked, usually without cause.

It didn't matter. They could talk about it all later, when Michael took him home. For now, he just desperately wanted Aaron to be OK. And to try and heal the rift that had opened up between them.

Chapter 25

Shaking from unspent adrenaline, his hands white-knuckled on the steering wheel, John skidded the van to a halt. He scowled at the sign. Druid's Heath. Maybe white-robed geezers had once done pagan rituals up here. Sacrificing virgins or whatever. But they were long gone now.

The only people you were likely to encounter these days were fly-tippers. The sort of semi-organised criminals you'd do well to steer clear of unless you had a burning desire to get acquainted with the business end of a baseball bat.

Ahead, wooden gates painted in clashing shades of pink and orange barred his way. Beyond, the algae-slimed roofs of long-abandoned trailer homes.

He got out of the van and snipped the padlock shackle with a pair of bolt cutters. Beyond the gates, the wasteland beckoned. Fire-blackened circles of glass-strewn dirt. Kids' ride-on toys, the red and yellow plastic sun-faded. Piles of rusting white goods from which corrugated hoses and power cords snaked away as if even they wanted to leave this depressing place. Burned-out wrecks of cars, to which he would shortly be adding a new stablemate.

He pulled up beyond a tumbledown shack, its tiled roof collapsed in on itself. Doors and windows shot, smashed or blown out by the fierce winds that occasionally swept across this unlovely part of the West Midlands.

From the back of the van he retrieved a heavy jerrycan that seemed to writhe in his grip as its contents shifted. He began sloshing it over the seats, the dashboard, the tyres, blinking as the heady petrol fumes wafted into his face.

A scrap of grey cloth stuck in the grille caught his eye. He plucked it free. The kid's school trousers. John wrinkled his nose. Christ, he'd fallen a long way since leading patrols in the sandbox. But he'd protected his kids. He had to cling onto that. It was all he had left.

The empty jerrycan went back inside the loadspace. His fingerprints were on the system. No sense in leaving such a simple clue for the local plod.

Unlike in the movies, he didn't have a Zippo. Even if he had, he wouldn't have wasted it by chucking it in through the open side window. A lighted matchbook would do just as good a job.

The match heads flared with a hiss. He caught the sharp tang of burning phosphorus. Not a bad detonator. He'd seen a defused IED in Helmand where the trigger used a couple of ounces of the stuff.

He flicked the burning matchbook through the driver's window. The petrol ignited with a soft *whoomp*.

He backed away and stood watching as the orange flames devoured the interior. The heat warmed his face. It was time to end it. Killing kids? He hadn't signed up for this. Not in Afghanistan. Not here. But somehow it had happened, hadn't it?

The petrol tank went up with a sharp bang. Oily black smoke coiled overhead. The wind caught it and blew a sickly cloud right into John's face. His breath caught in his throat and once again he felt himself sliding, slipping back to the horrors of the war.

He turned to go before the flashback could dig its claws in.

And yelped in shock, pulse racing.

Her face, framed by short dark brown hair, flickered in the reflected orange light of the blaze behind him. Her eyes danced, tiny orange fires in a face otherwise devoid of emotion. In the firelight, her red leather biker jacket seemed to be made of blood, held in place by some demonic force.

Her sidekick was bad enough. But *she* was the one John truly feared.

He'd only met her once before. And he hadn't enjoyed the

experience. It was like talking to a robot. A robot who saw people as things. To be used at a whim and disposed of just as easily as a fast-food wrapper.

'You messed up, John,' she said, stepping closer, seemingly impervious to the fierce heat cooking all moisture out of the air. 'You were supposed to kill the boy.'

He was scared. But he couldn't let her push him around any more. It was time to stand firm.

'I did! I hit him dead-on. I saw him in the road. Bleeding.'

'No, John,' she said in that dreadful cold voice of hers. 'You fucked up. Because Aaron Taylor is now lying in a hospital bed. So maybe you'd like to explain to me what went wrong. And please don't tell me you had an attack of conscience, because it's a bit late for that now, isn't it?'

He tried to hold her gaze. 'I never said I'd kill a kid.'

She cocked her head, amused, as if a pet dog had tried to curry favour by imitating his mistress's speech.

'I think that's *exactly* what you did. You took the order, and you took the money that went along with it. And it's not like you haven't done it before, is it? I know all about your court martial, John. I read every word of the judgement. Harsh, I thought, but fair.'

It was just like the first time. Her words were sharper than a bayonet. She could find the exact path to slide the blade in between your defences, right into your heart.

'That was a stitch-up,' he blurted. 'They needed a sacrifice and they chose me. Anyway, the dad must have got the message, yes? I mean, OK, the kid's not dead, but he got a good smack.'

She stepped closer, her teeth gleaming whitely in the shifting red light. John could feel the heat unpleasantly close on his back and shoulders.

'We didn't pay you to give him "a good smack", John,' she said insistently, raising her voice over the roaring flames. 'We paid you to kill him.'

The kid's terrified expression just before the van hit him flickered across John's vision. He squeezed his eyes shut, but it didn't help. Opened them to find her calmly studying him, like a scientist examining a new specimen. He'd almost rather have had her bawling and screaming like an enraged regimental sergeant major. Jesus, what was *wrong* with her?

'It's gone too far. *You've* gone too far,' he said. He swallowed nervously, backing away from this slender young woman who dressed like a biker and radiated an intense dark energy. 'I served my country fighting evil. I may be nothing more than an addict now, but I still have some of the values they instilled in me in the army. Courage. Duty. Honour. Please don't ask me to kill a kid again, because I won't do it.'

Her mouth quirked to one side. He'd never seen her smile before. The sudden change in her expression was unnerving.

'John, love, you drove a two-tonne van at a schoolchild this morning in an attempt to murder him. It's a bit late to be spouting off about honour now, don't you think?'

Her face flipped back to stony calm. Like switching masks.

She stepped towards him and placed her hands flat on his chest. Pushed. Lightly at first. Then harder. A proper shove. He stumbled backwards, his boot heel catching on a stone half buried in the dirt.

The heat scorched the back of his head, and he raised a protective hand. Felt the heat there, too.

Why didn't he just push back? He was taller than her by a good five inches. And he was bigger. Heavier. Stronger. He didn't know why. Only that deep down, she genuinely frightened him.

'Please…'

She shoved him again. He thought he could smell fabric burning. Was it his own clothes? The camo jacket igniting like the cloth in a petrol bomb?

He had to do something. Or soon he'd be burning as merrily as the van.

'Stop!'

He pushed her back.

She sidestepped, grabbed him by the left arm and pulled, sending him sprawling over her leg, face-down into the glass-speckled dirt. Something exploded behind him with a sharp crack like rifle fire. He flinched.

She crouched in front of him and lifted his chin with a sharp-pointed nail. 'Your medical records say you're suffering from PTSD.' She stroked his cheek with a fingertip. 'But however much you suffer with that, I promise you, it's nothing compared to the agony of losing both of your children. How would you cope? Would Ness even allow you to attend the funeral?'

She jerked his chin higher, digging her fingernail painfully into the soft place beneath his jaw.

'No. You're in too deep to start claiming you've got scruples.'

Then she stood. She stared down at him, those fire-flickered eyes searing him down to his soul – or what was left of it.

'Finish the job.'

She stalked off, leaving him on the ground, so close to the flames he could smell the hairs on the back of his head shrivelling in the heat. But he didn't get up until she was out of sight.

He was much too scared for that.

Chapter 26

Bracing herself for the confrontation she was about to provoke, Annie put her coffee mug down on the kitchen counter with a clink. She glanced at Isla, who was frowning at an algebra worksheet, pencil clicking against her lower teeth.

'I don't want you to go to Dad's tonight.'

Isla's head jerked up. The scowl, never far from the surface of her beautiful, unmarked fifteen-year-old complexion, transformed her from studious schoolgirl to wolverine in a flash.

'What? You know it's his day to have me.' She folded her arms, her go-to gesture of defiance ever since she'd been two and a half. 'I'm going and you can't stop me.'

Despite her defiance, Annie still caught the tremor of anxiety in her voice. She felt awful. Because however much *she'd* fallen out of love with Grant, she knew Isla treasured her relationship with her father. Annie would never willingly deprive her of that. But this was even more important. She *had* to make Isla understand the danger she was in. Somehow without referring to her escape from the stalker the day before.

'I know it's Dad's night, Isla. But you have to trust me on this one. I want you here where I can'– *Yes, what exactly, Annie? What the hell do you tell her?* – 'keep an eye on you.'

Annie had been expecting a teenaged eyeroll – after all, Isla had mastered the full repertoire. So her daughter's reaction surprised her.

'Look, Mum, I know you're worried about me. I'll be honest, that creep yesterday really frightened me. But I'll be at Dad's, won't I? Safe. It's not like I'm sneaking off to some crack den.'

Yet even as Isla negotiated, something behind her eyes betrayed her. Annie knew that look. She was hiding something.

'Where *are* you going, Isla? Not to some club with Naomi, I hope. I've told you before, you girls are far too young to be going clubbing.'

Isla shook her head. Offered a peacemaking smile that Annie almost bought.

'I'm not going clubbing with Naomi, Mum. I promise.'

Almost bought. Annie shook her head.

'I don't care *where* you're going, it's a no from me. I want you to call Dad, or I can. I want you here tonight, with me.'

Isla's temper, never far from the surface, flared. But her eyes glistened, too.

'No way. It's Dad's night to have me. It's his legal right, and I want to go. You have to let me, Mum, please.' She swallowed. 'He'd still be here with us if you hadn't thrown him out. I need to keep seeing him.'

Annie bit back a rejoinder. Her brilliant, frustrating, beautiful, stroppy, vulnerable teenage daughter had backed her into a corner. Nothing for it but to tell her the truth and deal with the consequences later. It wasn't fair to burden a child with so much, but she could see no other option. She *had* to keep Isla close to her, even if it meant worrying a girl already struggling with her mental health.

She took a deep breath.

'Isla, lovey, I need to tell you something, and it's going to be scary, but I want you to know I'm not going to let anything happen to you. Someone, I don't know who, not yet, but they've ... well, they're blackmailing me, or, I don't know, maybe that's the wrong word, it might be extortion, but ... Oh God ...' She wiped away a tear that had swollen painfully like a spot in the corner of her eye. 'Isla, they told me they'd kill you unless I paid them. I'm worried that guy yesterday was part of it. That's why you can't go to Dad's tonight. It's too risky. I'm sorting it out, but I'm not there yet. Please, love, you have to stay here with me.'

Isla's face stilled.

Annie held her breath. How bad was it going to be?

Her daughter's lips curved upwards. She snorted. Then she laughed. And couldn't stop.

'You're joking, right?' she wheezed, dabbing at her eyes. 'A murder plot? What the hell, Mum? This isn't some true-crime podcast, this is Harborne. I mean, this is desperate, even for you. I'm going to Dad's, OK?'

Blindsided by Isla's response, Annie's mouth worked, but nothing emerged. So many things she wanted to say, yet none likely to work against the force of her daughter's contempt.

Isla's phone chimed. She looked down.

'Saved by the bell,' she said, before sliding off her bar stool. 'That's Dad. He's outside. I'll see you tomorrow.'

And just like that, she was gone, and Annie could only stare after her – the last good thing in her life.

Annie had defied her parents to marry Grant. And look how that had turned out. Her best friend had been cruelly taken by cancer. And now Isla, her precious girl, was being threatened.

Alone in the kitchen, she gripped the cold granite counter with both hands, her mind a mess of whirling fears and doubts. Grant didn't believe her. Isla didn't either.

How could she keep her daughter safe when the only other person who believed she was in danger was the woman who'd threatened to kill her?

Chapter 27

The pizza place was noisy, crowded with youngsters, but Grant didn't mind. He liked the crazy vibe of the place. And it was Isla's favourite. Had been since she was a little girl.

He swallowed a mouthful of his meat special, chased it with a swig of Coke.

'So, your mum's been acting weird lately, don't you think, Isles?' He rolled his eyes. 'Just when you want her to be cutting you a bit more slack, she goes all Tiger Mom on you.'

Isla nibbled the point of her slice. Didn't seem to find his quip as funny as he'd hoped.

'She's just worried about me, Dad, that's all.'

'Yeah, but you're a big girl. You can take care of yourself.'

She looked worried for a second and her eyes slid away from his, checking her reflection in the window, he guessed.

'I guess. Look, maybe we should get going. I don't want to be late for Josh.'

'Sure, hon. Let me just grab the bill.'

Five minutes later, Isla checking her phone beside him, he pulled away from the kerb in his two-seater convertible. He'd wanted to get a red one, then told himself that was maybe just too much of a cliché. He'd gone for British Racing Green with a white stripe instead.

Isla was meeting her boyfriend, Josh, in the Bullring, the huge indoor mall in the heart of Birmingham. Grant pulled over into a bus stop outside Primark on Moor Street, blipping the throttle before twisting the key to silence the sporty little car's engine.

Isla leaned across to kiss him quickly on the cheek before clambering out – 'God, this stupid car is so low' – and walking across the wide pavement to stand beneath the store's gleaming metal facade.

Grant hung on, just to make sure Josh wasn't going to stand his little girl up.

A tall lad of maybe seventeen or eighteen descended the steps to Isla's right, kissed her on the lips and slid an arm around her waist.

Grant watched indulgently. Kids in love, so sweet. Like he was at their age. Isla was so lucky to have him for her dad. At least *he* remembered what it was like to be carefree, to be young. Unlike Annie. Jesus, the woman was so uptight you could play her like a snare drum.

He snickered at his own joke. But the feeling didn't last. What would he do once Isla was eighteen? Once she'd gone to uni? Because despite his best efforts, he knew that was her destination. He'd be on his own in that poky little flat. He used to live in bloody Harborne, for God's sake!

His phone pinged. A message from a girl he'd super-liked on Tinder. Emily. Cute. Into festivals.

He smiled, messaged her back.

When he looked up again, Isla and Josh had disappeared into the night.

Chapter 28

Annie swiped away tears of frustration as she tried for the fifth time to complete the online cash transfer from her ISA. She needed the funds before she could even attempt to set up the standing order.

But every time she started anew, her fingers would start shaking and she'd mistype a detail.

With Isla gone, she'd turned on the TV for company but had been oblivious to the local news until the presenter started talking about the accident that morning. She looked up and leaned forward, her finances forgotten for a second.

The picture cut to a female police officer. Her petite frame was bulked out by all that equipment they seemed to wear these days. The caption at the foot of the screen said her name was PC Dawn Jaeger.

'We are keen to speak to the driver of a white Ford Transit van who struck Aaron Taylor at 8.35 this morning on the Westbourne Road. The van is likely to have significant damage to the front end. If anyone watching has seen such a vehicle, I would ask them to get in touch with me at Birmingham Central Police Station, or via Crimestoppers.'

The director cut back to the studio and the frowning presenter.

'Traffic cameras picked up the van's number plate and this image of the driver.'

The screen filled with a pixelated but still clear image of a man with sparse long hair flowing over his shoulders. He appeared to be wearing an army jacket of some kind. But the detail that shrieked from the TV screen was the hideous blackish-purple bruise spreading from his left eye all the way across to his temple.

As Annie stared at the image, her stomach dropped and sweat broke out all over her body. He looked ... *familiar*.

Was this the man who'd followed Isla? And scared her half to death? If it was, what did it mean? She paused the TV. Found her phone and opened the photo Isla had AirDropped her. Neither picture was pin sharp, but she was certain it was the same man. The bruise was identical in each image, as was the camouflage jacket.

Her breath was coming in shallow gasps and she pulled at the neck of her blouse. Heat welled up from her chest and she felt faint. She took a quick gulp of wine, coughing as it hit her windpipe by accident. But the jolt of alcohol did the trick and she managed to force down the dizzy feelings.

She texted Isla and then clutched her phone, staring at the screen, willing a grey bubble to pop up indicating a reply. Nothing. Not even a pulsing set of three dots in the bottom left corner. She called next, the last resort of the desperate parent.

It went straight to voicemail. Isla's sassy outbound message.

'Hey, it's Isla. You know what to do and when. Luv ya!'

The sound of her daughter's voice drew stinging tears.

'Shit!' she shouted into the empty living room.

She was out of options. She'd have to call the one man she'd walk over broken glass to avoid.

But Grant rejected the call.

She tried again. Surely even Grant would realise she needed him if she was prepared to call twice.

Call rejected.

Moaning softly, Annie leaned forward, cradling her head in her hands. She felt as if the floor beneath her feet was giving way, sending her tumbling down a helter-skelter into a very dark place indeed, where bad people kidnapped innocent teenage girls and hurt them. And not just girls, either. It looked like they'd tried to murder Aaron Taylor, too.

Sweat broke out on her face, her chest. Even the insides of her arms felt clammy. How big was this thing that had swept over her and Isla like a tsunami? Were there even *more* victims out there?

She caught her breath as an idea occurred to her. She could visit the boy in hospital. Talk to his parents. Ask if *they'd* received a video and threats, too.

But first she had to get that payment sorted.

She returned to her banking app, and this time successfully transferred the money into her current account. Concentrating furiously, she set up the standing order. The app told her it was working.

Holding her breath, she watched the spinning circle pulse through pink, purple and green. Finally, it stopped. A green tick appeared and the app emitted a cheerful ping. She sighed out of sheer relief. She'd done it. Isla would be safe for now at least.

She got up and grabbed her jacket. It was time to visit the hospital. A sudden upwelling of grief rocked her. The last time she'd gone to Queen Elizabeth's, it had been to sit with Juliet during one of her final chemotherapy sessions.

Tears flowing freely at the memory of her friend's cancer-ravaged body, she left the house, slamming the front door behind her.

Chapter 29

Isla hadn't been lying to Mum earlier. The creep with the black eye *had* scared her. But she wasn't going to let him stop her seeing Josh.

When she was out with Josh, she felt safe, free of the bloody buzz. He was gentle, not like that idiot Ronan. And he was a good listener. She could talk to him about her mental health without feeling like a freak. About how she worried she might lose Dad. Even though he did stuff like take her out for pizza and give her the Glasto tickets, he was obviously more interested in Melissa than her.

Beside her, Josh was rolling a cigarette. She held her fingers out. He frowned, just for a split second, then handed over the narrow cylinder of expertly twisted paper.

'If you like them so much, you should learn to roll them yourself.'

She pouted, before taking a quick puff and blowing a smoke ring into the cold night air.

'Don't need to, do I? That's what I've got you for.'

Josh shook his head. Smiled. God, he was so hot. None of the other girls had a boyfriend like him. Naomi's boyfriend was so young, only a year older than her, whereas Josh was nineteen.

They all wanted to know if she was doing it with him. She wasn't. Didn't need Mum to tell her that shagging an older boy when she was underage was like taking the expressway to a world of trouble. But there were other things they could do. Besides, adults were all so hung up on sex. Obsessed with it. What she and Josh had was special. It went deeper than just shagging.

They had a *connection*.

She smiled. Hugged his arm a little tighter.

He turned and smiled.

'What?'

'Nothing! Just enjoying being out with my boyfriend, that's all. Is that OK?'

He shrugged.

'I s'pose so. What do you want to do now? Another pub? That ID I got you works like a dream, doesn't it?'

She shook her head, tugged him into a narrow side street, checking out her reflection in a darkened office window as they turned.

'Nope. Got a better idea. There's a new club opened. The Iron Foundry. I got a DM about it from a mate on Instagram. Know it?'

He shook his head. 'I don't really do clubs. How about some food? We could get Thai?'

'I had pizza with my dad. Come on, Joshy, I really wanna go. What's the matter? Scared you'll get carded?'

He smiled.

'I'm not scared of anything. Except possibly your terrible impressions. Where is this club, then?'

'Down here,' she said, pleased to have got her own way. 'You'll love it, I promise.'

She dragged him down the alley to a plain steel door set into the grimy brickwork. No sign: only rubbish clubs needed to advertise. A lone man in black jacket, jeans and boots stood guard. Her tummy flickered with nervousness. Maybe he'd spot her fake ID. Should they go to a pub after all?

Too late.

He scrutinised their faces. Isla hoped he was going to let her in without checking her ID while asking for Josh's. No such luck.

'ID?'

She smiled brightly as she flashed the fake student card Josh had given her.

'Eighteen, yeah?' the bouncer said. 'Date of birth?

She stared him boldly in the face, ignoring the squirm of anxiety – this was more than just the buzz – and recited the date she'd memorised. It was the easiest way to fail the bouncer test: claim you were old enough then mess up the date.

He nodded her past him. He spent longer on Josh's ID, really checking it over and asking him a couple of extra questions. Isla grinned.

Pushing through the heavy door, she descended the narrow staircase, her boot heels clanging on the perforated metal treads. The light was provided by dim industrial-looking lamps screwed to the painted brick wall, which was sweating like human skin.

Behind her, Josh grumbled about the stink of the place. It was true, it was rank. Cold metal, mouldy concrete and a sort of stale water smell. But that was part of the experience. The way it would all change once you hit the dance floor.

At the foot of the staircase she turned left along a narrow, low-ceilinged corridor. Exposed pipes ran along the wall at head height, burbling and hissing as if filled with steam. The only illumination came from red lanterns bolted into iron cages every couple of metres. The distant thump of the music and the chemical smell of dry ice made her heart beat faster. She patted her pocket and strode on.

'Is it much further?' Josh asked from right behind her, searching for her hand and squeezing it in his.

'Through that door there,' she said. 'Not long before we can dance.'

On the other side of the matte-black steel door, they entered a dark lobby. At the far end, black velvet curtains waved gently to and fro. The music was louder now. A proper banger. Plenty of bass she could feel in her insides. A heavy riff that got into her head and made her want to give it all up to the DJ.

'Isla, this was a mistake,' Josh said anxiously. 'We should go. Come on, please.'

He tugged her hand, but she pulled it free. What was wrong with him? This was *the* club to be seen at. Apparently Tü Carly had been in after they played the O2 Academy. No way was she backing out now. Naomi would be so jealous. Not that that was why Isla was here. She wasn't *that* shallow. But you know, a side benefit.

She turned to Josh. He did look a bit pale. And his forehead was shiny with sweat, even though they hadn't even hit the dance floor yet.

'What's the matter, babe? You look like you're going to throw up? Is it your blood sugar? We should get you a Coke, maybe something to eat.'

She reached up to touch his forehead, but he slapped her hand away.

'No!'

She snatched her hand back, stunned by his flash of temper.

'Josh! What the hell?'

His face crumpled. Like he might actually cry. Behind them a group of clubbers entered the darkness. They had matching light-stick necklaces and they reeked of weed. Laughing hysterically, they pushed past Isla and Josh and flung the velvet curtains aside, admitting a gust of hot sweat-and-perfume-scented air.

'I'm sorry, Isla. I didn't mean to hurt you, it's just…'

'What? *Tell* me.'

'I'm claustrophobic, OK?' he blurted out. 'And to be fair, I'm not a massive fan of the dark either. There. I've told you. Happy now?'

Her heart melted. Was that it? Jesus, *everyone* had mental health issues. It was like part of your Gen Z identity. How come he was embarrassed about *that*? It was kind of endearing, though, she had to admit. Her older boyfriend, needing her to protect him from the bogeyman.

She reached out a finger and booped him on the tip of his nose. Looked up into those beautiful warm eyes and pushed his hair clear so she could see them properly.

'Stick with me, babe,' she said in a deep, serious voice. 'I'll protect you.'

She took his hand in hers. With her other hand, she reached into her pocket and took out the little baggie with its precious cargo. Extracting a blue pill stamped with a smiley face, she slipped it onto her tongue, then kissed him deeply, sliding the E from her mouth into his.

'This'll take all your fears away and replace them with joy,' she whispered, before kissing him again.

Chapter 30

Her gut churning with fear, Annie kept trying Isla's phone on hands-free as she drove to the hospital.

Where was she? Had something happened? Even if she was out clubbing with Naomi, surely she could at least send a quick message to say she was OK?

Riven with fears for her daughter's safety, she arrived at Queen Elizabeth's. Three vast circular glass towers loomed. Clad in grey, white and blue panes, they had the monumental look of the sterns of ocean liners. Below them, a sprawling horizontal fascia with the hospital's name in huge white capitals.

She parked and strode past two fruit and vegetable stalls to the main entrance. Its sweeping curved roof and expanse of glass resembled an airport terminal. As she hated flying, this did nothing to calm her fragile mood.

After learning that Aaron Taylor had been transferred from A&E to an orthopaedic ward, Annie rushed to Level 4. This was crazy, but she had to know if she was right. If she and the boy's family had been sucked down into a dark vortex of blackmail and threats to murder their children.

As she neared the ward, pulse bumping uncomfortably in her throat, she tried to come up with a way of asking what she wanted without being dismissed as a crank. But everything she tried sounded more insane rather than less. Finally, as she hugged the side wall to make room for a porter and nurse wheeling a patient in a bed, she decided that the truth would have to serve.

Another few steps brought her to the doors of Ward 410.

Facing her was a sign above a dispenser advising her to 'Use the gel'. Beside it, a poster instructing staff not to let people enter behind them, 'for patient safety and confidentiality'. An ID card reader similar to those in some of the university's departments. And a video entry phone.

She stuck her hands under the dispenser, received a cold spurt of hand sanitiser. She rubbed it in until her palms were dry, then pressed the button. Sucked in a quick breath.

'I'm here to see Aaron Taylor. I'm a friend of the family.'

'Visiting hours have finished, I'm afraid. They start again at nine tomorrow morning. Sorry, but you'll have to come back then.'

Annie panicked. Why hadn't she realised they wouldn't let people come in at any hour of the night?

'Please. I'm . . .' her mind raced, 'his godmother. I only just found out about his accident.'

A huge lie she hoped wouldn't come back to bite her. Ten seconds passed. The latch hummed. She was in.

She rounded a dog-leg in a long, featureless corridor and found herself in the quiet of a hospital ward at night-time. Staff in different-coloured uniforms – bottle-green, navy, turquoise, burgundy – walked purposefully from bay to bay, stopping at the nurses' station to hand in forms or blood samples. A display behind the desk flashed yellow on its topmost row as a matching bleep indicated someone had hit the call button.

Annie approached the desk. A harassed-looking young woman in a pale blue tunic looked up, offered a tired smile.

'You're here to see Aaron, right?'

'I've been so worried.'

The nurse nodded, eyes flicking between Annie and the screen in front of her.

'Side room 3, just down the corridor. His dad's with him.'

Annie thanked her and moved away, wiping her palms, clammy again, on her trousers. She'd lied to a nurse to get in to see a boy injured in a hit-and-run. Part of her wanted to turn and flee before the lie caught up with her. But she forced herself to keep walking. She *had* to know.

She paused outside the door, shook her head and pasted a smile onto her face. Wiped it off again. What was she thinking? Aaron had almost been killed. There was nothing to smile about.

She knocked gently and opened the door. Stifled a gasp.

In the white-railed bed, a boy lay hooked up to a couple of machines. The blue-white light turned his skin grey. His eyes were bruised and his nose was swollen around an ugly cut sutured with spidery black thread. For one nightmarish instant, Annie imagined it was her own child lying there before her.

A man stood up as she entered, closing the door behind her. Was this the boy's father? He had to be. Only a parent could look that shattered. Bags under his eyes, and stubble on his jaw that spoke of fatigue and inattention to his own needs. She knew how he felt. That desperate, dogged determination to protect your child at all costs.

'Can I help you?' he asked.

He sounded exhausted, but still wary. He glanced at her chest. At first, confused, she thought he was checking her out. Then she realised. He was looking for her NHS ID.

It was now or never. She inhaled quickly and spoke on the out breath.

'I'm not a doctor. My name is Annie Barnes. I work at the university. I am so sorry about what happened to your son.' She glanced at Aaron, who was sleeping. 'To Aaron. I saw it on the news. It's actually quite a coincidence, because I was in the traffic jam this morning after it happened. The accident, I mean.'

She swallowed. She was making a complete dog's dinner of the most important conversation she'd probably ever had. Focused on getting the words out as plainly as possible.

'I saw the photo of the van driver and I think he was stalking my daughter yesterday. She was so frightened she rang me to come and get her. I believe we are both ... I mean, both our families are being targeted by some sort of ...' She bit her lip. Now for the part where he'd either sink into a chair, shocked by her revelation, or throw her out. 'I know this sounds weird, but I think we're being targeted by an organised crime group.'

He frowned, swiped a hand across his face. His features settled into a hard expression.

'Look, Alice, was it?'

'Annie.'

'Annie, then. My son *was* almost killed this morning. But it was a road accident, not some gangland thing. He was hit by a moron who was probably texting instead of paying attention to where he was going. That's all. You need to leave. Right now.'

He stepped round the end of the bed. His jaw was set, his gaze unwavering. Annie's pulse was racing and she had to fight the instinct to flee. But she stood her ground. One more try. She was desperate.

'Please. Just … just hear me out. Has a woman contacted you to demand money recently? Threatening Aaron if you refused? If she didn't call you, did she call your wife?'

There. She saw it. The recognition in his expression. His eyes flickered up to the ceiling and back to hers. She'd struck a nerve, and now he'd tell her and they could work out what to do about this obscene threat to their children together.

But his face was suffused with anger, maybe even hatred. His fists balled at his sides, though she was relieved to see he kept them there.

'How dare you come here asking questions about my wife? Do you really work at the university? I didn't see any ID. Are you a journalist?'

He pushed the call button.

Annie backed away until she hit the wall. She held her hands out in surrender.

'Please listen. Our kids are in danger, surely you can see that?' she gabbled. 'You have to help me stop her. Did she demand money from you or your wife? You have to tell me!'

'Get the fuck out of my son's room.'

'But we're being targeted. We need to do something.'

He closed the distance between them to a few inches. He smelled of stale sweat and, oddly, sawdust.

'Get. OUT!'

Beside her, the door flew open. A forty-something woman in navy-blue tunic and trousers stood there, arms folded, glaring at Annie. In her hand, a walkie-talkie of some kind, chirruping like a trapped bird.

'You need to leave right now. This young man has been very seriously injured and you are endangering his recovery.'

She held the door wide. Defeated, Annie bowed her head and stepped through.

Into the waiting grip of a pair of burly security guards wearing ribbed sweaters, heavy boots and grim expressions.

Chapter 31

Annie staggered onto the pavement as one of the guards gave her a firm shove between her shoulder blades. Being strong-armed out of an NHS hospital like a Friday-night drunk added embarrassment and shame to the fear and confusion roiling in her breast.

Back in her car, cheeks flaring, she slapped her palm down on the steering wheel, hissing out a breath at the pain.

The way Aaron's dad had reacted when she'd asked him about demands for money was proof enough. She was sure of it – they were connected by the threats to their children. Yet for some reason, he hadn't wanted to admit it. Why? Surely there was strength in numbers? Or if not strength, at least the idea that two heads were better than one. Because, frankly, alone she was fresh out of ideas. And scared. Very scared.

She started the car and pulled away, calling Isla again as she rejoined the traffic on New Fosse Way. Again it went straight to voicemail.

As she listened, she willed Isla to interrupt herself with a cheerful 'Hi, Mum! What's up?' But the message just played out, to be followed by a bleep.

A blast on the horn from an oncoming yellow car startled her. She'd drifted halfway across the centre line. Its panicked driver was flashing their lights, half blinding her.

She swore, heaving the wheel over and regaining the safety of her side of the road as the other driver blew past, the horn screaming in a descending howl as they crossed.

Heart pounding against her ribs, she made a sudden decision. She wasn't going to go home, to sit drinking wine, worrying and calling Isla every five minutes. She'd go direct to Grant's and collect her daughter herself.

Hang the divorce settlement and the custody rights section. Let Grant take it up with the judge if he wanted to. Annie would have a few choice words of her own about his lack of communication and inattention to the basics of good parenting.

But when she arrived, Grant's flat was in darkness. No reply from the entryphone, into which she shouted that Isla's safety was at risk. That surely would have had him responding, however much he'd been enjoying rejecting her calls.

Feeling powerless, frightened and very much alone, she returned to the car and settled in to wait for either Grant or Isla to make an appearance. She wanted more than anything to call the police, but the threatening female voice sounded its ominous warning in her head like a refrain.

If you call the police, Isla will die.

Chapter 32

Beautiful.

Everybody at the Iron Foundry was just so *beautiful*.

The boys. The girls. The ones who'd rejected all of that binary stuff in order to go their own way. Beautiful. She'd never felt so alive, so, so … alove. Haha. Not a word.

Even her anxiety had decided to take a holiday. She hoped the buzz was somewhere nice and sunny. A beach somewhere hot. Maybe she and Joshy could go on holiday in the summer once all the exams were out of the way. The thought of exams caused a momentary flicker of nerves deep in her belly, but she focused on nice things like Ekaterini told her to and they went away again.

Isla danced, letting the love wash through her, smiling at everyone moving to the beat around her. So cool to be free of all that grief at home and worrying Dad would go somewhere far away and she'd never see him again. It wasn't even Mum's fault, she knew it deep down, but that story about people threatening her wasn't helpful. Even that guy following her was probably just some mixed-up addict or a wino looking for a connection or just a couple of quid for a coffee.

She followed Josh as he weaved his way through the dancers to the bar, staring straight into a pretty stream of pinky-purple light that swept the dance floor like a searchlight from space picking out all the beauty on earth. Even climate change couldn't stop it. And for once thinking of all that wasn't even a teeny bit sad – they'd find a way.

Someone touched her lightly on the shoulder, the contact setting off electric sparks right on the surface of her hot, slick skin. She turned lazily, arms above her head, to smile at the stranger.

'Oh hey, Ronan, nice shirt. This is so cool, isn't it, do you love the music, I think the DJ's crushing it, don't you?'

Ronan nodded enthusiastically. Put his hands on her waist. His palms were hot, her skin molten like volcanic lava.

'Dance with me?'

'Sure,' she agreed readily, loving his soft, beautiful smile.

She closed her eyes and swayed in place, and time slowed down or maybe speeded up and then Ronan was kissing her and she opened her eyes with a start.

'Don't, Ronan! Don't spoil it, let's just dance.'

He didn't answer. Instead he spun away from her, whipping all the way round till he was facing away from her.

Rude.

No, he wasn't being rude, it was Josh, back from the bar with two bottles of water. He didn't look very happy, in fact he looked really pissed off with Ronan, mouthing something Isla couldn't hear. No, baby, she wanted to say to him, don't kill the mood.

Then Ronan was gone.

She felt panicky and the bliss of her high was turning sour. The colours dulling from pinks and purples to greys and browns. She needed to reassure Josh. He couldn't break up with her over a drunken snog. He couldn't!

'It was Ronan, Josh. I think he's drunk. It wasn't my idea. I'm sure he didn't mean anything.'

'It looked like it meant something to him.'

Oh God, Josh was really hurt. What had she done?

'I swear. He's just this wannabe gangster. He's such a loser. You're my boy, not him, OK?'

'You mean that?'

'Of course I do. A hundred per cent.'

Josh smiled and handed her a water. 'I know, Isla. It's fine. Come on. You wanted to dance, so let's dance.'

Her spirits lifted, she smiled up at him. Yes, it was going to be fine after all. She took a massive swig of her water, then stretched out for Josh's hand, and as she led her gorgeous, cute and, OK, maybe a little bit of a scaredy-cat boyfriend deeper into the centre of the dance floor, she screamed from joy. Pure joy...

...and she thinks to herself, *I am safe here and this is what love feels like*. And she raises her arms above her head and sways as that deep groove winds itself around her brain and her spine all the way down every limb and into her feet, and then she's kissing Josh passionately and he smells sooo good and *Look at me*, she wants to shout, *I am Isla Madeleine Barnes and I am worth it*, and she dances like she'll never ever be sad or anxious ever again and she feels the love as everyone turns their eyes towards her...

The tattooed young woman behind the bar watched the young girl dancing. She recognised the symptoms. Sweet, really, how a little pill and some drum and bass could make your worries fly away.

The trouble was, they always came back.

Chapter 33

Annie woke with a start. She jerked upright, then fell back as the seat belt dug painfully into her collarbone. Her phone was ringing. She'd fallen asleep in her car. She checked the dashboard clock: 11.41 p.m. Her cheek was wet. She'd been dreaming of Juliet. The two of them laughing in a bar. Juliet had been healthy – round-cheeked and beautiful.

As she struggled to find her phone, she looked up at the flat. Still dark. Where *was* Grant? And where was Isla?

A flash of light from the side of her seat caught her eye. She retrieved her phone: it must have slipped out when she was dozing. No messages from her feckless ex-husband or her daughter. But who was calling her this late at night?

No caller ID. She swallowed. The blackmailer again. Her pulse started racing. With a trembling hand, she accepted the call and raised the phone to her ear.

'Hello?' she said quietly.

'Mrs Barnes?' A young woman. Scottish. 'Mrs Annie Barnes?'

'Yes. Who is this?'

'My name is Melanie,' the woman said. 'I work for Santander in the fraud department. Is everything all right?'

Annie's pulse began to slow down.

'What? Oh, yes. Sorry. I thought you were somebody else.'

'OK.' A pause. 'Well, I'm calling you because we detected suspicious activity on your account earlier this evening.'

'But it's twenty to midnight!'

'It's a twenty-four-hour operation. Santander takes financial crime against our customers very seriously.'

Annie glanced up at the flat again. Still dark.

'Yes, but I don't understand. What do you mean, "suspicious activity"?'

'First I need to take you through security. Let's start with your memorable date.'

Annie was about to give Isla's date of birth, then stopped abruptly. Who was to say the woman wasn't part of the extortion gang?

'I'll call you back,' she said. 'Sorry, but you could be anyone.'

She hung up, googled the bank's details and rang the number for the fraud department.

A different woman answered.

'Hi, this is Ella. How can I help you?'

Annie explained about the call she'd received. The woman agreed that it might sound suspicious and that she'd been right to call back if she was worried, but then reassured her that it was all perfectly above board. She took her through the usual tedious rigmarole of remembering secret numbers and giving details of her first pet.

'So what's this all about?' Annie asked finally.

'Earlier today, you attempted to set up a standing order to a bank in the Cayman Islands for one thousand pounds a month, is that correct?'

Annie's insides sent up a warning flare.

'I didn't "attempt" to do anything. I *did* set it up. The app flashed up a green tick.'

'Yes, well it would have done. Just to show you'd completed the form correctly. But international transactions, especially regular payments, get flagged to us and we have to investigate. It's all part of our duty of care to customers. As of now, the payment is on hold.'

'It's genuine, I swear it. Listen, you have to approve it by midnight. This is really important.'

Annie checked the clock again: 11.46. Plenty of time to clear up the error.

'Why by midnight, Mrs Barnes? Has someone you haven't spoken to before asked you to make this payment?'

She tried to stay calm, even though her breath was coming in short little gasps. At least this wouldn't be a lie.

'No.'

'OK, well I need to take you through some questions.'

'Look, I appreciate your concern, but I'm afraid I really don't have time for this. Can you just approve the standing order, please?'

'It's for your own protection, madam,' the woman said primly.

Annie's right hand was shaking. She switched to hands-free and dropped the phone into her lap.

'Fine. Ask your questions. But please hurry.'

'Can I ask what the money is for?'

She blanked. What could she say? A charity? Offshore gambling? A family member in the Caymans?

Inspiration struck. Her lie earlier about her relationship to Aaron Taylor.

'It's my godson. He's doing voluntary work there and I'm supporting him financially. His parents are very poor.'

'OK, well that sounds very kind of you. Did your godson ask you to set up the standing order?'

'No. I offered.'

'OK, that's good. And has anyone told you to lie to us about the payments or to keep them a secret?'

'No.'

She glanced at the clock. 11.49. Ten minutes left. Surely they'd be done soon?

Question followed question. To each one, Annie answered with the 'I'm not a gullible fool' option: 'yes' or 'no' as appropriate.

Finally it was over.

'Thank you for your patience and your understanding, Mrs Barnes. It's our job to make sure you aren't the victim of financial crime.'

Annie forced herself to stay calm, however much her stomach was churning and her ears were ringing.

'I understand, and thank you. So you can approve the standing order?'

'Yes, of course.'

She could have wept with relief. She picked up her phone to end the call. But the woman was still speaking.

'I just need to contact our international department. It shouldn't take long. Are you all right to hold?'

'No! I mean, for how long? This is quite important. They … my godson, I mean, he needs this money quite urgently.'

'Oh, it shouldn't take long. A few minutes. I'll be right back.'

Overloud classical music blared through the speaker, making Annie flinch. Panicking, she looked at the dashboard clock again. 11.57.

Oh Jesus, this couldn't be happening. She twisted round in her seat, looking back down the road, then ahead. Up at the flat windows, back at the phone. No lights on, no messages, no sign of Isla. This was it, then. They'd taken her. They'd taken Isla and they were going to kill her. All because Annie had wasted time when she should have been paying them off straight away.

11.58.

Her stomach rolled again, as if she'd eaten something bad.

11.59.

'Mrs Barnes?'

'Yes?' she gasped, clutching the phone so tight the edges hurt her palm.

'That's all done for you. Was there anything else I can help you with tonight?'

How about a couple of Valium and a stiff whisky?

'No, you've been very helpful. Thank you.'

She dropped the phone into her lap and sat there shaking.

A loud knock on the window startled her. She reared up and looked sideways, into Grant's puzzled face.

She opened the window.

'What the hell're you doing here?' he said, breathing alcohol fumes into her face.

Annie climbed out, not wanting to be at a height disadvantage to Grant. Or Melissa, for that matter, who was standing behind him in a dress so short there'd be no need to hoick it up to have a pee.

All of a sudden, the humiliation he'd inflicted on her when he'd shagged Vicky Hill flooded back. Those sideways looks in the playground. The whispers she could still hear. Her cheeks flared as if it had happened that morning. Then anger took over. How *dare* he?

'Where's Isla?' she shouted.

Grant patted the air.

'Keep your voice down, Annie. You'll wake the neighbours.'

'Where is she, Grant?'

His eyes slid sideways towards Melissa. But she was clearly unwilling or unable to help him out.

'She's ... she's ...' His eyes slid sideways and a grin spread across his face as he pointed past Annie's shoulder. 'Over there!'

Annie spun round, and there was Isla. Weaving down the centre of the road, smiling and singing, eye make-up smeared all over the place and clearly off her face on some pill or other. Annie ran to her.

'Oh my God, Isla,' she exclaimed, hugging her fiercely. 'Where have you been? You *did* go to a club, didn't you? After I told you not to.'

Isla offered a dreamy smile.

'Sorry, Mum. I love you, though. Can we go home now, please?'

Annie read Grant the riot act, then bundled Isla into the back seat and drove home. By the time they reached the end of their road, she'd calmed down. No harm had come to Isla, and the standing order was in place.

The danger was over. For now, at least.

Day Four

Chapter 34

As Lucy bent over Aaron's bed and stroked his cheek, Michael smiled with relief. She wasn't dead after all. Everything was going to be OK. Then she turned and stared at him, her eyes ablaze.

'You need to take better care of Aaron, Mike. I mean, look at the state of him.' Her eyes darkened to black and her lips drew back from her teeth. 'He looks like fucking DEATH!'

He woke with a start, crying out, drenched in sweat, and pushed himself upright in the armchair they'd wheeled in for him to sleep on. Lucy was still there, in the corner, mocking him. His heart jerked in his chest. He scrubbed his eyes and looked again. It was just a shadow on the wall.

Panting, he got to his feet and crossed to Aaron's bed. Laid the backs of his fingers against the boy's cheek. It had turned a kaleidoscopic mix of blues, purples and reds, but it was cool to the touch. Aaron mumbled in his sleep. Michael bent closer, but the sounds were just nonsense words.

He checked the time – 5.21 a.m. Sleep wouldn't come now. He went to make himself a hot drink. As he stirred the scalding but otherwise revolting hospital coffee, his son's insistent claim assailed him again. *Some weirdo tried to kill me. Why won't you believe me?*

Was it possible? Could the van driver have been targeting him deliberately? Trying to murder him? Aaron had been there, Michael hadn't. Nor had PC Jaeger. He tried to approach it logically, practically. What did he actually know?

Some idiot had appeared out of nowhere and almost killed Aaron. And Dawn – that was what the cop had insisted he call her, even though he couldn't help but think of her as PC Jaeger

– had told him they were investigating. But she made it sound routine. Just some low-level criminal who'd nicked a van and didn't want to get caught, most likely.

Aaron had said the guy was following him. Giving him an evil look. But the idea that he'd been targeted was ridiculous. After all, who would want to murder an eighteen-year-old schoolboy? This wasn't London. Or Manchester. Sure, Birmingham had its rough spots, but that was precisely why he and Lucy had chosen Harborne. It was just Aaron's overstressed imagination trying to impose order on chaos.

He shook his head and took a cautious sip of the coffee. He'd been down this kind of rabbit hole once before, with Lucy. Making up fantastical scenarios because accepting the truth was too painful. In all of them, the doctors had made a mistake. *We're sorry, Mr and Mrs Taylor, the MRI was malfunctioning. It's just migraines.*

He'd lost Lucy, and he'd come to terms with that. Not good terms, but he was functioning. He couldn't compromise that, or his fragile relationship with Aaron, by giving in to anxiety about murder plots. And as for that woman bursting in like that. She'd probably just got out of the psych ward. One of those sad cases off their meds and pouring out their paranoid fantasies to complete strangers.

He shook his head. Said, 'No,' aloud, several times. And went back to his son's bedside.

Three hours passed, and then, after a great deal of form-filling, Aaron was discharged.

After sliding the passenger seat all the way back, Michael helped him climb up into the Ranger's cab, juggling crutches and a small green plastic carrier bag of pills. What had the nurse called them as she handed them over? TTO, that was it. Tablets to take out. Sister Danni had explained what they all did, and the various doses. Painkillers, mostly.

That was it. Apart from a recommendation to check in with

the GP in a week or so and to come back to A&E immediately if Aaron experienced double vision, unexplained stomach pains or severe headaches that didn't respond to paracetamol. A miracle really, the discharging doctor had said, just like Sister Danni. Put it down to teenage physical resilience and a whopping great dose of good luck.

Sitting up high in the Ranger's cab, Michael usually felt invulnerable. But today, bringing Aaron back home after a night's observation, he'd never felt so powerless.

He shoved these intrusive thoughts down for now.

'How are you feeling, mate?' he asked, easing the pickup carefully onto a roundabout, triple-checking for white Transit vans veering crazily into their path.

'Bit stiff. I keep finding new places that hurt.'

'Yeah, Sister Danni said you might feel sore for a few days as the bruises come out. And that leg, well, it's not the worst kind of break but it's bound to be a bit painful, right?'

Aaron nodded ruefully. Scrunched the plastic carrier bag on his lap with a crackle.

'Lucky for me I've got more drugs here than Joe Barras.'

'Joe Barras?'

'School dealer.'

Michael shot a glance to his left.

'At the college?'

'Everywhere! It isn't like when you were at school.' He heard the unspoken line – *in the olden days*. 'Kids do stuff.'

'Yeah? Well, we did stuff, too. Your old man even smoked a bit of dope back in the day.'

'Dope? What is this, the seventies?' Aaron laughed, then winced and clutched his side. 'Ow, my chest.'

'It's going to hurt for a while. Nothing to be done with cracked ribs, either. They don't even bother strapping them these days.'

Bantering gently, both avoiding anything too sensitive, they negotiated the traffic and the damaged parts of their relationship.

'We'll need to get you set up for home-learning for a few days,' he said. 'Do you want me to speak to the college?'

'Could you?'

'Of course. It's not as if they don't have the resources, not after lockdown. The doctor said you should take a week off minimum, but if you need longer, that's cool. I'll square it with the school. I'm sure they'll just be glad to hear you're OK.'

'Thanks.' A beat. 'Dad.'

Michael flicked his head round, but Aaron had turned away to look out the side window. His ears hadn't deceived him, though. Maybe things were going to be all right between them. He hoped so. It was just the two of them now.

He looked ahead. Fear flashed through him. Waiting at a side street, a white Transit edged forward, its front wheels tiptoeing across the dotted white lines marking the limits of its right of way.

Fear curdled Michael's good mood, and he leaned on the horn before swerving away from the van. As he passed it, he looked across Aaron to the driver, a black guy with a heavy beard and a look of outrage on his face, hands upraised.

'What the hell?' Aaron exclaimed.

'Sorry. I saw the van and, you know…'

Aaron whipped his head round. 'Oh. I get it. Maybe let's just get home in one piece, though. One car accident is enough, yeah?'

He was going for a bantering tone, but Michael caught a note of fear just beneath the surface. Forcing himself to smile, though it felt like his cheeks might simply fracture, he nodded and drove on. Aaron had called it an accident, presumably to reassure him. But his fears were rising like an incoming tide. What if the lad was right? What if the woman at the hospital wasn't a psychiatric patient at all? No. He was just overreacting. He'd been summoned to Aaron's bedside by the police. He'd barely had any sleep. Then there'd been that awful nightmare about Lucy. He just needed to get a decent cup of coffee inside him. And a grip.

He checked the mirrors. His pulse rate spiked. How long had the white van been following them?

He swung the wheel hard over and screeched into a side street without indicating. As Aaron swore loudly, clutching his damaged ribs, Michael checked the mirrors again. Sighed. The van was gone.

His right leg had started trembling, making it hard to keep his foot steady on the throttle. Somehow he made it back to the sanctuary of their gated estate without any more incidents. As he pulled up in the drive, his phone rang.

'Yes, Chris, what is it?'

'Can you come in, Mike? We've got a tiny bit of a crisis developing here.'

'Can't you handle it? I've just got back from the hospital with Aaron.'

He looked at Aaron, rolled his eyes, mouthed, 'Work.'

'The thing is, Mike, there's been...' Chris cleared his throat. 'Well, there's no easy way to put this. There's been a fight. Couple of the guys got into it on the shop floor. I managed to separate them, but I could really do with some help. You know HR isn't my strong point.'

Michael sighed. 'I'll be there as soon as I can. Just... hold the fort until then, yes?'

He turned to Aaron, who was easing himself down from the Ranger's high cab, cast stuck out in front of him.

'Mate, I am so sorry. I'm going to have to go in.'

'It's fine. I'll just get some rest till you're back.'

Michael shook his head. 'No. I'm not leaving you on your own. I'll get auntie Jodie to come over.'

Aaron looked outraged. 'I'm eighteen. I don't need a babysitter.'

'She won't be babysitting,' Michael said. 'Think of it as a... concierge service. She can make you a cheese toastie, get you comfortable. You know she loves you like you were her own.'

'I'll be fine.'

'I know you will. I just want to know there's someone here with you.' He stepped closer and took his son by the shoulders. Stared into eyes in which for a fleeting second he saw Lucy's proud gaze. 'I nearly lost you yesterday, Aaron. Please let me do this. Just so I can go to work and bail Chris out of yet another mess without worrying about you, too. I love you, you know.'

Aaron stood passively, overtopping Michael by an inch or so. Then he nodded, smiled quietly. 'I love you, too. And, you know, thanks. For having my back.'

Michael smiled back, with love, but mostly, just this once, with relief, too.

Maybe things were going to be OK between them after all.

Chapter 35

Annie gripped the steering wheel with her left hand.

She used her right to scrub at her eyes, which felt as though the Sandman had run out of his usual materials and used powdered glass instead. The dashboard clock read 8.25 a.m. If they made it to Isla's appointment at the Oaks on time it would be a miracle. And all because Isla had lied to her the previous night.

Annie had sat up half the night while Isla came down off the drugs before falling into a deep and apparently peaceful sleep. She, on the other hand, had only dozed fitfully, waking every ten or fifteen minutes to check on her daughter. Somewhere after 5 a.m., she had finally succumbed to fatigue, only to sleep right through her alarm.

She tried to resist the urge to shout. It was just sleep deprivation, she told herself. And Isla was hardly the first teenager to experiment with drugs and lie about it to her parents. Then she remembered Grant's drunken, mocking cry as she'd hauled Isla into the car to take her home. *Oops. You've done it now, Isles. Mum's in one of her moods.*

That did it. Her anger at the previous night's antics resurfaced like a slumbering volcano erupting.

'How could you have been so stupid, Isla? I told you I wanted you with me so I could keep an eye on you, and what do you do? Go swanning out to a club. And you lied to me about it, too.'

Isla folded her arms. 'I didn't lie. You asked me if I was going clubbing with Naomi and I said no. Because I wasn't.'

Annie glanced across at her. Isla's lawyerly little tactics sometimes worked. She even admired her for them. But not this morning.

'Who *were* you out with, then?'

'Just friends. It was fine.'

'But you'd taken something, love, hadn't you? Your pupils were huge.'

'Mum, please. Look, I accidentally took two of the pills they prescribe me at the Oaks, that's all. I went a little woozy but I was fine.'

Annie had no doubt she was lying. But after the relief at getting the standing order sorted, she felt she could afford to cut her daughter a little slack, just this once. And, after all, she *was* fine. Or at least no worse than she'd be without having taken something.

Drawing up in front of the Oaks, she stepped out into the cold autumnal air and stared up at the clinic's logo, applied to the flat brick face of the building in sage-green letters two feet tall.

If there ever had been oaks here, they'd been chopped down a long time ago. The area in front of the three-storey yellow-brick building was taken up entirely with the car park, stuffed today, as on every one of their previous visits, with high-end 4x4s, sleek German saloons – both bigger and more expensive than hers – and even, today, an angular scarlet sports car. From the looks of it, something Italian.

Charitably, she'd call the style of the building 'functional'. On days like today, severely sleep-deprived and disinclined to be charitable, she'd call it as she saw it. Ugly. An ugly building full of therapists and their patients trying to undo even uglier things, from eating disorders and panic attacks to self-harming, anxiety and depression.

They entered the calm interior, signed in and took their seats in the waiting room. Soft ambient music and a calming floral scent filled the air. Around them, well-dressed women and a lone man in a business suit looking uncomfortable sat in cream leather armchairs. Beside them, teenage children, all of whom appeared to be wishing fervently they were anywhere else but here. Heads down, listening to music like Isla, picking skin from their fingertips, chewing hair, fidgeting with little plastic gizmos.

So much misery in such a privileged generation. Annie felt despair for them. How had it happened in one of the richest countries on earth that they couldn't even keep their children happy? Was it lockdown? Or something deeper, more pervasive? Something to do with the relentless and insidious pressure of social media?

A thirty-something woman with sharp cheekbones and large, quizzical eyes popped her head around a pale wooden door. Ekaterini, Isla's therapist. Friendly, smart and, in other circumstances, someone Annie could have imagined being mates with.

Ekaterini smiled at Isla, who sensed her gaze even though she'd got her head down as her thumbs danced over her phone screen.

'Isla? Ready?'

Isla nodded, got to her feet and entered Ekaterini's office without a backward glance.

Annie sighed. Checked her own phone, then, irritated for reasons she couldn't quite fathom, stuck it in her bag again.

She desperately wanted to protect her daughter, but she had to acknowledge that Isla was growing up fast. Too fast, maybe. And yes, Annie had been just the same at her age. God, the rows she'd had with her own mum. Everything had been a battleground, from the length of her school skirt to the character of her boyfriends.

But nobody had been stalking her back in 1997. It was a simpler time. No smartphones. No internet, not really. Definitely no social media. She and her mates used to sneak off to the pub and even the odd club. They used to compare themselves against pictures of models or the in-crowd at school, but they weren't constantly having to measure themselves against every girl in the entire world.

Staring at the closed door of Ekaterini's office, she wondered what Isla was saying about her. Could imagine all too easily.

Controlling... No freedom... Always in my face... Threw Dad out... I feel so alone.

Worst of all, she might be telling Ekaterini that Annie was even trying to frighten her into staying at home with some crazy story of blackmailers trying to hurt her. How she couldn't even enjoy a night out with her bestie.

In the silence of the waiting room, her own best friend's face floated up from Annie's subconscious. Not the pain-ravaged one, or the drug-sedated one, but the laughing girl she'd got to know just after graduating. God, the times they'd had. She sniffed, reached into her bag for a tissue and blew her nose.

A movement in the corner of her eye made her turn.

A woman of about her own age settled into the armchair Isla had vacated. Annie gave her an appreciative glance. Flawless make-up that must have taken an age to apply. Immaculate nails: white-tipped pink ovals that Annie could imagine clicking on the keyboard of a brand-new MacBook. Gems that had to be real diamonds sparkled on her ear lobes and at her throat. Was she the owner of the Italian sports car outside?

She leaned over and Annie caught a whisper of her perfume, something expensive and musky.

'Self-harming?'

Annie pulled her head back.

'I'm sorry?'

'Cora has panic attacks. Its's awful. She can hardly breathe, poor love. How about you? You're Isla's mum, aren't you?'

'I ... I'm sorry. I don't want to talk about my daughter right now.' She got to her feet. 'Excuse me.'

The woman tutted, shook her head and went back to her phone.

Annie approached the reception desk to ask for some tea. The woman in the neighbouring seat was dreadful. Talk about oversharing.

With a freshly made cup of tea in hand, she moved to a different chair and took out her phone again. Stared at the screen with all those inviting little red circles with white numbers. All those notifications. All those comments, likes and shares.

Her finger hovered over the Facebook icon. She was about to begin a process that would take up most of the hour, methodically visiting each social media platform in turn.

She frowned. Withdrew her fingertip.

Oversharing.

Had *she* been oversharing? About Isla?

Dread settling over her like a clammy grey cloak, she started scrolling back through her Facebook and Instagram posts for the last couple of years. Hundreds of posts, all mentioning her daughter.

The pictures spun by, and with each new image, Annie's own anxiety deepened.

Here was Isla in her taekwondo outfit.

And here they were on the sofa: *#BingeingRealHousewives.*

Isla and Naomi making faces for the camera: *Isla and Naomi: a girl needs her bestie!*

She placed her phone back in her bag with a trembling hand, a horrifying sense of guilt descending on her. You put yourself out there, on Facebook, on Instagram. It was normal. You bared your soul, from triumphs to tragedies, and your friends showed they cared. You got the little pats on the back, the messages of sympathy and support – *You got this hun x* – that made you feel, just for that moment, like you weren't alone.

But all the time, skulking in the shadows on the other side of your screen, predators were lurking, sucking up your life, feeding off it, turning it to their advantage.

Yes, now she knew how the blackmailer had found out so much about Isla.

Annie had told her.

Chapter 36

Michael ran upstairs to his home office, shaking his head at the prospect of dealing with two brawling workers. He grabbed his bag, almost spilling its contents as the strap caught on the bottom and upended it. Swearing, he stopped to refasten the flap, then headed for the door, glancing out of the window as he crossed the room.

Something was moving outside the house. Just a shimmer in the light beneath a tall birch tree, a change in intensity. But he caught it all the same.

He peered down. And saw him. Definitely a man. Loitering across the road. His head was turned towards the house, although his face was in deep shadow. Alarmed, Michael stepped back hurriedly.

Aaron was ensconced in his room and Michael's sister Jodie had just arrived, so there was no immediate danger, but it was unsettling all the same.

Or was he just being paranoid? After all, he'd almost crashed twice on the way home from the hospital, seeing danger in random white vans whose drivers were completely innocent.

Edging up to the window from one side, his back pressed flat against the wall, he peered round the window frame and down at the far side of the street. He was sure now that he'd either imagined it, or the poor guy had just stepped out for a cigarette. His wife probably wouldn't let him smoke indoors. He smiled. But it didn't take, and his lip trembled with tension.

The man was still there. Only now he'd moved out from the shadows and was looking at the house. It was him. The guy from the CCTV images. Dark bruising spreading over half his face.

Long, lank hair, scruffy beard and that flak jacket. Oh God, it was the guy who'd tried to murder Aaron. Aaron hadn't been imagining things. The woman at the hospital wasn't crazy. She'd been telling the truth all along. And now he had proof.

Enraged, Michael ran for the stairs, hurtling down them three at a time, almost falling as his leading foot missed a step before rushing out the back door.

He slipped out of the garden gate into a little lane that ran behind all the gardens, knocking an overhanging branch heavy with last night's rain that sent a shower of icy droplets down onto the top of his head. Keeping his tread as light as possible, he made his way along the lane until he emerged from a gap in a hedge on the corner.

A high, curving brick wall gave him a limited amount of cover. He edged his way along it, praying that none his neighbours would spot him and call out a greeting. Or, more likely given the collective anxiety about the threat of 'undesirables' disrupting their estate's peace and quiet, asking if everything was OK.

Which it absolutely, positively was not.

Not in any way.

It was time to act. Time to confront this intruder and if necessary beat the truth out of him.

He stepped out from the shadow of the wall and began walking on the balls of his feet towards the man. Ten yards. He strove to keep his breathing under control, though his pulse was skittering. Seven. His vision dimmed momentarily. He blinked it clear. Five. He bunched his fists. Three. Two.

His foot clipped a pebble, which clattered along the tarmac.

The guy whirled round, eyes narrowed.

Michael's heart thumped in his chest and a roaring in his ears blotted out all other sound. For a second, he thought the prowler was going to attack him. But instead he spun round and ran.

'Stop, you bastard!' Michael yelled, and sprinted after him, teeth gritted as he summoned every ounce of strength to close the gap.

But the guy was a strong runner and was soon drawing away from him.

Arms pumping, Michael tore after him. Little by little, as they pounded down the centre of the road, he gained on his quarry. Spurred on by his anger, he found an additional burst of speed and caught up with him at a sloping T-junction.

He threw himself forward and grabbed onto the man's trailing leg in a clumsy rugby tackle. The two of them tumbled to the ground in a flailing mass of tangled limbs. The impact as he thumped down onto the tarmac drove the breath from Michael's lungs. But seconds later he was back on his feet and chasing his man down again. The guy must have hurt his leg in the collision, because he was favouring his right now.

They were nearly at the edge of the estate, and although the entrance from the main road was gated, the far side was simply bordered by a small copse of yew, sycamore and birch. If the guy reached the trees, his chances of escaping would increase dramatically.

Time was running out. Michael's breath was coming in searing cold rasps as he strained every muscle, every sinew. With just yards to go, in desperation he stuck out a foot and tripped the man, who went tumbling head over heels before coming to rest on his front.

Michael reached down and yanked him to his feet by the back of his camo jacket.

'Who the fuck are you?' he yelled, spinning the guy around.

Lights flashed white in his vision as a bomb exploded in his left temple. He moaned with the reality-altering pain of it. The guy had a punch that would fell an ox. Michael staggered back and lost his grip. He swung wildly, felt his fist glance across bone. His knuckles cracked ominously, and pain speared up from his fingers into his forearm.

The guy reared back, hand up to his bruised face, eyes wild. He attacked again, lunging forward, dodging another of Michael's punches before jabbing a bladed hand into the soft part of Michael's throat.

Michael's hands flew to his neck, which felt as though it was clamped in a vice. The pain was intense, burning, panic-inducing. He couldn't breathe. He staggered back, struggling to draw a sip of air down his damaged windpipe.

The guy lunged again.

'Stay back. Don't make me hurt you,' he hissed.

Crouching in an attempt to shield his throat, Michael lashed out a boot and connected with his opponent's right knee. The man cried out before delivering a rabbit punch to the back of Michael's neck. Momentarily stunned, Michael fought to stay on his feet as black curtains swung closed over his vision. He felt panic overwhelm him as the air he'd dragged into his lungs was expelled in a painful gasp.

Sinking to his knees, he raised his head and could dimly make out the man's hunched form sprinting into the woods. And freedom.

Stunned by the speed and violence of the attack, Michael made his way on unsteady legs back to the house.

As his breath, and senses, returned, he broke into a run.

Chapter 37

'Ekaterini is such a pretty name,' Annie said as she indicated for a left turn. 'I've never asked you before. Is she Greek?'

'Her parents are. I think she was born here. Why?'

She took a breath. Offered up a little prayer to whichever God protected worried parents.

'I don't want to pry, lovey, but did you talk about that man who followed you?'

'It's private, Mum. I wish you wouldn't keep sticking your nose into my business.'

'I'm not, love. I'm just, you know, concerned. Because—'

'You're trying to stop me seeing Dad. Please, Mum, I know you don't love him any more, and I get it, OK? I really do. But *I* love him. If you're worried about me, I understand. But I'm nearly sixteen. I can manage my relationship with him without you trying to protect me.'

From somewhere deep down, where Annie hoarded her reserves of parental patience like a dragon guarding its gold, she drew up a precious coin. She clutched it tight and said nothing beyond a quiet 'Let's just get you to school, shall we?'

She was feeling a little calmer since the bank had approved the standing order, but her nerves had been shredded by the events of the last few days. And there was still the huge problem of finding the criminals before her money ran out. She'd feel a lot more comfortable knowing Isla was at least trying to keep herself safe.

'Please come home straight afterwards. On the safe route. And check all around before you cross the roads. Even at the crossing. Please, Isla.'

'Fine. Can we just leave it, Mum? I'm getting a headache.'

Five minutes later, as Annie brought the car to a stop outside Edgbaston High School, her phone rang. Her pulse began racing as she checked the screen. No caller ID. Isla had her hand on the door release, but Annie placed her own on her daughter's leg.

'Wait! Just for a second.'

Isla slumped back into her seat. Annie put the phone to her ear.

'Hello?' she said quietly, not liking the frightened tremor in her voice.

'Is that Annie Barnes?'

The voice was male. She sagged in her seat. And he sounded nervous, not aggressive or smug like that horrible woman.

'Who is this, please?'

She scanned the view out of the windscreen. Saw no suspicious-looking men holding phones to their ears. The caller replied in a low, level voice that she found strangely reassuring. She felt a glimmer of recognition, too.

'My name is Michael Taylor. I'm Aaron's dad. You came to his room at the hospital yesterday.'

He sounded out of breath. Flustered, almost. And his voice was really croaky. She turned to Isla.

'It's OK, love. Sorry, it's, um, work. Go, go! And be careful, yes? Love you.'

Isla smiled briefly, flicked a hand in a quick wave, then got out, closing the door with a muted thunk. The car sealed itself back into hermetic silence.

'Are you still there, Annie?' Michael asked.

'Yes, I'm still here.'

'Good. Because I had to work really hard to track you down.' He paused, and she heard him drag down a deep, shuddering breath. What was *wrong* with him? 'We need to talk. Can you come to my house?'

Why was he suddenly so eager to see her? He wasn't a part of it, was he? No, how could he be? They'd almost killed his son. But she needed to press him.

'You're saying you believe me now? Only last night you made it quite clear you thought I was off my head.'

'I know. And I'm sorry. But what you said about people demanding money from us, well, I started thinking, and ... Look, something just happened that convinced me. I don't want to say more on the phone. Can you come? I'll explain everything.'

He gave her the address. She knew where it was.

She raced away from the kerb.

At last, an ally.

Chapter 38

As soon as the tall steel gates had opened wide enough, Annie powered through the gap and into the Chamberlain estate.

She parked and took a moment before getting out. She realised she knew nothing about Michael and his wife, beyond the fact that their child had also been threatened, almost killed, by the faceless criminals extorting her. And that they obviously had enough money to live in one of the best addresses in Harborne.

She looked up at the front of the house. Its design was at odds with the others on the street, and, for that matter, most of those in Harborne as a whole.

They, like Annie's own house, were mostly late Victorian or Edwardian villas. Red brick, like so many of the buildings in Birmingham. Graced with little details like stained-glass panels in the front doors, wide bay windows and ornate terracotta mouldings.

But the architect who'd designed the Taylors' house had obviously drawn inspiration from Miami, or maybe Los Angeles. Mind you, if they'd been hoping to recreate that spirit of soaring post-war US optimism, they hadn't reckoned with the low West Midlands skies. The white render looked grey in the diffuse sunlight leaking through to ground level.

Outside in the cold, damp air, she blipped her fob, walked up to the front door and rang the doorbell. Michael answered at once, as though he'd been waiting on the other side for her.

'Hi,' she said, suddenly embarrassed as she faced the man she'd confronted at the hospital.

She held out her hand and they shook. He had warm hands, a firm grip. He released hers quickly, smiling nervously.

'Hi, Annie. Come in, let me take your coat.'

She shrugged it off and let him take it from her, the two of them almost colliding as he tried to move past her to hang it on one of the hooks behind the door.

'Sorry, sorry,' he said, smiling more naturally now as they stumbled around each other. 'Let's go into the kitchen. Coffee?'

'Please.'

She followed him down a wide hallway hung with tasteful black and white photos of him with an attractive brunette, presumably his wife, and between them Aaron, smiling at the camera from beneath a floppy mop of dark curls.

She glanced in through a doorway at a beautifully decorated room in which a buttercup-yellow chaise longue took pride of place beneath a reading lamp. Car magazines were scattered on the floor alongside an open pizza box. A couple of long-necked beer bottles sat on a low glass-topped table. TV remotes were scattered across its dusty surface. A third bottle lay on its side on the carpet. Odd.

To get to the kitchen she had to step past a huge black gym bag from which blue and white kit spilled in an untidy heap. A waft of sweat-scented air hit her as she passed it, and she wrinkled her nose, dubbing the smell 'unwashed sporty teen'.

She wondered whether Michael's wife was away, maybe on business. How else to explain the bachelor-pad atmosphere pervading the house? She couldn't imagine herself, or any woman, being content to allow her house to descend into this near-squalor. When Grant used to leave his dirty clothes on the floor, she'd find him and make him clear them up.

She turned back to check the set of pegs. Saw only men's coats and jackets. No heels on the shoe rack, either. No women's shoes at all, not even a pair of flatties. Intuition kicked in, hard. There was no woman here. Hadn't been for a while. A divorce? Curious, but not wanting to pry, she framed an innocent-sounding question.

'How is your wife coping after the hit-and-run?' she asked as she walked across to a set of sliding doors that gave onto a big garden.

Michael turned away from the coffee machine to face her. In his eyes a sadness that went beyond the shock of almost losing his son. She knew what he was going to say before he said it, wished she could retract her question.

'Lucy died last year. May. A brain tumour.'

'I'm so sorry. I feel awful for asking. That must have been dreadful.' Annie swallowed. Felt a tear prick as she remembered Juliet's.

'I lost a good friend to cancer last year. It's so hard to watch someone you love suffer.'

He heaved a loud sigh.

'Honestly? It was pretty bad. For Lucy, for me. Especially for Aaron. He took his mum's death really hard. But I'm the one who should be apologising. You were only trying to help yesterday and I treated you appallingly. I'm sorry.' He held his hands out from his sides, the palms towards her. 'It's not an excuse, but Queen Elizabeth's is where Lucy spent her last days. It holds some pretty unpleasant memories. Things have been kind of rough since then. Work's been full-on and Aaron needs a lot of extra love. In fact his aunt's upstairs with him right now playing computer games.'

'Look, let's put the "sorries" behind us. I don't mind telling you, Michael, I've been terrified about what these people might do to Isla. Then when I saw about Aaron on the TV, I just lost it.'

'Agreed, but let's get coffee sorted first. I can't function without it.'

After Michael's admission, Annie felt herself becoming more comfortable in his presence. She felt she should offer some of her own story in return, while he worked the coffee machine. He handed her a coffee then started on one for himself.

'I'm a single parent, too. I divorced my husband just over a year ago.' She felt a blush creeping over her cheeks and took a sip of coffee as cover. 'Grant was . . . well, not to put too fine a point on it, he was screwing around behind my back. I'd just, you know, run out of road, but Isla took it hard. She's fifteen-going-on-twenty-five and she blames me. To be honest, there are times when I wonder whether I should have made more of an effort to keep the marriage going, for Isla's sake. It's been so tough on her since Grant and I separated.'

Suddenly aware that she was at risk of her new least-favourite activity – oversharing – and with a stranger to boot, she withdrew a little. After all, how much did she really know about the man opposite her? She noticed the watch on his left wrist. A Rolex. So he had expensive tastes.

He must have caught her looking at the fancy timepiece.

'Lucy ran a small chain of hairdressing salons across the city.' He pulled his shirt cuff back and held the watch up. 'She gave me this for my fortieth – it was her best year ever. She said it was a treat for supporting her in the early days. I always had cheap ones before.'

She felt bad for intruding on his grief. But she pressed on. She had to be sure she could trust him.

'Why did you sound so out of breath when you called me? And what happened to your neck? Those bruises weren't there last night.'

'The guy who almost killed Aaron was spying on us this morning. From across the road. I chased him. I almost caught him, too, but then he lamped me and the lights went out for a second.'

Annie took another nervous sip of coffee. If the guy was still coming after Aaron, that meant the gang were really out to get him.

'You poor thing. But you're all right?'

He shrugged. 'I'll have a few bruises. But that's not the problem. The thing is, Annie, you were right. *Are* right, I mean. I think some evil people are out to get us and our children and I don't know what to do about it. I mean, this is terrifying.'

'I feel that way, too, if it's any consolation. What changed your mind about talking to me?'

'Apart from being attacked by the guy who tried to kill Aaron, you mean?' He went for a lopsided grin. Didn't pull it off. 'A few days ago, I discovered Lucy had been paying a thousand pounds a month by standing order to a bank in the Caymans. It didn't make any sense until you came to see me last night.'

Annie nodded, relief that she had a friend mixed with fear that this was far from over.

'That's exactly what I've been told to do, unless I want to see Isla dead.'

Michael looked as though he might throw up. The colour leached out of his face, throwing his dark stubble into sharp relief.

'I cancelled the standing order on Monday. I almost got Aaron killed,' he murmured, clenching his fist.

Sensing she could trust Michael, another parent terrified by the thought of losing his child, Annie reached out towards him. Unsure if the gesture would be welcomed, she held back at the last moment from touching his whitened knuckles. But she understood his pain all the same. Because it was the same as her own.

'No, you didn't. That's on them, Michael. Them. Not you.'

'So what did they do to you?' he asked.

She told him about the deepfake video, the call at the conference, the man with the black eye following Isla. Michael's gaze never left her. When she finished, he sat back and scrubbed at his face with both hands.

'My God. Poor Lucy. She went through all of that too, and she never told me.'

'They probably told her not to. Made more threats against Aaron.' She flashed on the black and white family photos in the hall. 'Aaron's an only child, right?'

'Yeah. From Lucy's first marriage. We didn't manage to have kids of our own.'

'Isla is, too. I think they target victims that way to make it even easier to control us.'

'But what can we do? Do we go to the police?'

Annie's stomach turned over with anxiety. 'No. The woman who called me told me explicitly not to. We have to take them seriously, Michael, after what happened to Aaron.'

'But what *do* we do, then? They're criminals, and they're threatening to kill our kids.'

Michael's eyes were pleading. She realised he was expecting her to have answers because she'd made the initial approach. She was about to say she didn't know, which was true. But then, from somewhere deep inside her, somewhere quiet but powerful, a thought bubbled up. And with it a sense of resolution.

'We can track them down and expose them. *Stop* them!'

'Stop them how? We're talking about our children's lives here, Annie.'

She hesitated. Her gut was churning. She fought down the panicky feeling, aware that to succeed they'd need more than just the will to make it happen.

'We're their parents. We'll do whatever it takes.'

Michael sighed, swiped a hand over his face.

'Look, Annie, don't get me wrong. I admire your attitude. But "whatever it takes" is hardly a plan, is it? We've got nothing.'

She reached out and grabbed his hand.

'Listen to me, Michael. They made a mistake yesterday. A big one. They got careless and they lost control of what's happening. And now the police are involved, even though we didn't call them. If they've made one mistake, they might make another. This could be our only chance. Don't you see that?'

Pulling his hand away, Michael took out his phone.

'That's not a plan either. We have to call the police.'

Annie shook her head violently.

'No!' she said, too loudly. Then, more quietly, 'No. We can't. We can't take the risk.'

'We could ask for protection. For the kids. This is high-level crime, Annie. Stalking, extortion, attempted murder? They'd have to take it seriously.'

'They *should* take it seriously, I agree. But what evidence do we have? I deleted the email, although I'm trying to retrieve it. Anyway, we can't risk Isla and Aaron's lives.' She voiced the thought she'd been trying to avoid giving any credence to, even though it had been turning over in her mind since that first terrifying call. 'Suppose they've got someone on the inside? Of the police, I mean. Crime gangs bribe cops all the time, don't they? Or threaten them or their families. Even if we *could* get someone to listen, how do we know the blackmailers wouldn't get to hear of it? Then we'd be exposed. They'd come for our children.'

Michael spread his hands wide.

'Well, what *do* you want to do then? We need something concrete. Something specific.'

Annie picked at a fingernail, drawing blood. Looked back up at him. She couldn't quite believe what she was about to say. Because she'd figured out what she meant by 'whatever it takes'. But she knew she'd never have the courage to do it alone.

'We have to go after them ourselves' she said. 'Track them down, identify them, get proof they're the ones who've been blackmailing us and trying to kill our kids, and then, yes, go to the police with the evidence.'

His brows knotted. He didn't say anything for what felt like minutes.

'You're not serious? You want to take on an organised crime gang? Annie, are you insane?'

Annie knew she wasn't mad. What she was was a woman – a mother – out of ideas except this one. She knew how it sounded. And if Michael had been the one to suggest it, maybe she'd be the one raising doubts. But the more she thought about it, the more determined she became. She had another try at reassuring him.

'I'm not talking about some sort of big confrontation. But

they wormed their way into our lives. Maybe we can find out about them the same way. We can do it remotely. They'll never know. I honestly think it might be our best chance of keeping our children safe.'

Michael stared at her. She watched his eyes, the way they flicked left and right as if even now he was alert to the possibility of intruders. She held her breath as she waited for his reaction.

When he finally spoke, it was in a low, grating voice.

Chapter 39

'So how do we go about it?' Michael asked. 'I spend my days answering emails from timber mills, talking to customers and trying to stop my workers knocking lumps out of each other. I've never done anything remotely like this before.'

She nodded grimly. So it was really happening. They were going to try and outwit a bunch of criminals.

'Me neither. But I do work with money. And however anonymous the account, however distant or uncooperative the bank, money always leaves a trail. These people have a bank account in the Caymans. Somewhere there's a bricks-and-mortar building, with computers, staff, customer records. We have the account number. The name of the bank.'

'Could we, I don't know, hire someone?' Michael asked. 'A private eye?'

It sounded faintly ridiculous when he said it out loud. She pictured a man in a snap-brim hat and a scruffy raincoat, then erased it. In the Caymans? More likely a Hawaiian shirt and cargo shorts. Asking questions, getting himself noticed.

'I think that's too risky,' she said. 'Surely they'd be expecting it?'

'What about one of those specialist accountants? Someone who could trace the money back from the Caymans to here,' Michael said.

'I've got a feeling they all work for the police. Besides, I can't imagine they'd be cheap.' A thought occurred to Annie. 'But *you* could do it. You could say you wanted to move some company funds offshore. You could ask the bank in the Caymans if they have any other clients in the UK. Maybe if you got something out of them, *then* we could hire an investigator.'

Michael frowned. 'I suppose it could work.'

Then Annie had another idea. Something that gave her genuine hope, without endangering Isla and Aaron.

'We're missing the obvious here, Michael. We've got Isla's photo from when that man followed her. Plus the one from the CCTV when he hit Aaron. So we know it's the same guy. Why don't we put it out there on social media? If we get a hit, we can trace him, and from him we might find a link back to the blackmailers.'

He nodded thoughtfully.

'The guy I chased, he didn't look so sharp. Tough, yes, but more like hired muscle. It's a good idea.'

It was a plan. Not a great plan, but the best they had.

Michael excused himself, saying he had some work calls to make, leaving Annie downstairs in the kitchen, her MacBook open before her. She logged on to Mumsnet, typed out a short message and posted it, adding the photo Isla had taken of her stalker.

This individual followed my daughter on Monday, scaring her badly. Has anyone seen this man? Maybe you know him?

She added a final sentence.

Please help keep our kids safe.

There. That ought to do it. She posted similar messages on Facebook and on her local WhatsApp group. Then she waited, fingers knotting around each other as she stared at her post, willing someone, anyone, to reply. Her stomach fizzed with sudden anxiety. What if the blackmailers saw it?

Too late now. And anyway, they were too confident to worry about it. That was their Achilles heel. She prayed fervently that she was right.

She gasped. Someone was typing. A single response. As she was reading, another one came in. Then another, and another. From a handful to a steady stream.

Oh, God, how absolutely awful for you! Why can't these men just be normal?

So sorry. Don't know this guy but he looks a total nonce. Sending love for you and your daughter xoxoxo

People like him should be castrated and then hanged. Perverts. Where are the police?

I havent seen a cop on the streets round our way for years. Too busy worrying about criminals rights. What about our rights and our kids?!?!

The answers varied in emphasis and inventiveness when it came to summary justice, but none contained anything even remotely useful. Annie shook her head and snapped the MacBook shut.

Maybe Michael would have more luck with the bank in the Caymans.

Chapter 40

Plates and cutlery clattered. Empty crisp packets popped. The dining hall echoed with the laughs, jeers and conversations of a hundred or so students.

Someone dropped a tray and the resultant ironic cheer caused one of the teachers eating at their separate table to stand and bark out a sharp request for order.

A brief silence ensued. People were happy enough to go back to their phones anyway. Isla included. Naomi nudged her.

'Do you want to hang out after school?'

'Can't. My mum wants me to come straight home. "And use the safe route, Isla",' she added in a wicked parody of her mum that had Naomi snickering as she took a selfie.

'OK, babes, laters.' Naomi got to her feet. 'Gotta run. Lacrosse practice.'

Isla nodded. She'd been a bit mean about Mum. But in reality she didn't mind going straight home. The encounter with the creep had sent her anxiety skyrocketing and she felt safer there, even if Mum didn't get home till six or even later.

She nibbled a final bite from her half-eaten low-fat halloumi and falafel wrap, sucked the last few drops from her carton of no-added-sugar cranberry juice and dropped her trash in the bin as she left the dining hall.

She headed towards the library. She had some Spanish home-work to finish. Head bent to her phone, checking which girls she followed on Instagram had changed their looks, she collided with someone, also head down.

'Hey, watch out!'

She looked up.

It was Ronan. His face was a mess. Black eyes, a split lip and a big bruise on his jaw on the left side. He backed away, eyes startling white against the mottled purply-green of the surrounding skin.

'Just leave me alone!' he said, holdings his hands out.

'What the hell happened to your face? You look like someone beat the crap out of you.'

He scowled, then winced and touched the bruise on his jaw.

'Is that supposed to be funny, Isla, 'cause I'm not laughing.'

'Of course not! I mean it. What happened?'

'Someone beat the crap out of me all right.' He jabbed a finger at her. 'Your psycho boyfriend.'

She gasped. No. It couldn't be. Ronan was trying to break her and Josh up because she'd refused to go out with him. Blaming Josh because some rando got a rage on. Probably 'cause they'd bought dodgy drugs off him. Another thought occurred to her. A faint memory. Hazy.

'Is this because you tried to kiss me at the club?"

'That's when he did it, for sure.'

She shook her head. 'Josh would *never* do that. He wouldn't hurt a fly. You're just jealous. And anyway, it's not as if you're exactly a stranger to bullying, is it? Or making stuff up about people. I seem to remember you got suspended last year because you kicked the crap out of that new kid. And what about that time you said you could get us all into the Modesto88 after-party? We all rocked up at midnight and that stupid fat bouncer told us where to go. This is just another one of your sad little lies. You probably did it to yourself.'

She turned around and headed in the opposite direction, heart pounding. The library would have to wait.

Ronan shouted after her.

'You should be careful around that nutcase, Isla. He's dangerous. I could report him to the police for assault, you know.'

She hurried on. He wouldn't. They'd probably smell the weed and arrest him instead. She tried to smile at the idea of Ronan in handcuffs, but the image didn't cheer her.

Chapter 41

If he'd heard about this from a neighbour, he'd have been first in line with a shouted curse and a baseball bat.

A dirty, dishevelled man in shabby, stinking clothes climbing over a fence into a back garden where kids played was a legitimate target. But they'd be looking at things all wrong. Because John had fucked up with his *own* targets, hadn't he? After getting snapped by the Barnes girl and then failing to kill the Taylor boy – twice – he was out of options.

He hooked a boot over the top of the panel, hauled himself up and over and dropped onto the lawn on the far side. Stripes. A tiny part of him was glad the new guy had maintained them. Ness never could see the point when John got the mower out, even using a pegged string to get the lines straight.

He pushed the thought away. Because he had one final bit of business to attend to in Birmingham. The pain he felt as he contemplated what he was about to do to his children was agonising – worse, even, than holding Corporal Heather Jones in his arms as she died. But it needed doing. Best get it over with clean and quick.

Then he could leave Birmingham and their filthy clutches. He'd have to square it with the woman first. If she wouldn't see reason, there were other ways he could free himself from her claws. He might be a train wreck of an ex-soldier, but he'd received the finest training in the world. And he remembered a few things. He just needed a bit of time to prepare. He'd make a call. Arrange a meet.

But first, his kids.

He peered round the old apple tree that provided decent cover even without its leaves. The kitchen lights were on, but he couldn't see Ness. Maybe she was upstairs, or out running an errand. Didn't matter. He'd talk to her when she got back, and in the meantime, who was that sitting at the table, a brightly coloured box of cereal in front of him? Little tyke.

He snuck up the edge of the garden, keeping low so any nosy neighbours wouldn't see him, until he reached the back door.

Through the glass, he watched Benji spooning Cheerios into his mouth. He knocked softly on the glass with a bent knuckle. Benji looked round, and when he spotted John, his face broke into a wide, gap-toothed smile.

He jumped down from his chair and opened the door.

'Daddy!'

He jumped into John's arms, and just like that, every worry, every care, every hateful black mood that poisoned John's waking and sleeping hours evaporated like diesel spilled onto a hot desert road. He hugged his son close, smelling his hair.

'Hey, Benji, how have you been? You're getting so tall.'

Benji leaned away from him.

'I am one hundred and six centimetres tall, sir,' he said, freeing one hand and snapping off a half-decent salute.

'And you've lost a couple of teeth, too.'

Benji poked his tongue through the gap at the front.

'Where's Ruby?'

Benji tipped his head towards the door. 'Upstairs. Mum's washing her hair.'

John nodded. He was disappointed not to see his daughter. But this? Being with Benji, just the two of them? It was good.

'Hey, I'm sorry I missed your birthday,' he said, talking around a sudden lump in his throat. 'Did you have a fun day?'

Benji's eyes brightened. 'Oh yeah! It was awesome. Alex got me a drone. Do you want to see it?'

A bitter taste coated John's tongue. He swallowed. Wanting to shout that no, he didn't want to see Alex's present.

'That's OK, mate. Maybe later. Listen.' He set Benji down and crouched so they were eye to eye. His throat tightened and he felt a sudden urge to cry. He fought it down. 'I've got some news. It's not great, but I think you're grown up enough to hear it. I need to go away for a bit. You see, it's a special overseas mission.'

Benji's eyes widened. 'Top secret?'

John felt the lump in his throat growing. Went for a smile that he thought he pulled off. 'Yeah, classified. Eyes only.'

'Are you going to fight the Taliban again?'

'Not this time.'

'Who, then?'

'Uh, Somali pirates. We're going to disrupt their supply lines.'

'Real pirates?' Benji asked, the wonder written all over his face.

John shook his head. 'Not the kind you mean. But they're properly evil, Benji. And Daddy's going to be taking them out.'

'With Heather?'

John swallowed hard against a sudden crippling upsurge of grief and guilt. He'd never been able to tell Benji or Ruby what had happened in the sandbox. About why their daddy left the army and joined a private contracting firm before getting kicked out of that outfit too, for brawling, for drinking. And, to put a tin hat on it, for decking his squad commander. How from there he'd spiralled down through one badly paid doorman job after another until his current – he shuddered – *employer* had offered him that strange but lucrative first job a year or so ago.

'Yeah,' he croaked. He cleared his throat. Tried again. 'Yes, that's right.'

Benji screwed his face up in a comical snarl. 'You'll kill them all. The British Army is the best fighting force in the world. And you're their best soldier.'

John had to smile. Where had little Benji learned to speak like a recruiting sergeant? Oh, right. Of course. His old man.

'That's right. So, do you want to know the details of the mission?'

Benji nodded frantically. 'What guns are you going to shoot? Do you have to wear body armour? Are you in charge? Are the pirates really dangerous?'

The kitchen door opened and Ruby burst in, her hair wrapped in a towelling turban.

'Daddy!' she squealed.

'Hey, pipsqueak, how's my favourite girl?'

'Ruby, go back upstairs,' Vanessa said, in a voice that brooked no dissent. 'You too, Benji.'

'But I'm talking to Daddy! He's going away on a secret mission. To fight pirates.'

Ness shot John a look that would penetrate tank armour.

'Is that so? Well, go and get changed anyway.'

'But Mum—'

'But nothing. Off you go, or no screen time until tomorrow.'

That did it. With all the ill grace only a six-year-old child could muster, Benji stumped off after his sister, slamming the door behind him.

Vanessa folded her arms and glared at John.

'"Secret mission"? Really?'

He spread his hands wide. 'It was a little white lie. Benji thinks I'm still in the army.'

'Er, no. He doesn't. He only gets like that when you show your face. He can't get over the fact you left us. His therapist says it's a coping mechanism.'

'His therapist? Why the hell are you taking him to a therapist? There's nothing wrong with him.'

'No, John. We're not getting into this again. Not now. Not ever. Why are you even here?'

'As it happens, I *am* going away.' He invented a lie on the spot, something to salve his wounded pride. 'For work. I got a job. A good one.'

She stared at him in that way she had. Halfway between an

X-ray and a rifle round. Maybe they taught it to women at a secret training course before they got married.

'I see. This job, does it involve stalking teenage girls?'

Shame flashed through him, heating his skin. 'What? No! Of course not!'

'No?' Her voice rose. 'Because a woman on Mumsnet posted your photo and said you'd been following her daughter. What the *hell* have you done, John?'

'Nothing!'

He took a step back as she advanced towards him, her eyes hard, sharp points in a white face. She couldn't have seen the local news about the hit-and-run, he thought, as his back hit the edge of the countertop. She'd have pulled a knife from the block by now.

'Get out! Get out, get out, get out!' she screamed.

He retreated down the hall, wrenched the front door wide and fled into the street, hands clapped to his ears, her curses filling the air around him, bursting like grenades overhead.

What the hell was happening? Why was it all tearing itself into pieces just when he'd decided to get his shit together? He ran down the street with a single thought revolving in his overstressed brain.

I need to see him. I need to end this once and for all.

Chapter 42

Arriving at work late after her visit to Michael, Annie cancelled her morning's meetings and shut herself away in her office.

She'd almost given up hope of finding anything helpful online about the criminals targeting her, Michael and who knew how many other families. She felt numb, blank, unable to focus. Hunched over her laptop, she started again. After another fruitless hour, she tweaked her search terms and pressed enter.

The results flashed up on the screen. Her breath quickened. This was it!

A blogger in nearby Tamworth had posted about a pair of scammers – a man and a woman – who'd charmed their way into a woman's home and then stolen a thousand pounds in cash.

Her eyes skittered down the page until they snagged on a detail.

Mrs Morgan told me that the woman 'seemed so nice. You never think a white-haired old lady is going to be a con artist, do you?' Given that her male partner was also in his seventies, according to their latest victim, they seem to be a new example of what this true-crime reporter is dubbing 'Silver Scammers'.

She tried another search, subtly altering the wording and order and adding speech marks for good measure.

'Extortion + death threats child + Caymans'

Google replied at once.

No results containing all your search terms were found.

What had her very first tutor at uni told her whenever she got stuck?

First principles, Annie. Instead of building on flawed research, start afresh. Go back to the beginning and do it all again. The human mind is a wonderful machine, but you have to give it a little kick now and then.

She started with the *Birmingham Mail*. The website had an archive going back three years and nothing on any blackmailers. But was that all their material, or did they have stuff they'd never digitised? Certainly the School of Computer Science still had paper records kicking around, although Letitia was always going on about how they really ought to devote some resources to it. Fat chance when there were always higher-profile projects clamouring for the same funds. Was the *Mail* in the same boat?

She called the paper and asked to speak to the librarian, if they had such a thing.

'That'll be Julian,' the receptionist said. 'Though he likes to be called Chief Knowledge Officer. Putting you through.'

The line clicked and warbled for a couple of seconds.

'Knowledge Management. This is Julian.'

The man who answered sounded as if he wore a cardigan with leather elbow patches and smoked a pipe. Fussy. A bachelor. She pictured a cluttered office with a photo of him cheek to cheek with a terrier of some kind.

She introduced herself and gave him the story she'd concocted.

'I'm researching non-violent crime in Birmingham and the surrounding towns. Do you have any articles going back further than the three years on your website?'

'Do I have ... ?' She heard a dry, papery sound. Realised he was laughing. 'How does one hundred and fifty-five years sound? Some of them are a bit dusty, mind.'

Annie quailed at the thought of a mountain of yellowing

newspaper stretching up to the ceiling of a very large, dimly lit warehouse. Struggled to inject a brightness into her voice she wasn't feeling.

'It sounds amazing. Actually, I'm mainly focusing on the last ten years.'

It was true. She'd decided based on nothing more than her guess at the female blackmailer's age.

'That's a bit better then. They're not online, but I have got a prototype database humming away down here in my lair.' He chuckled. 'There's a basic search function, too.'

'Could I come and see you? Today? Now? It's rather important, I'm afraid. I...' she hesitated, 'I have a deadline.'

'Tell me about it,' he said. 'Come whenever you like. I'm not so busy I haven't got time for visitors.'

Half an hour later, she was sitting at a PC in the basement level of the *Mail*'s red-brick building on Brindley Place.

Julian turned out to be in his early thirties and dressed in Superdry from head to toe. He'd shown her how to query the database, brought her a coffee and left her to it. His only request: that she mention him in her final research report. She hoped he wouldn't be too disappointed if he ever discovered she'd been guilty of a minor deception of her own.

She tried her original, broad search query.

Birmingham blackmail extortion man woman con artists

Maybe she'd become too used to the split-second operation of Google, but when she hit the return key, all she got was an hourglass icon jerking around a quarter-turn at a time.

Her belly was packed tight with butterflies, though they still had space to flap their wings. Was this thing ever going to wake up, or had she crashed it?

The hourglass paused, mid-turn, then vanished altogether, to be replaced by a message.

Her pulse rate picking up, she clicked the link and found herself staring at a list of headlines, the first of which sent her mind spinning, half overjoyed, half terrified.

5 January 2022 // Local businessman blackmailed over website scam

Heart thumping, she read the article. A young woman had lured a man to a hotel room with the promise of extramarital sex via a website called Discreet Encounters. Once there, the tables were turned. A male partner emerged from the bathroom and threatened the man physically, and money was demanded in exchange for silence.

CCTV pictures showed images of the pair. The female was hard to make out clearly behind oversized sunglasses and a low fringe, but the male had looked up at the camera. His face was perfectly framed. Youthful, blandly good-looking, with Byronic curls flopping over one eye that he presumably thought made him appear cool. Jesus, he only looked about eighteen.

She found it hard to sympathise with the victim of this particular blackmail. He only had himself to blame. But she made a note anyway.

She tried the next link.

23 August 2019 // Police warn dog owners, 'petnappers' active in Birmingham

A young woman and an equally youthful male partner had been returning dogs lost in suspicious circumstances and demanding bigger rewards than those offered by the bereft owners, citing 'travel expenses' after finding the beloved pet many miles from home.

In a chilling comment on their ruthlessness, one owner who'd sent them packing after refusing to pay revealed: *Pablo went missing a second time a few days later. My husband found him in the woods at the back of our house. He'd had his throat cut.*

Apparently the poor animal had suffered further injuries, which the *Mail* had declined to describe, 'as this is a family newspaper'.

She was about to skip to the next article when a phrase jumped off the page, stopping her dead.

Mrs Boatwright said the young woman was cold and ruthless. 'Literally like she was enjoying being cruel. She used this sort of slogan, like a gameshow host or something. "That's the deal. Take it or leave it." '

Annie sat back and swept a hand over her face, which had flashed all over with clammy sweat. She'd heard that phrase herself. At the conference. The bitch had used it on her, as well. It was the same woman. It *had* to be.

Over the next ninety minutes, heart pounding, she read and reread all nineteen articles. In the final piece, the reporter concluded, in a paragraph tagged on the database copy as '[SBC: SNN]', that the pair of blackmailers, as she called them, might have been involved in extorting parents of vulnerable children, although she had no definitive proof.

Annie went and found Julian.

'Can you tell me what SBC-colon-SNN means, please? One of the articles was tagged with it.'

He smiled up at her.

'"Submitted but cut: speculation not news". Our editorial code is very clear on reporters adding their own opinions into news pieces. Strictly *verboten*.'

She thanked him and asked if she could have printouts of the articles.

Five minutes later, with the sheaf of paper secure in her bag, she was back on Brindley Place again.

She felt sick. Yet somewhere deep down, she felt relieved, too. From everything she could piece together, the blackmailers were not part of some octopus-like crime gang with far-reaching tentacles. They were just – *just!* – an opportunistic couple with a talent, if you could call it that, for inventive and callous methods of forcing people to pay them to stop their life-shattering activities.

She called Michael.

'I think I know who they are. Not their names, but they've been doing this for almost ten years. The *Mail* ran a whole series of articles about it. It's not organised crime, it's just two people. A couple.'

'Thank God you found something, because I got the brush-off from the bank. Privacy, confidentiality, data protection, you know, the usual. So, look, if it's just a couple of blackmailers, maybe we *should* go to the police. They've got the resources, after all, and it sounds like these two are already on their radar.'

'No! I told you, no police. It doesn't matter if it's only two of them. They tried to kill Aaron and we still don't have any evidence. We can't risk it.'

Her phone vibrated before she could tell him any more. An alert from Mumsnet. She had a private message.

'I'll call you back,' she said.

The Mumsnet member called herself VanessunDorma. Her message sent Annie's pulse stuttering upwards.

I saw your post about the man who followed your daughter.
I am so sorry about this, but he's my ex-husband. His name
is John Varney. I don't know where he lives. He might even
be homeless these days. But he hangs out with a bunch of
addicts and whatever. Try Waterstone Lane Cemetery. Good
luck. Sorry again about your daughter. I don't know what else
to say.

The message filled Annie with a weird mix of elation and anxiety. Stomach squirming unpleasantly, as if she had a big presentation to give to a roomful of donors, she tapped out a quick thank you to VanessunDorma and then called Michael back.

'I think we've found the van driver.'

Chapter 43

Her red leather biker jacket creaked as she hunched over her keyboard.

Grace was desperate for a sympathetic ear. Poor cow's parents were holding the line over the pill. Ironic, really, given that her yummy-yoga-mummy wasn't nearly so uptight about posting about her daughter's mental troubles on Mumsnet.

Not her problem. More like one more branch on her magic money tree. She gave it another shake.

listen grace u cant let them tel u what 2 do
there are ways u can get round them

like what

tell your doctor u get really bad period pains but your mum is strict catholic

will that work

i dunno but worth a try

what if she tells my parents

Maya smiled lazily. Time to bait her hook.

u wanna meet up irl for coffee we could talk bout it

She waited. Grace was thinking about it. That was OK. She had time. And a few tricks up her sleeve. Jack typed again.

its ok im happy just chattin like this gotta go x

She signed out. Grace would suggest it herself next time. And then they could take their relationship to the next level.

Her phone rang. Caller: Richard Bodden. Profession: bank manager. Location: Cayman Islands.

'Yes?'

'Miss Kinton, I trust you're well.'

She hated this. All the frills you had to stick onto your conversation just so you could get what you wanted. But she could play the game well enough. Pretending to be someone else.

'Very well, Richard. And you?'

'Oh, you know, mustn't grumble. Although my tennis elbow does from time to time.'

She laughed briefly. Haha. Other people's jokes puzzled her.

She employed a phrase she thought might resonate with the stuffy banker.

'To what do I owe the pleasure?'

'Well, Miss Kinton, it would appear someone is trying to gain information about your account with us. I hasten to add our cashier divulged nothing. But when she enquired after the gentleman's own identity, he became evasive and then hung up.'

She bit her lip. Who'd had the nerve to start poking their nose into her business? The answer presented itself at once: Michael Taylor. First he cancelled the standing order, now he was calling the bank. She doodled a straight razor on the pad beside her keyboard. Noses poked out too far could find themselves cut off.

'You're sure he learned nothing?'

'Of course. Our clients' privacy – *your* privacy – is sacrosanct.'

'Keep it that way.'

She hung up.

She was still considering what to do about the unwanted attention when the door to the flat opened.

'Guess what?' Ollie asked.

She turned.

'I'm not in the mood. Just tell me.'

He grabbed a half-drunk can of Coke off the desk, took a swig, then threw himself down into a chair.

'Our friend John's only gone and got himself outed on social media as a paedo.'

She spun round to face him.

'He's done *what*?'

'The new one, what's her name, Annie Barnes? She's put a not-very-nice post on Mumsnet telling all her bougie friends that poor old John's a predator. Asking them to be on the lookout.'

His smirk infuriated her. Him being the way he was had its uses, but his inability to see risks irked her.

'I'm sorry, Ollie, do you think this is funny? Because from where I'm sitting, it looks like a massive fucking problem.'

He finished the Coke, crushed the can one-handed and tossed it into the bin on the far side of the room.

'All I see is a bunch of bourgeois mummies getting their collective Fairtrade bamboo knickers in a twist about a nonce stalking their precious little kids.'

She stared at him in disbelief. How could he not see the threat facing them? A threat that could upend the life they'd spent years building.

'Do you not get it, Ollie? They're trying to get to us through John.'

She rocked back in her chair. None of their marks had ever fought back before. They all did what they were supposed to and obeyed the rules. Paid up and got to live their nice little lives. But now two of them had started *breaking* the rules. First Taylor, and now Barnes, acting like an undercover cop on Mums-bloody-net.

Maya rubbed her tattoo as an unwelcome thought occurred to her. Surely they hadn't dared to team up, had they? Against her?

What the hell was she going to do? Maybe it was time to test out an idea. One she'd been mulling over for a while.

'We could disappear,' she murmured, with a soft, encouraging smile. 'We've got enough money to live on for years. Maybe for ever if we invest it.'

Something happened to his face. Every trace of glib charm melted away, like a wax mask being burned off by a blowtorch. Beneath the mask, an ugly, animalistic expression disfigured his handsome features. She'd seen this side of him before, but it didn't mean she liked it. He was useful, but in all honesty, as he'd got older and bigger, faster and more impulsive, he'd begun to scare her. Just a little.

He jumped up and took a step towards her. Grabbed the arms of her chair and leaned over her, pushing that predator's face close to hers. She could smell the sweetness of the Coke on his breath.

'If they want to fight back, that's fine. I'm getting bored of all this fly-by-wire shit. I want to do things for real. Out there,' he added, momentarily freeing his right hand and pointing at the window. 'I can shut them up. I can frighten them so badly they'll call you for permission to take a shit in their own homes. Just let me.'

As she looked up into his eyes, flashing with violence that was never far from the surface, she imagined herself a scientist meeting a new species of animal deep in the jungle, where the dangerous things lurked. All teeth and talons, rippling muscles, bunched haunches. Ready to spring, and bite, and tear, and kill.

Maybe it would be fun to let him loose among the marks. It was an enjoyable, but brief, fantasy. They had to be smart, not savage.

'I know how much you'd enjoy that,' she said, 'But how long do you think it would be before the cops caught you? Ever hear of DNA? Fingerprints? Forensics? Do you really want to exchange a few minutes of pleasure for spending the rest of your life in a prison cell?'

It was a cruel but necessary question. He backed away as if the arms of her chair were suddenly red hot. His eyes lost their animalistic fire. He wrapped his arms around himself and looked every inch the lost boy she'd known before.

He paced in front of her, side to side, shaking his head and muttering low and indistinctly. The image of a caged tiger came to her.

She stood, went to him. Caught him on his next return pass and drew him close. She stroked his cheek and pulled his head down so she could kiss his forehead. He stilled, breathing heavily, as the fight gradually went out of him.

'Trust me,' she whispered into his ear. 'I'll look after you like I've always done. You know that, don't you, Ollie?'

His head nestled into the crook of her neck. His stubbled chin grated a little against the exposed skin there as he nodded his assent.

As she stroked his hair, she remembered when her little brother hadn't even needed to shave.

Chapter 44

He felt naked. Vulnerable.

He tugged his hood down over his eyes.

Everyone he passed was staring at him. No, not *at* him. *Into* him. Like his skin, his muscles, organs, bones were all made of glass and they could see right into his soul.

Not a pleasant thing to look at, he thought.

The encounter with Ness had really hurt. All he was doing was spending some time with his kid, and she'd treated him like dirt. Worse than dirt. Like a nonce. A paedo! He'd done stuff he wasn't proud of, sure. Who hadn't? But that? No. Never.

It was all that Barnes woman's fault. He hadn't even hurt the girl. Just given her a scare. Following orders like a good little soldier. His bruised face burned with shame. How had it come to this?

Normally, the city felt like somewhere he could disappear into. Hide among the other down-and-outs, the cast-offs society had no use for any more. Addicts, winos, headcases.

And veterans like himself, strung out from what they'd seen in foreign wars. Mates blown to pink mist in front of them or torn apart like rag dolls. Civilians machine-gunned by Apaches following crap intel. Or tortured and killed by the Tali, their corpses left in the dirt or hanging from cranes as a warning.

But tonight it felt like hostile territory. He felt exposed. Like they were watching him. Hacking into street cameras, CCTV. Tracking his every move. He hustled along, keeping to the dark side of the road, where some diligent vandal had smashed the lamps in every single street light.

Ahead, a few of the people he'd got to know in his new life were clustered around a shopping trolley they'd turned on its side and topped with a broken piece of plywood to serve as a table. Two-and-a-half-litre bottles of Frosty Jack's cider clustered in the centre. At 7.5 per cent, not the strongest, but Iceland was cheap and they didn't try to chuck you out before you'd made your purchase. So all in all, a decent bet for low-price, high-strength oblivion.

He added two four-packs of Stella he'd bought as he walked into the city centre from Ness's.

'Nice one, Johnno,' an older man, also a veteran, said. 'You going to join us, then? Tam got a twenty today off some rich bloke. We're having a party.'

John looked at the cans. Imagined the fast hit of the alcohol. Then shook his head.

'I can't, mate. Sorry.'

He needed to be clear-headed for what he had to do. He hunched his shoulders and pulled his hood down further. Kept walking.

He reached Fazeley Street around 11 p.m. Lots of places in Birmingham that used to be rough had been smoothed over. Gentrified, that was what Ness called it. Gastropubs and canal boat rides where the main activity used to be drowning cats or chucking old bikes into the stinking green water.

But this part of Digbeth seemed to have missed the memo. And nestled into an elbow of the Digbeth Branch Canal was the spot he'd selected for his rendezvous. The Banana Warehouse.

During the day, the broken-down red-brick and corrugated-iron structure was a magnet for tourists. They'd rock up, take their selfies then bugger off again. But when the sun went down, it lost whatever post-industrial charm it might possess and reverted to its true identity as a scary, stinking, rat-infested shithole.

When he reached its shadowy embrace, he headed inside. Nobody in tonight, which was just as well for what he had planned. Better not to have any witnesses. Around the mould-darkened walls lay thin, stained sleeping bags and mounds of newspaper and cardboard – shadowy echoes of their former users – contributing their own aroma to the foul stench of decay, disease and human waste.

With the place to himself, he wandered across the puddled concrete floor and stared through the smashed windows at the canal bank. A greasy, rotting stench coiled off the water and infiltrated his nostrils, making him wrinkle his nose and turn away. Were there any tourists who'd want to risk a boat ride here? Unlikely, he thought, unless they fancied catching dysentery.

It was time to make the call. The cheap burner phone's plastic case was unpleasantly warm in his hand as he punched in the number he'd committed to memory.

'It's me,' he said, when it was answered, angrily.

'What the hell are you doing? That phone's for incoming calls only. Specifically, *my* calls.'

John was in no mood to be lectured about standard operating procedures. Things had escalated way beyond that.

'Never mind that. I want out, and I need money. Proper money. *Walk-away* money. You've got to come and meet me.'

'Oh, I've got to, have I?'

'You don't *have* to. But I need to get away. I could always go to the cops, tell them what I know. I'm sure they'd find somewhere warm for me.'

A long pause.

'No. Sorry, John. No need to be hasty. Where do you want to meet?'

'The Banana Factory in Digbeth.'

'Wait there.'

John smiled. Turned out he still had it after all. He shivered. The place was colder than Helmand in January. He gathered some scraps of wood and cardboard, threw it all into an empty oil drum.

He tossed in a match and stared into the leaping flames. For once, no flashback. Just a welcome image of the old John, the *bad* John, going up in smoke.

Not long now, Johnno, and we'll be free.

Chapter 45

'Hi, lovey,' Annie said breezily, trying to ignore the fluttering in the pit of her stomach. 'Save what you're doing. I'm taking you to your dad's.'

Isla looked up from her laptop, her smile betraying her true feelings. She was delighted, even though she was trying hard to look nonchalant.

'Really? But it's not his day.'

Annie smiled. It felt as though the effort might split her cheeks from the corners of her mouth all the way back to her ears.

'Well, it'll be a nice surprise for him, won't it?'

'But he might not be in,' Isla said, though she was already shutting her laptop and reaching for her school bag.

'He gave you a key, didn't he?'

'Yes.'

'Well, then, you'll be fine, won't you?'

'OK, I just need some stuff from my room.'

Annie texted Grant to let him know of her change of their usual arrangement. He replied immediately.

No probz. Melissa's here. The girls can hang out together.
We'll order in sushi. Good to see u being bit more flexi too :-)

Annie resisted the urge to chuck the phone at the wall. Besides, it wasn't the iPhone she wanted to see hitting exposed brickwork at high speed.

Isla clattered back down the stairs a few minutes later, a rucksack slung over one shoulder. Annie slammed the front door closed behind her and double-locked it. Twenty-five minutes later, she was driving away from Grant's and towards Michael's, half fired up, half petrified at the thought of what they were embarking on. But it was for the children's sakes.

They had to go through with it.

Chapter 46

Even with Michael by her side, Waterstone Lane Cemetery gave Annie the willies. Picturesque in the daylight, with its two-tier curving catacombs cut into the hillside, the Victorian necropolis was creepy as hell after dark. As they peered into the recesses in the earth wall, she tried not to picture the bruised, combat-jacketed man coming at her with a long knife. But however spooky it was, there was no sign of Varney.

The same was true of the improvised encampment in the wooded centre of the vast Bordesley Circus roundabout Michael had suggested they try next. Yes, there were homeless people there, warming their hands over a small fire of boxes and what looked like wooden fence posts, but they either didn't know Varney or didn't want to give him up to strangers. Annie couldn't blame them. Not really.

'You cops?' asked one young woman with track marks visible on the insides of her arms.

An older man beside her, grey beard fastened into a narrow tail with silver beads, shook his grizzled head.

'Nah. They're too well dressed for the filth. What are you?' he asked Annie, stepping closer and giving her an aggressive stare. 'Journalists, is it? Sky or whatever? Bit of poverty tourism for the masses?'

'No, we're just—'

Michael took her arm.

'We're friends of John's. We're worried about him.'

The man looked him up and down.

'Friends.'

'That's right.'

'And I'm the Pope. Maybe you better piss off before I call the Vatican guards.'

He whistled loudly, a piercing screech that set Annie's teeth on edge.

'People took a wrong turn,' he called as a trio of young men detached themselves from the darkness around the fire and ambled over.

Michael held up his free hand.

'No need for any trouble, lads. Your man here's right. We just got lost. Have a good evening.'

They descended the grassy slope off the roundabout and darted across the road, earning an angry blast from a Jaguar hitting the busy junction at speed off Coventry Road.

'City Centre Gardens?' Annie asked, panting as they reached the safety of the pavement.

Michael shook his head.

'I've got a better idea. There's a soup kitchen in Digbeth. There's always lots of people there. Maybe we could buy the information we need.'

She raised her eyebrows. 'How do *you* know where the city's soup kitchens are?'

He shrugged. 'I helped set this one up. Used to volunteer there before Lucy died. I don't really have the time now, what with Aaron and everything.'

She smiled at him. Realising she didn't really know that much about him despite the way they'd been thrown together.

'I think that's amazing.'

He shook off the compliment.

'My mum always said we should help those less fortunate. I mean, she didn't have much, she brought me up on her own, but she'd always give to charity, stop and chat with beggars, you know?'

Annie nodded. 'Your mum sounds like a lovely person. Is she…?'

'She was seventy-one last month. Lives in Sutton Coldfield. Grows prize dahlias.' Michael cleared his throat. 'Let's see if her advice pays off, eh?'

Ten minutes later, he parked the pickup on Fazeley Street, under a railway bridge. A passing train – one of the new electric ones – rattled and screeched overhead as they climbed out, leaving behind it the seaside tang of ozone in the air.

This was a largely deserted neighbourhood of warehouses, small industrial units and derelict housing. Britain's second city it might be, but away from the bright street lights and the bars, restaurants and retail outlets of the centre, Birmingham felt as cold and forbidding as many far lower down the urban pecking order.

Annie told herself the bright smears of spray paint tagging the exteriors of the run-down buildings were street art, not graffiti. Maybe on the side of a gallery in the Jewellery Quarter, that self-deception would have flown. Here it felt like whistling in the dark.

The soup kitchen, on a vacant corner lot where Fazeley Street crossed Pickford Street, was housed inside a converted single-decker bus. Hissing patio heaters warmed picnic benches at which a couple of dozen people sat with trays laden with stew and potatoes, wraps and sandwiches, mugs of tea and bowls of steaming pudding drenched in custard.

The counter was staffed by two young women in baseball caps and an older woman wearing a bright green, black and white batik headscarf. This matronly figure bustled about, bantering with her customers and occasionally tossing out salty remarks if she spotted anyone trying to push in to the queue.

Michael led Annie to the side of the counter and called to the mother hen.

'Hi, Comfort, busy night?'

She looked down from her elevated position. Annie watched her expression change rapidly through surprise to joy to concern.

'My Lord, it's Michael Taylor, as I live and breathe. We haven't seen you down here for so long. How is poor Aaron? I saw his picture on the news. That awful man.'

'He's pretty banged up, but he's young, you know? He's already itching to be back at school.'

She gave him a searching look. 'How are you coping, my love?'

'You know, doing the best I can for him.'

'Well, that's all we can do for our kids, eh?' She turned to Annie. 'And who is your friend?'

'I'm Annie,' she said, stretching out her hand.

Comfort shook briskly.

'Pleased to meet you, Annie. So tell me, what brings you out on a cold night like this to the St Mungo's mobile soup kitchen and food counter? Are you here to volunteer?'

'Not tonight, but I'd like to later on.' Annie glanced at Michael. 'We just wanted to talk to some of your customers.'

'Well, be my guest. It's a free country. But whether they'll talk to *you* or not is another story. Private people, you know?'

And with that she went back to dishing up, chivvying her two young assistants and dispensing homilies from the Bible along with the stew.

The first few people they asked stonewalled them. Annie began to wonder if John Varney had some sort of power over these people. They certainly seemed keen to distance themselves from him. Or maybe they'd heard about his crimes. Seemed understandable you'd want to keep your distance from a man willing to kill a child.

Side by side with Michael, she approached a man in his thirties on the edge of the group, sitting by himself and wiping a thick hunk of bread around his plate.

'Hi,' she said. 'Can we join you?'

He looked up. Fixed large brown eyes on her. Not aggressive. Straightforward, maybe. He echoed Comfort's words.

'It's a free country.'

'We're looking for someone, and I was hoping you might be

able to help us find him. I don't want to sound patronising, but I'd be happy to pay you for your trouble.'

'I don't want your charity.'

Embarrassed, Annie stilled her hand in the act of reaching for her purse.

'Oh no, of course not, I'm sorry.'

'What's his name, this bloke you're looking for?'

'John. Varney. He has long hair. A beard. Wears a camouflage jacket. Right now he's got a huge black eye, here.'

She touched the left side of her face.

He nodded. 'I know him. Ex-army. PTSD, I think. He was here about half an hour ago. You know the Banana Warehouse?' Michael nodded. 'He was heading that way.'

Annie and Michael got up to leave. Michael reached into his pocket and fished out a twenty-pound note.

'No charity. Call it payment for services received,' he said.

He held it out until the man took it with a nod and a 'Thanks.'

This time of night there was no traffic. Annie still crossed Fazeley Street at a run, heading towards the narrow side street on which ancient cobbles broke through the tarmac. Michael behind her, she hurried on towards the forbidding tumbledown structure.

Standing in front of its rust-scabbed double doors, she shivered, and not just from the cold penetrating her padded jacket. Someone – the landlord, she assumed – had bolted perforated steel plates to the doors. But the impressive-looking lock hung askew, leaning out from the splintered wooden frame and rendering the metal reinforcement useless.

Fear rippled through her as she contemplated entering the darkness beyond the door. Her palms were sweaty and she couldn't suppress the squirming anxiety in her belly.

What the hell were they doing? If John Varney really was ex-army and suffering from PTSD, wouldn't that make him even more unpredictable? Even more dangerous? It had seemed like a logical plan at Michael's, and even in her office. Track him down, confront him, force him to give up the names of the people who'd hired him. But what if he had other ideas?

What if he had a plan, too? Lure them to this deserted neighbourhood. Get a mate to send them into a crack den, or whatever the hell this place was. And then what? Pull a knife. A gun? What were they thinking? Her breath was coming in rapid, shallow gasps and she felt as though she might faint.

No, wait. He couldn't have lured them here. That had been the tip-off from his wife. Or had it? VanessunDorma was just a Mumsnet user name. It would be child's play to hack your spouse's account. She might even have shared her details with him.

'Ready?' Michael said, making her jump.

Another petrifying thought flashed through her, sending the butterflies in her stomach into a maddened panic to break free. What if Michael was involved? No, he couldn't be. His son had almost been killed. She was losing it. Seeing threats everywhere, even from the one man she knew she could trust.

She looked at him. Really *looked*. Saw only concern. Maybe a hint of fear, too.

'We don't have to do this, Annie,' he said. 'We can back off now. Think of something else.'

She thought of Isla's terrified phone call. *There was a man f-following me.* And that man, that bastard, was inside this shithole shooting gallery. Nobody threatened her little girl and got away it.

She steeled herself. 'Come on, let's do it.'

She pulled the door wide and stepped into the blackness.

Chapter 47

Trying to ignore the rapid-fire thrum of her pulse, Annie crept inside the warehouse. A fetid stench of human waste and stagnant water invaded her nostrils, and she was seized with a violent urge to vomit. She let out a breath and then inhaled through her mouth, trying not to think of particles of God-knew-what passing between her lips.

The warehouse had to be thirty yards across. At the far end, a fire blazed up from an oil drum. His face seeming to writhe in the shifting glare of the flames, John Varney was arguing loudly with a tall young man.

The firelight, tinged by thick black smoke, barely lit the two men. Annie and Michael, crouched in the lee of a pile of broken crates, were shrouded in shadow.

What now? Should they hang back and risk allowing Varney to hurt the young man? Or rush in and risk getting into the middle of a fight? She turned to Michael. Tilted her head towards the two men. Raised her eyebrows.

He shook his head.

That was fine by her. Her heart was bumping painfully in her throat and she doubted she could walk, her legs were trembling so violently.

Varney was pacing back and forth, though he kept his eyes on the young man at all times. He was gesticulating, waving his hands in the air. Then he turned suddenly and advanced. Raised his fists and shouted.

'What do you mean, no? I just told you what's going to happen. It's not up to you any more. I've killed men with my bare hands.'

He levelled a finger and aimed it straight at the younger man's face. 'Don't make me go down that road again.'

Annie felt cold terror clouding her mind. If they didn't do something soon, he was going to hurt the young guy. Maybe even kill him, like he'd tried to do to Aaron. But her muscles were paralysed. Michael was frozen to the spot, too, his eyes wide.

The young man was smiling nervously, fear pasting the inappropriate expression onto his face, looking everywhere but at Varney's distorted features.

He backed away, hands held out in supplication.

'Look, I'm sorry. I misjudged you, OK? How strongly you felt about things. That's on me. But there's no need for violence, John. Maybe we can work something out.'

'I told you what I need. That's all there is to work out. I want enough cash to disappear.'

'Yeah, but how much are we talking about? You must have a sum in mind.'

Varney paused. Annie held her breath. It was going to be all right. Like they said, every man had his price.

'A hundred grand,' he said.

The young man pulled his head back, firelight gleaming on his jawline.

'A hundred ... John, mate, that's a lot of dosh. I could probably find twenty-five, but that's it.'

Varney pushed his face forward.

'You two are loaded. You can afford more. I want a hundred.'

'Come on, John, that's not a negotiating position. Maybe I could go to fifty, but I'll be in trouble with the boss. You know it.'

'Fifty?'

'You could disappear for sure with that kind of money. Cash in hand? No questions asked? You could go anywhere. Get yourself a place. New clothes. The works. You'd be a different man. Maybe Vanessa would even take you back.'

Varney hesitated. But Annie knew he was going to take the deal. Then the young man would leave and she and Michael could get what they came for.

'Fifty grand and I'm out. Free and clear?'

'As a bird.'

He looked up at the filthy roof. Then back at the young man. 'OK, then.'

'Thank Christ! I thought you were going to do me some serious damage. I'll go and get your money straight after this.' The young man smiled, took a hesitant step forward. 'Look, John, we did some good work together. Let's not end as enemies.'

He held his arms wide.

Annie held her breath. He was insane. Leaving himself open to an attack.

Varney said something, but too quietly for her to hear. Was it a threat? She reached out and clutched Michael's forearm, unable to believe they were just going to crouch there in the dark and watch him claim another victim.

The two men closed, and miraculously Varney held his arms out too, stepping into the younger man's embrace and patting him on the back.

Annie relaxed. Thank God. It was going to be all right. Whoever the young man was, he'd worked some kind of magic and soothed Varney to the point where his anger had left him. Maybe he'd even be able to help them convince Varney to give up the identity of his employers.

As she watched, Varney jerked, hard and fast. Annie gasped. He'd stabbed the young man while pretending to accept his hug.

He stepped away, and she flinched, expecting to see him gripping a knife. But both his hands were empty. He looked down, eyes wide, mouth twisting, then back up at the young man. Slowly he raised his hands to his belly, across which a dark stain was spreading.

Annie couldn't make sense of the picture she was seeing. Time slowed down and she watched the look of blank incomprehension on Varney's face switch to a twisted rictus of agony.

He took his hands away from his stomach and held them up. The palms were slick with blood. Lots of blood. Annie almost cried out as she saw the tide of it washing down the front of his hoodie.

Then the young man laughed, loudly, breaking the spell.

In his right hand he brandished a long knife, the blade smeared scarlet.

Varney screamed, a cracked sound in the dark, and launched himself at the young man. But even as he closed the distance between them, Annie could see he was badly wounded. His face twisted again in pain and he screamed a second time, a plaintive screech she would never be able to forget.

The young man sidestepped and yanked viciously on his right arm, sending him sprawling onto the glass-strewn concrete. In a flash he was on top of him, knees pinning his arms to the ground.

'No, please!' Varney grunted.

The young man raised the knife, held it there so firelight glinted off the tip.

'Don't,' Varney sobbed. 'My kids. They need—'

The young man plunged the blade straight down into his chest with a sickening wet crunch.

Varney screamed for a third time.

The knife lanced down again, piercing his throat, releasing thick spurts of blood that arced into the air before splashing down all over his attacker.

Annie was balled up with fear, but unable to tear her eyes away from the horrific scene unfolding in front of her.

Varney was no longer making any noise, but still the knife rose and fell, rose and fell, hitting him indiscriminately, in the chest, the neck, the face.

And the whole time he was carrying out the frenzied attack, the young man remained impassive, concentrating on the job at hand like a butcher preparing cuts of meat.

Chapter 48

Annie clapped her hands over her mouth to stifle the scream that threatened to burst free. She'd just watched a man get stabbed to death.

But the action unbalanced her and she stumbled sideways, scraping her boot along the gritty concrete floor.

The young man whipped around. He climbed off Varney's blood-soaked body, head cocked, and looked straight at Annie, his eyes white in his bloodied face. She felt as though her bladder might let go.

But he made no move to advance towards her, and she realised that she and Michael were invisible. The darkness was deep and the light from the fire he was standing behind would be virtually blinding him.

She held her breath. If he came for them, they'd stand no chance. Somehow she knew that even against two opponents, this baby-faced psychopath would emerge triumphant, that bloody butcher's knife glinting in his hand as their corpses lay amidst the used condoms, broken glass and needles.

But he didn't come for them. Instead, he bent from the waist and gripped the hilt of the knife, which protruded obscenely from Varney's midsection. He pulled it free, and she felt her gorge rise as the blade screeched against bone. He wiped it on his trousers – pointlessly, she thought, given the amount of blood covering him – and then, as if he were nothing more than a selfie-taking tourist, sauntered out through a door at the far end of the warehouse.

Sickened, Annie scrambled to her feet, ignoring the agonising pins and needles that flared from toes to hip, and rushed towards

Varney's motionless form. Michael reached him first, Annie crouching beside him a second later, barely able to look at the horrific injuries the young man had inflicted.

Michael leaned closer and gently pushed two fingers into the soft flesh under Varney's jaw. Annie took Varney's hand in hers and squeezed, felt a brief answering pressure.

'Oh my God, Michael. He's alive.'

'He's got a pulse. Weak, but it's there. We need to call 999. We can't let him die here.'

She nodded. Even though an ambulance would mean police, too, what else could they do?

She looked down into Varney's ruined face. His left eye fluttered open.

'Hey,' she said softly. 'You're going to be OK. We're going to call an ambulance.'

His lips worked, but no words emerged. He turned his head aside and coughed. A great gout of dark blood poured from his mouth, streaming onto the floor. His body convulsed, and for a second his pain-racked eyes locked onto Annie's and she caught the fading light of his humanity.

Then they fluttered closed and he was still.

Michael pushed his fingers back into Varney's neck, searching for a pulse, but from the way he sank back onto his haunches, Annie knew it was too late.

'My God, Annie,' he said, his face drawn. 'He's dead.'

She burst into tears, unable to control her emotions any longer. Michael drew her into his arms as she buried her face in the crook of his neck. She sobbed uncontrollably, kneeling in a pool of another human being's blood and knowing she would never, ever be able to erase the horror of this night for as long as she lived. Finally, he eased her away from him. Tilted her chin up.

'We have to go,' he said.

She nodded, and tried to speak, her voice clotted with snot and tears.

'I know.'

She stumbled past the corpse, the oil drum in which the flames were dying and the broken-down doors.

Outside, she gulped down breath after cold breath. But the bloody, smoky stink of the warehouse clung to her.

She pulled out her phone.

'What are you doing?' Michael hissed.

'We have to report it.'

'I know. But from a call box. That way it's anonymous. By the time the police get here, we'll be long gone.'

She nodded her agreement, and they fled, ducking into the shadowed yard of a motor-parts wholesaler when a solitary car cruised by, its headlights sweeping the street.

As they reached the pickup, Annie paused and looked back towards the warehouse. She and Michael were in way over their heads in a brutal, ugly place, with no way back to where normal families lived, going on holiday, taking silly pictures, sharing meals around tables, arguing about homework or where to order takeaway from.

They'd fallen through the surface into a world where lies, violence, pain and death were all that counted.

Chapter 49

She was trawling Facebook, searching for her next victim.

Would it be Laura, with her faux-modest post about the simple, unspoilt Tuscan village where she, Roly, Tim and Penny had been 'lucky' enough to spend a month? Or how about Sara, who was feeling 'blessed' that her darling Mabel had passed her Grade 8 piano with distinction? Helen looked promising. Struggling to support 'poor Tabitha', who was battling an eating disorder.

A hank of black fringe obscured the screen. She hooked it out of the way of her thick-framed plastic glasses.

Where would she be without their empty narcissism and boasts about their kids' never-ending achievements? Their perfect homes? Their mutually satisfying marriages? Even while their 'soulmate and best friend' was arranging to bang pretty, blonde, sexy Tilly's brains out in some five-star hotel room with complimentary toiletries from Jo Malone and a warm chocolate cookie on check-in.

Talk about a kid in a sweet shop.

She shucked off her red leather jacket and slung it over the back of her chair. Hunting always made her hot. Sensing a stranger's gaze, she looked up from her laptop.

'I love your tattoo,' a woman at a nearby table said.

Maya looked down at the rope and half-knot, then back at her neighbour, who was smiling expectantly.

'I don't care.'

Flushing, the woman went back to perusing her phone.

Maya bent to her laptop again. She didn't need validation. People only praised you before dumping on you. *Oh Maya, you look so pretty. But we can't go shopping now after all. Mummy has to meet her friend.*

Yeah, right. More like her dealer. Bitch.

Behind the stripped-pine counter, the barista called out another order.

'Charley!'

Maya rose from her chair, snapping the laptop's lid shut and shooting the nearby woman a look as if to say, *Touch it, lose your hand*. No fear on that score. Except possibly from the woman herself, who bent even closer to her own screen. Maya smiled to herself. Collected her coffee.

Once more engrossed in other women's lives, she took an exploratory sip of the coffee and tapped out a short reply to the post about Mabel's Grade 8 distinction and how it had been worth all the bullying over practice.

So happy for you. Not easy being strong for your kids. People call us pushy and selfish, but we only want what's best for them.

There, let her mull on that for a while.

Her phone vibrated. A message from Grace. This should be interesting.

wanna meet up

where and when

tk maxx bullring 11am sat

cool

Maya hesitated. Just for a moment. But she trusted her instincts. Which, had Grace been able to understand them, would have had her fleeing the online world like a mouse coming face to face with a snake. Poor Grace. She typed again.

luv u xox

She held her breath. Three pulsing dots. Grace was typing.

luv u 2 xoxo

Maya's pulse never really did much beyond tick over like an idling car engine. But here, now, with Grace taking that tentative next step in their relationship, it wandered up just a little. Soon she could start pulling information from her, intimate stuff, feeding off Grace's excitement at finally meeting her friend. Er, newsflash, Grace: not going to happen.

Maya had developed a tried-and-tested line: *Let's tell each other a secret we've never told anyone else.* And when she had enough, she'd vanish from Grace's life only to pop up in her mum's. She'd recently started posting about her fear that she wouldn't be able to cope when her 'darling Gracie' went to Spain on an exchange trip. *Fear?* The stupid woman was about to discover the true meaning of the word.

The café door banged wide, admitting a gust of freezing air. Maya's neighbour whipped her head round, ready to shoot a look at whoever had let the heat out. When she saw who had entered, and the look on his face, she turned back to her laptop. Maya smirked. Silly cow did well to trust her instincts there.

Ollie came over to her table, smelling strongly of apple shower gel. No jacket. Just a thin white T-shirt and a clean pair of jeans. He pulled out the chair facing her, scraping its legs across the floor with a squawk, and plonked himself down. His mouth twitched. She knew that look. He was hiding something. Something he was proud of. Her pulse flickered upwards again. What now?

'I did what you wanted,' he said. 'Took care of John.'

A flash of something unpleasant rippled through Maya. She knew she didn't really experience emotions like other people. But there was something there. Not fear. Not exactly. It was more like ... apprehension.

Ollie was normally reliable. Yes, he occasionally went a little too far, but nothing that couldn't be folded into the basic blackmail demand. A memory of a hotel room in Bristol swam into view.

She leaned forward and dropped her a voice to a low murmur. 'What have you done, Ollie?'

'Like I said, I took care of business.'

'And that means what, exactly?'

'Let's just say I don't think our ex-military friend is going to be causing us any more trouble.'

His right knee was jiggling up and down and he kept running a hand over his hair. He was hyper, adrenalised, like he'd just done a big fat line of coke.

Then she saw it. Behind his ear. A spot of blood. He must have missed it when he'd showered. That feeling of apprehension deepened, tendrils of icy cold needling into her gut.

She stood, leaned over him, glaring down into his face, sending the smug smile scurrying for cover. Only she could produce that effect in him.

'Get up, we're going,' she said, grabbing her jacket.

He wrinkled his nose. 'I only just got here.'

She planted her hands on his shoulders and pulled. 'We're leaving.'

Ollie got to his feet and allowed Maya to frogmarch him out of the café and round the corner into a dark alley. The wind knifed down it between the walls.

She shoved him against the grimy brickwork and pushed her face into his.

'What have you done?' she asked, knowing already the answer he'd give her.

He shrugged. 'You know what I did, Maya. I had to. I mean, I didn't *want* to, if that's what you're thinking. It was self-defence. *He* went for *me*. He had this massive hunting knife. I managed to get it off him and, you know, I got lucky.' He stared down into her eyes, his own deader than she'd ever seen them. 'Look at it this way. It's just one less thing for us to worry about. Now can we go, please? I'm freezing my bollocks off.'

Maya shook her head in utter disbelief. Yes, Ollie had his moments. But this? This was different. She needed to make him understand.

'Why, Ollie? There was no need. We had him just where we wanted him. You could just have reminded him about his precious bloody kids.'

'It doesn't matter,' he said petulantly, twisting away from her grip. 'I sorted it, it's done. End of.'

'But that's just it, isn't it? It isn't the end of *anything*. Your DNA will be all over the place. The body, the scene. And if the police link that back to the guy you attacked in Bristol, we're screwed.' That insistent little thought forced its way up again. She framed it as a question. 'Do you *want* to break us up?'

She bit her lip, regretting her choice of words. But Ollie, for all his bluntness, knew her too well.

'No, Maya, I don't. Do you? Is that what you're saying?' He pushed his face closer to hers and dropped his voice to a predatory murmur that set the hairs on the nape of her neck prickling. 'You better not be saying you want to stop my fun. Because that would be a really, *really* bad idea.'

'Forget it, Ollie. Let's go home.'

Something happened to him then that Maya couldn't immediately process. His head twisted jerkily to the side and he took a step towards her, a look of thoughtful concentration deepening his eye colour to black. And then she had it.

He was considering hurting her. Murderous fire burned in those inky irises, and now she did feel fear – just a glimmer. It was the first time in a very long while. Since the cellar.

But this was Ollie. *Her* Ollie. He wouldn't really hurt her, would he? After all she'd done for him? How dare he, when she spent all her time protecting him? They were only standing here facing off in a piss-stinking alleyway behind a café because he'd offed the help.

He stopped with his face – pale and taut – a few inches from hers.

'You can't go, Maya. I won't allow it. I need you. And you need me.' His voice was a low growl. 'I don't know what I'd do if you tried to go.'

Maya looked down. His fists were clenching and releasing, but in that moment she knew she was safe, physically, at least. He'd come close, but his breathing had slowed and colour was already returning to his cheeks. But she needed to reach him right now, before he lost it completely. She couldn't afford for that to happen. Anyone who thought there was something off about her brother on first acquaintance should see him when one of his dark moods took him.

'What we've built together, Ollie? It's special. You know I would never leave you.'

'Yes, Maya. I do know that.' He pushed up his sleeve, revealing his rope tattoo. 'Give me your arm.'

She knew what he wanted and bared her own arm, aligning it with his so the two tattoos lined up, two halves making a whole knot. And she remembered the sting of the needle as they'd lain on parallel couches getting them done ten years earlier. The pain that had joined them was starting to signify something else for her now.

She pulled back a little.

'I'm sorry. Now hold still. You've got blood on you.'

She retrieved a tissue, licked the corner and wiped the spot of gore from behind his ear.

He nodded, smiled.

'Thank you, Maya. Now come here.'

The cold tendrils of fear retreated into her spine as she allowed him to enfold her in his arms. His grip was strong and unyielding. No softness to it. More like a hold than a hug.

He was getting harder and harder to control. What if she couldn't manage it the next time?

Day Five

Chapter 50

Gripping the kitchen counter as if she might otherwise fall off the world, Annie tried to forget the nightmare. The grinning young man baring his teeth as he plunged a dagger into John Varney's chest.

Isla had a full day's study leave, so Annie dropped her round at Grant's, managing the drive on a combination of super-strength black coffee, two Pro Plus tablets and a prayer.

As she rang the doorbell, she dropped the bombshell she'd been planning since the previous day.

'I want you to put the Find My app on your phone and I want access so I can see where you are.'

Isla's eyes widened. She was half grinning, as if she couldn't believe what she was hearing. Annie waited her out. She needed to know she could find Isla any time she wanted while she and Michael attempted to take down the blackmailers.

'What? Are you serious? I'm not doing that.'

'I'm keeping you safe, Isla, that's all.'

'But Mum, I'm sixteen.' She looked down. 'Almost.'

'Please, lovey, do it for me. Hopefully it won't be for long.' Maybe the nuclear button would work. 'I don't want to have to ground you, but…'

Isla's resistance crumbled. 'Fine.'

'I mean it, Isla. I'll check, and I'll come back and fetch you if it's not there in ten minutes.'

After securing a promise from Isla and Grant that she wouldn't leave the flat, Annie drove into work, where she headed straight to the kitchen for more coffee.

Her heart felt light, insubstantial, her pulse fluttering when she checked her wrists.

That poor man, dying in front of her and Michael. They'd found a phone box and called an ambulance and the police, but it didn't help the feeling that she'd crossed a line somewhere.

Her desk phone rang. It was Letitia's secretary. Annie didn't have an appointment. This couldn't be good.

'Could you come to her office, please?'

'Now?' Annie checked the time: 8.57 a.m.

'If you wouldn't mind.'

The line went dead.

She reached Letitia's office two minutes later. As she took the visitor chair, she could tell Letitia was gearing up for something. Her watery blue eyes were abnormally focused this morning. Her lips were compressed into a tight line and her hands were clasped on the glass desktop in front of her.

'How was your evening, Annie?' she asked.

Fear rushed through Annie like a tidal wave. How did Letitia know? Had it been her driving past when they took cover in the workshop forecourt?

She didn't have any more time to worry. About that, anyway. Letitia was still speaking.

'Dan Gao called me at half past six this morning to complain that you stood him up. What happened?'

A sickly flood of guilt washed over Annie as she realised what she'd done. In the heat of the moment, trying to track down John Varney with Michael, she'd completely forgotten about her dinner with the CEO of Gao Industries. Embarrassment and shame curdled inside her and she felt her cheeks heating up.

It would have been marginally less distressing if Letitia had gone red in the face, started swearing and banging the low-carbon glass of her desk with her bony fist. At least then Annie could have permitted herself the limited-value gift of feeling like she was the adult in the room. But where a male manager might have yelled, or, these days in academia, probably huffed and puffed, struggling to find a politically acceptable way to express his anger, Letitia merely stared at Annie coolly.

She had the best excuse in the world a mother could give: *I was trying to protect my child*. But how could she possibly say that without explaining about the blackmailers and exposing Isla to even more danger? Her mouth opened and closed wordlessly.

Letitia's lips parted with a click.

'Nothing?'

Annie's mind raced as she struggled to concoct something believable that was not an out-and-out lie.

'Letitia, I am so sorry this happened. It was Isla. You know she's been having problems since the divorce. Something triggered her last night. A TV show, I think. She had a panic attack. A bad one. I had to take her to A&E. I thought they were going to have to sedate her.'

Letitia sighed, scratched the tip of her sharp-pointed nose.

'This is a strategically crucial relationship, Annie. You know what's at stake here.'

'Of course I do, Letitia, but—'

Letitia rode over her.

'Do you have any idea the pressure I'm under? I have to show a profit, for God's sake! When did that become a thing?' She paused for breath. 'I rely on you, Annie. You're my right-hand woman. If your daughter was unwell, I understand you'd have to put her needs ahead of the school's. But you didn't even have the courtesy to call Dan and explain. Are you really telling me you couldn't find five minutes to do that simple thing?'

'I'm sorry, Letitia. I'll call him now. Apologise. I'll make it right, I promise.'

Calm restored as if her momentary outburst had never happened, Letitia nodded curtly.

'Good. Your annual review is coming up, Annie. I hope and

expect we'll be discussing your financial triumph, and not oppor-
tunities elsewhere in the university.'

Annie recognised a dismissal when she heard one. And a threat.

She spun on her heel and left. She needed to see Michael
urgently. Work would have to wait.

Chapter 51

Maya rubbed at her tattoo. Ties could bind, but sometimes they could strangle, too.

On the surveillance feed she'd logged onto, a teenage girl left her house to sit in the front of a big black BMW X5. Elspeth had an eating disorder and it was time for her first appointment with her therapist.

Her phone rang. She glanced at the screen and frowned. It was Bodden again, the manager of the bank in the Caymans. What did he want now?

'Hello?'

'Hello, Miss Kinton, I trust you are well?'

More small talk? She could do it, she just didn't see the point.

'Very well, Mr Bodden. And you? Your family?'

He had two children. She thought it best not to reveal that she knew their names. Their schools. Not yet, anyway.

'All good, thank you.' He cleared his throat. 'I'm afraid we've had a rather disturbing enquiry. About your account.'

'Go on.'

'We have received a Section 271 notice from a bank in the UK. Do you know what that is, Miss Kinton?'

Maya frowned. The bank manager's usual fawning tone had vanished, replaced by something harder-edged.

'You'll have to explain, Mr Bodden. You're the banker, after all.'

'A Section 271 notice is an inter-bank request made under the provisions of international anti-money laundering regulations. An HSBC branch in Birmingham has been advised by one of its account holders that a recently cancelled standing order to your account was in fact in response to a fraudulent request. They are

requesting full and immediate disclosure of your account's bene-
ficial owner as well as statements going back five years. Obviously,
we have said nothing thus far. But we will have to comply. Can
you help me out here? Why might the HSBC be concerned about
fraud on your account?'

He was being polite. Just. But Maya caught the note of danger
reverberating down the line all the way from the Caymans to her
flat in the Jewellery Quarter. Bloody Michael Taylor and his new
best friend were misbehaving. She needed to buy time while she
figured out how to snip off this loose end.

'Obviously all our dealings are entirely above board, Mr
Bodden. And frankly I am horrified at the thought that one
of our clients has come to so gross a misunderstanding of our
business relationship. I can assure you, *categorically*,' she added,
throwing as much emphasis onto the word as she could summon,
'that there is nothing fraudulent in our financial dealings, either
with our many happy clients or with you and your bank.'

'I am relieved to hear it. But still there remains the matter of
the Section 271 notice. These things can't be ignored, you know,
however much we might wish to protect our own clients' privacy.'

'Of course not. I understand,' she said. 'So don't ignore it. But
could you take a day or so to respond? I'm sure you are a very
busy man with a great many demands on your time.'

'I suppose we could manage a twenty-four-hour delay. But—'

'That's settled, then. Thank you, Mr Bodden. You'll have to
forgive me, I have another call coming in.'

After she'd hung up, she sat there breathing hard and feeling another jab of fear, the second in as many days. What was
happening? Everything was falling apart just when it should be
holding together.

Her fingers skittered over her keyboard. She brought up
Annie and Michael's call logs. Mobiles and landlines. Taylor had
called the bank. But there were no calls to the police. Either the
emergency number or the local stations. That was good. They

were still in line, just. Not only that: if they were keeping things to themselves, then they were still scared. And that meant they were vulnerable.

Another set of commands, tapped out with lightning speed, brought up the surveillance camera feeds from their properties. Barnes's Audi was parked outside Taylor's place. So they were together, were they? Probably scheming away inside, figuring out how to beat her.

She nodded to herself. They were about to learn a painful lesson.

Chapter 52

Tongue protruding between her teeth, Isla stared at the phrase at the top of the worksheet their Latin teacher had handed out. *Quid est punctum latine?*

On the line beneath, she dutifully supplied the translation.

What is the point of Latin?

He thought he could make his subject interesting with jokes like that one. Haha. A whole day's study leave sounded like fun until you got down to it. The key word, as Miss Stevens had pointed out the previous afternoon, was 'study', not 'leave'.

She shoved the worksheet away her. It spun across the table and see-sawed through the air onto the kitchen floor.

She checked her phone, even though it hadn't beeped to let her know she had a message. Nothing. They were all just heads down, revising. Or pretending to, anyway.

She took a selfie. Posted it. *#bludystudyleave*. She smiled at her own cleverness.

The TV was on with the sound down. She grabbed the remote and turned it up. Local news. It was showing footage of some sort of crime scene. CSIs walking about with cameras and clear plastic boxes. Cops and paramedics doing official-looking stuff.

The presenter said, 'Police are looking for a man and woman in connection with the murder of a local homeless man identified as John Varney. An eyewitness was able to give police a description of the woman.'

Her dad wandered in and popped the kettle on.

'Hey, munchkin, watcha watchin'?'

She smiled even though it was a bit lame to use old bits from when she was little. Then the smile slid off her face. Because as she stared at the face on the little telly, she felt cold inside, and sweaty, like a panic attack was coming.

She pointed at the screen. At the weirdly smooth CGI face – like the worst-ever anime.

'That's Mum,' she whispered. 'And the man she was with must have been Michael.'

He followed her pointing finger.

'Bloody hell! It is! Wait, who's this Michael?'

'He's like a new friend. His son was hit by a car on Tuesday. They've been working together on her crazy paranoid fantasy that I'm in danger. But the police want to talk to her, Dad. They say she's involved in a murder.'

The outraged expression disfiguring her dad's face frightened her.

'She's really lost it! Coming round here making all these accusations when her and her boyfriend—'

'I don't think he's her boyfriend.'

'Well, whatever he is, they cooked up this story to get you away from me, and now this?' He shook his head. 'No. Not going to happen. Where does he live?'

'I don't know, do I?'

'Doesn't matter. I'll find out.'

He snatched his car keys up from the table and stormed out, slamming the front door behind him so hard it made Isla jump.

Chapter 53

The doorbell rang, startling Annie. It rang again. And again. She bit her lip, fearing the worst.

She and Michael had just been watching the news and seen the e-fit picture of Annie. She pictured suited detectives with stern faces standing side by side. Somehow the police had tracked her to Michael's.

The ringing turned to hammering. Now Annie pictured an enraged psychopath, one fist bunched, the other clutching a knife. Her stomach flipped.

Michael checked the entryphone on the office wall.

He turned to her. 'Relax. I don't think it's the cops. It's just some bloke.'

'Let me see,' Annie said, joining him. She found herself looking into the furious face of her ex-husband. 'Oh God, it's Grant. We'd better go and talk to him.'

She followed him out of the room and down the stairs.

Michael opened the door. Then staggered back as the visitor barged his way in, punching him in the face. He grunted with pain and clutched his jaw.

'Grant!' Annie screamed. 'What the hell?'

Chest heaving, hair dishevelled, Grant stood over Michael, who'd sunk to one knee and was holding his free hand up to keep him at bay.

'You've really gone and done it now, Annie,' he shouted. 'You and your boyfriend here are wanted in a murder investigation? Have you lost your fucking mind?'

She ran at him and shoved him hard in the breastbone. He

stumbled back through the front door before catching his heel and sprawling on the front path.

Michael was on his feet again and standing beside her.

'You have no idea what you're talking about,' she shouted down at Grant. 'You need to leave. Now!'

Grant pulled himself to his feet. He aimed a finger at each of them in turn like a gun.

'This isn't over, Annie. First you accuse me of creating some deepfake video, then it turns out you're wanted for murder. I think it's pretty clear you're an unfit mother. Isla should stay with me until this whole thing is over one way or another. Maybe I should talk to my solicitor. Or the police.'

She put her hands on her hips, breathing heavily.

'*I'm* unfit? Well, *you* promised to not let her out of your sight. I see that promise didn't last very long. Anyway, are you going to move your stash of drugs first? Still keep them in the bedside table, do you? Maybe *I* should call the cops.' Seeing his frown, she rode her anger instead of fighting it down. 'No? OK, then, so unless a judge says different, the custody arrangement's going to stay exactly the way it is. And by the way? We didn't murder *anyone*.'

'You were on the TV,' he shot back. 'A bloody e-fit!'

'It's mistaken identity. Yes, we were there, Grant. We *witnessed* it. That's all. Now unless you really want me to dial 999, you have to go.'

Grant's eyes slid away from hers. She had him. Shaking his head, he backed away.

'I'm not going to let you get away with this, Annie. You're out of control.'

He spun round and marched off down the path before dropping into the seat of his ridiculous little sports car. The engine roared into life and he screeched away from the kerb, leaving a cloud of acrid blue rubber smoke in his wake.

Shaking his head, Michael ushered Annie inside again. They went into the kitchen while he made coffee.

'How's your chin?' she asked, touching the swelling that had popped out along his jawline.

He winced and jerked his head away.

'Sore, actually. Jesus, your husband's got a hell of a right hook.'

Annie felt awful, and the fact that Michael was trying to make light of Grant's assault just made it worse.

'I'll get something for it.'

After wrapping a tea towel around a bag of frozen peas and applying it to his jaw, she sighed.

'What the hell are we going to do, Michael? We're on the news now. And they've got my description. Should we go to the police first, before they come for us?'

He shook his head. 'What if they arrest us? Who'll protect Aaron and Isla then? We have to find these people on our own. I just don't think the cops will take us seriously unless we have real evidence.'

'But what about poor John? Isn't *he* evidence?'

'He's evidence of murder, yes. But thanks to our friend at the soup kitchen, the cops think we did it. They'll want to close down that lead before they start spending money on DNA analysis.'

'Yes, but if Grant recognised me, it won't be long before other people do. Maybe they'll get a description of you, too. Sooner or later, the police are going to be the ones ringing your doorbell.' She peered out the kitchen window at the street. 'They could be on their way here now. Or to mine.'

'Are you saying we should turn ourselves in?'

She shook her head, balled her fist.

'No.'

'What are you saying, then?'

Annie's phone rang, and she started, knocking her coffee cup over. Fear overwhelmed her. They'd tracked her already. Pulse racing, she put the phone on speaker and held it out between them as if it might go off.

'This is Annie,' she said tentatively.

'I know!' Deanna's infectious laugh filled the air. 'I called *you*, remember? Listen, I finally recovered that email. Some pretty hardcore encryption, but they didn't reckon with my superior tech chops. Plus, bonus time – ta-daa! – I got the IP address, too. Traced it, did some PhD-level geotargeting, and guess what? It's registered to commercial premises in Digbeth. I can send you everything I've got now if you like?'

Suddenly fearful that whoever was behind the scam had hacked her email, Annie reacted quickly.

'No! Don't do that. We'll come over to the university. And thanks, Deanna. You're a star. I mean it. A supernova. We'll be there as quick as we can.'

She exchanged a look with Michael, her pulse kicking into high gear. At last they had a real lead on the blackmailers. They were about to start fighting back for real. Then a frightening thought barged its way to the front of her mind, erasing all her optimism.

At some point, probably very soon, they were going to come face to face with the psychopaths who'd been tormenting them.

Were they ready for that?

Chapter 54

Michael slid his truck into a space outside a student property letting agency. Slumping low in her seat, Annie looked up at the window across the street. A flat above a kebab shop. Frowning, she checked the address on the sheet of paper Deanna had given her.

Even if she hadn't discovered the existence of the two blackmailers on the *Mail*'s website, the sight of the run-down terrace opposite would have killed the idea that she and Michael were facing an organised crime group stone dead.

Part of the guttering had detached from the eaves and now hung drunkenly over the left-hand bay window, its birdshit-smeared top crusted with clearly ineffective anti-pigeon spikes. Greying net curtains obscured the windows themselves. And a thick spreading fan of greenish muck slimed its way down the off-white stucco where the original cast-iron drainpipe had rusted through.

But whoever worked there had sufficient professional pride to have stencilled a company name in now-faded gold capitals on the windows.

L. H. MURRAY

TAX CONSULTANT, ACCOUNTANT, BOOKKEEPING

Michael turned. His mouth was a grim line. A muscle flickered under his left eye.

'This is it, then.'

Annie nodded. A shudder spiralled through her belly and into her chest, making her catch her breath.

'Yep.'

'Nervous?'

'A little.'

'A little? I'm shitting myself.'

That was a surprise. She'd had Michael down as the unflappable type.

'But you were so calm on the drive over.'

'I was concentrating on not crashing or running a red light, that's all.'

She wiped her palms on her thighs. 'I didn't want to look weak in front of you. I'm actually terrified,' she confessed. 'I just thought, you know, you're the practical one.'

Michael ran a hand over his face. Huffed out a breath.

'Look, Annie, I'd do anything to protect Aaron – and Isla. But after seeing John get killed by that maniac last night, well, it shook me up, I don't mind admitting it.'

She laid a hand on his shoulder. The muscle beneath her palm was hard, tight.

'Come on. Let's get it over with.'

Thirty seconds later, Annie Barnes was standing outside a building that housed either the answer to her prayers or her worst nightmare.

Chapter 55

Annie stretched out a trembling finger to ring the bell for the top flat. Then stopped. What was she thinking? Hardened criminals weren't exactly likely to just let her in.

She pushed the middle bell instead. Silence. Perhaps they were out. She let out a breath and was turning to Michael to suggest they come back later when the intercom crackled, startling her.

'Who is it?'

A woman's voice. Local accent.

Annie leaned forward. Put her mouth close to the grille.

'Amazon.'

The latch buzzed and clacked. Michael pushed the door inwards. The dingy hallway smelled of takeaway food. An impression solidified by the colourful printed menus piled haphazardly on a painted radiator cover. A naked light bulb dangled from a white flex, shedding sad yellow light over a narrow staircase covered in reddish-brown carpet so worn its fibrous backing showed through.

Now that they were in, Annie's nerves solidified into something more like resolve. They were past the point of no return. She took a deep breath and started climbing. She tiptoed past the front door on the middle floor. The woman expecting a delivery would be disappointed. Annie felt she could live with the deception.

At the top of the staircase, the hall dog-legged around a chimney breast and ended at a door panelled in its upper half with rippled glass. The company name was repeated here in more gold lettering.

Her heart was beating so fast she could feel it inside her chest, thrumming against her ribs and her diaphragm. No time to hesitate.

She raised her hand, knuckles bent, then stopped. What on earth was the point in knocking? They were here to extract information and stop criminals extorting them. She took hold of the doorknob, twisted it quietly, then drew back and shoved with all her might.

The door travelled inwards for three inches before jerking to a stop so sudden Annie knocked her arm painfully on the frame. A brass chain stretched tight across the gap.

Seconds later, a man's face appeared. He was in his mid-thirties. A couple of inches over six feet. Deep-set, suspicious eyes, but his overall expression was more frightened than angry. Was it the man from the *Mail*'s photo archive? With a few more years of stressful living on the clock? She couldn't tell.

He stared at her. Then beyond her, at Michael. Looking him up and down, too.

'What's going on? Who are you?'

Before she could answer, Michael leaned back and kicked at the door just below the knob. The flimsy lock sheared out of the narrow strip of cheap wood, the chain ripped free of its mounting, and Michael half charged, half fell into the room beyond. The man cried out, backing away, clutching the side of his head. Annie rushed in behind Michael, ready to scream, to fight tooth and claw to protect Isla.

The man retreated towards a desk from which the laminate was peeling along one edge. Hands aloft, wild-eyed, mouth open, his right cheekbone reddening from the impact of the door.

'What the hell's going on? I haven't done anything!' he shouted, as Annie looked around, hyper-alert for the nutcase from the previous night to emerge from a door, brandishing that wicked-looking knife. But it seemed they were alone.

Michael advanced on the man, grabbed his lapels and thrust him against the desk.

'Who are you and why are you threatening our children?' he yelled into his waxen face.

'Get your hands off me! I haven't done anything.'

The man struggled to regain his balance, grabbing Michael's forearms. Michael seemed possessed. Eyes blazing, he knocked the man's hands off, then wrenched him forwards.

'My son was almost killed the other day and I'm not in the mood for lies. So unless you want me to hurt you properly, you'd better start talking.'

He let go with his right hand and drew it back, fist clenched.

Something about the man made Annie believe him. He wasn't acting like a violent blackmailer. Maybe he *was* only a businessman. But Michael was also a father who'd kept a lonely vigil by his son's hospital bed. She feared for the man's life.

'Michael, no! He's terrified – look at him.'

Michael stopped mid-punch, though judging from his flaring nostrils and narrowed eyes, the effort to hold himself back clearly cost him. Annie relaxed. Michael shoved the man back against the desk and stepped away from him, chest heaving. Delivered a kick to a grey filing cabinet that left a huge dent in its side.

Heart pounding, Annie closed the distance between her and the man. She forced herself to speak calmly and slowly.

'My name is Annie. Are you Mr Murray?'

He glared at her.

'You just assaulted me. I'm calling the police.'

He reached into an inside pocket.

'No, you're not!' she shouted. 'Not unless you want to be arrested for blackmail. We know you sent that disgusting deepfake video. We know you sent John Varney to follow our kids. And we *know* you had him killed. So unless you want *me* to call the police, start talking.'

He shook his head. Refused to meet her gaze.

'I can't,' he mumbled.

'What do you mean, "can't"? We traced the email back to your PC,' she said, chest heaving. 'You're involved. We've got hard evidence. Look, just tell me what you know and I promise I won't call the police.'

Michael came back to join them, fists balled. She caught his eye, shook her head. She thought she had Murray where she wanted him. He was definitely hiding something.

'They'll kill me!' he choked out.

'Who?' Annie barked, suddenly tiring of being the good cop. 'Tell me or I'll kill you myself. We're trying to save our children's lives. Do you think we care about yours?'

Something happened to his body, then. His shoulders slumped. When he looked up at Annie, she saw the resignation in his eyes. He'd weighed up the options and settled on the least worst. Avoiding current danger was the only logical choice.

His words came in a torrent. Here was a man clearly relieved to be unburdening himself of both guilt and shame.

'It started three years ago. I was on this website. I'm not proud, but it was for married people who wanted affairs. There was this girl there. Tilly, her name was. Gorgeous, really. Red hair, bright green eyes. I arranged to meet her in a hotel, but it was all a scam. They were filming me. Her and this...' his eyes flickered and he looked at the ceiling, clearly reliving some highly unpleasant memory, 'this nutter. They said I had to pay them or they'd send the video to my wife. A thousand pounds a month. I said I didn't have that kind of cash just lying around. All our money is in joint accounts, so my wife would notice it. They said I had to find it one way or another or they'd ruin me.'

'But you couldn't pay,' Annie prompted, already seeing where the story was headed. Just another kind of blackmail.

He shook his head.

'They said they'd give me a week to sort it, but when they came back, I still didn't have it. I thought of everything, even considered taking it from client accounts, but I'm an honest man. You have to believe me.'

'You work for people who threaten children, who try to *murder* children,' Michael growled from behind the accountant, startling him.

Lost in his shameful story, the man had obviously forgotten Michael was there.

'They said they'd had a change of heart,' he said bitterly. 'They said they'd write off my debt if I let them use my computer to send the occasional email.'

'And that's all you do for them?' Annie asked.

'That's all, I swear.'

'Give us their names, then.'

'I don't have them. I asked once, and she... she just told me never to ask again unless I wanted *him* to hurt me.' He shook his head, clearly recalling some horrifying interaction with the blackmailers. Then his eyes widened. 'But I can show you her photo. Her profile one, I mean, off Private Liaisons.' He gestured at the PC. 'May I?'

She nodded and swapped places with him.

He stabbed at the keyboard, typing clumsily with two fingers. Then swung the monitor round to face Annie.

'That's her. That's Tilly.'

Annie leaned closer. Peered at the photo.

The young woman calling herself Tilly – Annie was sure the name was as fake as the video she'd sent her – stared out of the screen with a sultry gaze, above a brief bio in which she claimed to be a personal trainer who loved cats, rom coms and no-strings fun.

She wore a lacy white cami and leaned towards the camera. The look was pure seduction: russet-coloured hair piled up on her head, emerald-green eyes Annie thought were probably coloured contacts, and bright red parted lips. God, why were men so predictable?

She scrutinised Tilly's come-hither look, and then it hit her with such force she gasped in shock. Hiding behind the up-do,

the make-up, the pout and the cleavage was a woman she recognised.

'I know her.'

Michael leaned over her shoulder. His face turned white.

'So do I.'

Chapter 56

For once, the tide of teenagers with mental health issues had subsided. A little.

Taking advantage of the lull, Sandy, the older of the two receptionists, turned to her colleague.

'I'm going to take a quick break, Ellie. I didn't have time for breakfast this morning.'

The younger woman smiled accommodatingly.

'That's fine. I can handle things here. Anyway, I don't want you passing out right in front of me. Think of all the paperwork I'd have to complete.'

Laughing, Sandy got up from her chair. 'You're a sweetheart.'

She patted Ellie's shoulder, then headed off towards the lift that would take her to the staff restaurant.

Maya watched Sandy's back as she left the softly lit seating area. All the way until she was out of sight. The few mothers left sitting in the low armchairs were engrossed in their phones. Of course they were. Some she was already friends with. Others she was merely observing. For now.

She felt a sudden urge to scream at them, 'Look around you! Look what you've done to your children!' But that would be wholly inappropriate for helpful, friendly, breezy-yet-compassionate Ellie, so she said nothing. Instead, she pulled out her current burner phone and called the number she'd taken down from the TV news that lunchtime. The female detective who'd spoken on camera. It was time to get rid of Annie Barnes.

'Major Incident Team, DC Singh speaking.'

Maya turned her back on the mothers and dropped her voice.

'Hi, yes, my name is Olivia. You're the one to call about that murder at the Banana Warehouse, aren't you?'

'That's right. How can I help you, Olivia?'

'It's that woman in the ... you know,' she faked a little hesitation, 'photofit?'

'We call them e-fits, but go on.'

'Sorry. Anyway, I recognised her. Her name is Annie Barnes. She works at the university. I can tell you exactly which department.'

A note of suspicion crept into the detective's voice.

'Great. But let's just get a few details from you first, Olivia. Is that all right?'

'Oh, sure. I mean, whatever you need.'

'Thanks. Let's start with your surname.'

'It's Clinton, like the president?'

'And your address?'

Maya gave her the number of a house on Woodbourne Road, the most expensive street in the city. Pictured the detective's raised eyebrows. Even if she worked until she dropped, she'd never be able to afford to live there. A minor cruelty, but still enjoyable.

'Right. So, this Annie Barnes. You said you have her work address?'

'Yes. It's the School of Computer Science. It's on University Road West. Right opposite Queen Elizabeth's Hospital.'

'That's great, Olivia, thank you. Can I just ask, how do you know her?'

Maya suppressed a grin as she gave a deliciously on-point answer. 'Hot yoga. I'm her teacher.'

'I see. Well, thanks again, you've been most helpful.'

She hoped the detective would check out her story. There really was a hot yoga teacher named Olivia Clinton who lived in Woodbourne Road.

They followed each other on Instagram.

Chapter 57

Michael's well-used truck stood out among the spotless SUVs parked outside the Oaks. A working man's vehicle among play-things.

Together he and Annie raced through the glass doors and up a flight of stairs, arriving breathless at the first-floor reception. The woman tapping at a keyboard behind the desk looked up, momentary surprise quickly replaced by a professional smile.

Annie knew her by sight. Sandy. A perfectly groomed example of that cadre of efficient, no-nonsense female functionaries that included Letitia's secretary.

'Hello, Mrs Barnes. And Mr Taylor.' She frowned. 'I'm sorry, I don't think we have either Aaron or Isla down for an appointment today.'

'There's a young woman who works here with you,' Annie said, holding out her phone displaying the Private Liaisons profile picture of 'Tilly'. Her hand was shaking. 'That's her. I can't re-member her name.'

Somewhere behind the reception desk, a door banged. Sandy looked round, tutting.

'The photo?' Annie prompted.

Sandy scrutinised it much as Annie herself had done earlier.

'My goodness,' she exclaimed, frowning. 'Is that Ellie?'

'Is she in today?'

'Well, yes. But—'

'Where is she?' Annie asked.

Sandy looked towards a corridor and a wall sign listing various corporate functions.

'She's in the admin office. We're a little quiet today, so she said she'd do some database work, reconciling client files.'

As Annie and Michael rushed down the corridor, Sandy called after them.

'Wait! You can't go in there!'

Annie slowed at the first door they came to. *Finance.*

Michael ran past, to the second. *HR.*

She passed him and stopped dead at the third. *Admin.*

She grasped the door handle, ready to confront the woman who'd been tormenting her and Michael for the last three days, threatening Isla, almost killing Aaron. This was it. They were nearly home.

She took a deep breath, shot Michael a strained smile. And burst in.

The room was empty. Unattended computers sat at each of the three desks. On two of the monitors, screen savers displayed the clinic's logo bouncing around the screen like a corporate game of video ping-pong. On the third, a database query screen glowed brightly.

And in the far corner, a grey fire door with a pushbar stood open, admitting a cold, dry wind.

Annie rushed over to the metal fire escape and looked over the railing. Apart from a mother and daughter walking arm in arm towards the front door, the car park was deserted.

She turned to Michael, sick with disappointment.

'We're too late.'

Chapter 58

Maya streaked through the car park and out through the clinic's gates before wheeling sharply right and sprinting away up the road.

That was way too close for comfort. How had they found her? They were targets. That was all. They weren't in charge. She was. For once, she wished Ollie had been there to frighten them off. But now it was too late.

She vaulted a low hedge and cut through someone's huge front garden before emerging from a gap in their fence onto a side street. A glance over her shoulder reassured her. Taylor's ridiculous pickup truck was nowhere to be seen.

Slowing to a walk, she ducked behind a signboard at the entrance to a private school and reached into her shoulder bag. The woman who emerged a minute or two later had long blonde hair and carmine lips. Oversized sunglasses and a vape. She puffed out a huge white cherry-scented cloud and strolled on her way. Not a care in the world.

She called Ollie.

'Meet me at the flat in twenty. We need to talk.'

Smiling with satisfaction, she ended the call. It was time to put an end to Barnes and Taylor's interference once and for all.

Chapter 59

Filled with despair at their near-miss, Annie marched back to the reception area full of troubled kids and their worried parents.

In that moment, she saw the blackmailers for what they truly were. Cold-hearted predators who lived off ordinary people's love for family, their emotional frailty and, yes, their weaknesses.

She spotted a woman wearing a lanyard and a manager's blazer talking in hushed tones on the desk phone at reception.

'Excuse me, I need to ask about one of your receptionists.'

The woman frowned and gestured with her free hand at her phone, as if Annie was perhaps sight-impaired or just stupid.

'I'm on a call,' she mouthed.

Annie stabbed the switch hook button. 'Now you're not. I need to talk to you.'

The woman's outraged expression faded as she took in Annie's stance, arms folded, eyes boring into hers.

'My office,' she said curtly, glancing over Annie's shoulder at the faces turned their way, social media forgotten in favour of the real drama playing out in front of them.

With the office door closed behind them, the woman gestured to a pair of visitor chairs. Annie shook her head. She and Michael remained standing.

'She calls herself Ellie, but I doubt that's her real name,' Annie said, trying and failing to control her breathing. 'I want to know everything about her. When she started work here, where she lives, contact number, the lot.'

The woman sat behind the desk, favouring Annie with a look combining pity with officiousness.

'I'm afraid I can't do that. We are legally, corporately and *morally* obliged to respect our employees' rights to confidentiality and privacy.'

It may have been true, but it was also unwise. Annie gave in to her temper.

'I don't care about their rights! This woman is mixed up in a scheme that is extorting money from *your* clients. In murder, for Christ's sake! Now, either you tell us what we want to know or I go public that the Oaks is shielding blackmailers and murderers.'

The woman blanched beneath her flawless make-up.

'There's no need for anything like that. At the Oaks, we pride ourselves on—'

Annie held up a hand. 'Again, not interested. When did Ellie start work here?'

'A few months ago. August, I think. I don't really know that much about her. She's actually legally employed by an agency. She only works here a couple of days a week.'

'We need her personnel file.'

From somewhere, the woman excavated a shred of professional dignity.

'Which, as I think I mentioned, is confidential. We could release it to the police, but only if they have a correctly drawn-up warrant.' She folded her hands on the desk in front of her and, chest rising and falling, locked eyes with Annie. 'And *I* don't care whether *you* like it or not.'

Michael stretched out a hand and touched Annie lightly on the arm, startling her. She'd forgotten he was there.

'Come on, Annie,' he said. 'We need to find another way to get to her.'

She let him steer her out of the office and felt a pang of guilt when he apologised to the probably traumatised manager as he closed the door behind them.

She turned away, and her heart lifted as suddenly as it had fallen. Was there another way to find Ellie?

On a noticeboard headed 'Your Caring Oaks Staff', colour

photos of all the clinic employees were arrayed according to their roles. And there on the second-to-last row was a photo of a smiling young woman, no distracting make-up, coloured contacts or blazing red wig to fool the casual observer.

'Ellie Morris' was average-looking. Brown hair cut in a simple bob. Clear skin. A pleasant smile that stopped short of her hazel eyes. Whatever her actual name, Annie knew that this was what she really looked like.

She snatched the photo down and tucked it into her bag.

'Let's go,' she murmured to Michael.

As they rushed back to the truck, she vowed she would track down 'Ellie' and her psychopathic boyfriend. After all, they'd almost caught her today.

Perhaps she should have tempered her optimism with caution. But she was on a roll.

They had the upper hand now and she intended to keep it that way.

Chapter 60

As soon as Michael brought the truck to a halt, Annie jumped out and led him in a dash towards the School of Computer Science. She wanted to run the photo past Deanna, see if the brilliant young woman could find her through facial recognition software.

Then she stumbled to a halt, causing Michael to crash into her. She froze as she took in the scene fifty yards ahead.

Beside a marked police car, two uniformed cops in high-vis vests were talking to a couple of students.

'Turn around, slowly, and walk back to the car,' she said quickly. 'They've got my face, but we're too far away for them to recognise me.'

Walking on legs that felt like she'd just run a marathon, Annie took Michael's arm and led him back to the pickup.

Who could have tipped off the police? Grant? 'Ellie'? Someone at the university? It didn't matter. There was no point hanging about. Before they'd have a chance to explain about the black-mailers, they'd be in handcuffs and, shortly after that, a world of serious legal trouble.

Michael started the engine and pulled out of the car park before Annie had even strapped in.

She kept glancing in the door mirror as he sped away from the university.

It wasn't Ellie and her boyfriend who were on the run.

It was her and Michael.

Chapter 61

The apartment felt too small. Claustrophobic. A cage or – she shuddered – a cellar.

The screens, with their ever-changing CCTV views, their columns of numbers, scrolling social media feeds and messaging apps, suddenly seemed like windows looking in at her and not the other way round.

Everything Maya loved about the life she'd built for her and Ollie had turned sour. The scams had always been fun. Ever since that first time, when they'd scooped up a lost dog in Regent's Park in London and returned it to its distraught, cash-rich owners.

They'd moved on to kidnapping the pets themselves, then burgling houses. Maya would keep the owner occupied at the front door with a collecting tin and a tale about a new pets' charity, while Ollie broke in round the back and took whatever he could carry.

Discreet Encounters had followed, and then, after the near-miss getting reported in the papers, Private Liaisons. That was fun.

The latest and best scam, raising cash while sticking it to hypocritical, selfish, failing mothers, had seemed like it would carry them all the way. But now one of those mothers and her carpenter boyfriend had hurled a bucket of spanners into the works and she could hear the gears grinding and shrieking as the machine threatened to blow itself apart. From phoning Bodden in the Caymans to chasing her down at the Oaks, they were getting way too close.

She'd caught a lucky break today. If she hadn't happened to glance out of the window as they pulled up outside the clinic in that ridiculous truck of his, it would have been over.

Ollie came back in from the kitchen, swigging from a bottle of vodka, still frosty from the freezer. He sat in an armchair, perching right on the edge of the cushion. Wiped his mouth. Twitched. Wiped it again. Drank some more.

'I wish you'd calm down, Maya. You're making me nervous, and you know how much I hate that.'

'If I'm on edge, Ollie, it's because we've got a problem. Those two almost caught me. I could be in a bloody cell by now.'

He tipped the bottle to his lips again.

'Which is why I've got a plan.'

'Tell me,' she said, fearing the worst.

'You're not the only one who can think ahead. What we do is, we go round to their places and kill them all. Then it's back to business as usual.'

She glared at him. Was he serious? *That* was his plan?

'Don't you get it? We need an exit strategy.'

He frowned. 'What are you talking about? I just *gave* you our exit strategy.'

He'd never understand, she knew that. He pretended to, but in the last few days she'd seen that side of him she'd never be able to control growing in strength. Killing John had been the last little step he'd needed to take. So it was down to her to make sure they both got away clean. It hurt, admitting defeat to Barnes and Taylor, but she could swallow that if it meant escaping.

'If we kill them without a plan ...'

'As I think I just said, Maya, I *gave* you a plan.'

'...a *proper* plan, we'll get caught, I guarantee it,' she said. 'And I have no intention of ending up in prison. We need to wind things up, Ollie. It's over.'

From the edge of the armchair, he looked across at her. And a thread of unease spun out from her gut. It was like being stared at by a crocodile. Dead, dark eyes that promised only pain, oblivion and death.

'I like this life, Maya,' he said, enunciating each word carefully. 'This life I've built. I like it very much. And I don't want to stop.'

'We have to, Ollie, don't you see?' Maya said, hearing the pleading note in her own voice, and hating it.

'No, I don't see. You're overthinking things. You don't need to do anything: I know you like to stay behind your screens. *I'll* do it. I'm *happy* to do it.'

She shook her head. Arguing with Ollie always carried an element of risk. And lately he'd been showing a lot more signs of independence. But she had to win him round. Their lives depended on it.

Maybe she could reach him by going back to those early days when everything was less complicated, even if still deeply unpleasant.

'Do you remember when they used to bully us at school, Ollie? When we had the wrong uniform? Or Mum forgot to pay the gas bill so we couldn't wash properly?'

He frowned. 'Don't try to distract me, Maya. I know all your tricks, remember?'

'Do you?' she insisted.

'Of course I do. Little shits. Calling us skagheads because she was an addict. I soon stopped them, though, didn't I? They weren't laughing at us then.'

'No, they weren't. And when we were split up after she died. In care, I mean. I had that trouble with one of the foster fathers. You sorted that, too, didn't you?'

A sly smile stole across Ollie's features. It was working. She began to relax.

'Sent him to A&E, didn't I?'

She smiled. 'You did. You saved me, Ollie. But now it's my turn to save you. We have to stick together like we always have. I need you to trust me. You'll get to have your fun, I promise. Just not yet.'

He tipped his head on one side. Not for the first time, she

found herself wondering what exactly went on behind those lifeless eyes of his. He pursed his lips. Making her wait. A minor cruelty of which they were both capable. Perhaps because she knew his tricks just as well as he knew hers, it didn't bother her. She just needed him to agree.

Ten seconds passed. Finally, he nodded. Just a little.

'Fine.'

Maya smiled at him. She'd won him round. She always did. And when she'd worked things out, she'd let her brother have such fun he'd never argue with her again.

Chapter 62

Michael cornered so fast the tyres screeched, forcing Annie to lunge for the grab rail. Once he'd righted the vehicle, she started picking at the problem they'd almost just solved.

They'd been so close to confronting their blackmailer, she couldn't quite believe she'd evaded them at the last moment. And now someone had identified Annie to the cops.

How could this be happening? The previous week her main worry had been trying to pin Dan Gao down to a date and a final amount for his professorial endowment. Now she was trying to stop Isla and Aaron from being murdered, witnessing a psychopath stab a man to death, and, to top it all, being hunted for that very murder herself.

Whatever else was going on, there was one fact of which she was sure. One duty she'd fulfil above every other.

'I need to get Isla,' she said. 'She's with Grant. That's about as safe as wandering round near New Street station on her own at midnight.'

'The two of you should stay at ours. The cops aren't looking for me yet so it's the safest place for you.'

'Thanks. We will.'

'Would it be OK if you went in your car? I really want to get home and check on Aaron.'

'Of course. Drop me and then go. It's not fair on his aunt to leave her there alone if Ellie and her psycho boyfriend are after Aaron.' She covered her mouth, ashamed at herself for planting such a horrific seed in Michael's mind. 'Oh God, Michael, I'm sorry. I'm sure they're OK. I just meant—'

'It's fine,' he said grimly, accelerating towards a traffic light that had just shifted to amber and blasting across the junction as the cross-traffic began moving. 'We need to get the kids together so we can protect them.'

At the end of her street, he swung the wheel, setting the rear tyres squealing, and shot along Norfolk Road before slamming the brakes on outside her house.

With a quick smile, and an answering nod, Annie unbuckled and leaped out. She didn't even look round as Michael sped away from the kerb to the cacophony of the truck's powerful engine note, its blaring exhaust pipes and more tyre screech. A cloud of smoke drifted up the front path, setting off a bout of coughing that brought stinging tears to her eyes.

She fumbled out her front door keys and then dropped them in her haste.

'Shit!' she shouted.

On the second try, she got the door open and ran upstairs. She snatched a weekend bag down from the top of the wardrobe, grabbed clothes at random and stuffed them in. Added a washbag and ran back downstairs. Isla would have a few things at Grant's. They'd have to do.

She swiped her car keys off the hall table and was behind the wheel of her car seconds later.

Unlike Michael's old-school petrol-engined pickup, her car started and pulled away utterly silently. She'd left the radio on last time she'd driven it, and now the BBC Radio WM news faded up. '...still looking for a male and female, the latter now identified as Annie Barnes, a university business manager, in connection with the murder of ex-soldier John Varney.'

She stabbed the off button, swearing. They made it sound like she was the psycho when it was Varney who'd terrorised Isla and then almost succeeded in killing Aaron.

No time for that now. The recriminations could wait. Right now, she needed to collect Isla and take her to Michael's.

The route to Grant's was all 20 mph limits. Part of her wanted to mash the accelerator down and get to his flat as fast as possible. But all it would take would be one police car and the whole plan, shaky as it was, would come crashing down. So, gritting her teeth, she crawled along, even resorting to using the speed-limiter control.

Finally, shaking with frustration and pent-up anxiety, she parked outside Grant's and ran up the path. She held her finger down on the bell until, scowling, he let her in.

'What are you doing here? Shouldn't you be on the run or something? Or' – air quotes – 'helping the police with their enquiries?' He looked past her. 'Where's your boyfriend?'

She pushed past him and called out.

'Isla? Isla! Come on, darling, get your stuff, we have to go.'

Grant spun her round by her shoulder.

'Hey! What exactly do you think you're doing? You need to leave.'

'Our daughter's in danger, Grant. I'm taking her somewhere safe.'

He folded his arms. 'Not while you're wanted by the cops you're not. She stays with me. End of story.'

Annie shook her head, hardly hearing him.

'Isla!' she shouted. 'Where are you?'

A cold worm of fear had just uncoiled deep in the pit of her stomach. How could Isla not have appeared by now, if only to level a teenage death-ray stare at her interfering mother? This was a two-bedroom flat, not Birmingham Town Hall.

Where was she?

Annie ran from the kitchen into the spare bedroom. Grant had painted it a lurid pink and Isla had slung multicoloured fairy lights around the dressing table mirror, taping printed-out photos of her and Naomi around the frame. But apart from a scattering of clothes, there was no sign of Isla herself.

The master bedroom, then. Annie burst in, but Isla wasn't there either. As she scanned the room, her gaze tripped on a blue glass bong on the bedside table and a lacy bra slung over one bedpost. Poor Melissa would get tired of Grant before long, like she had.

She returned to the kitchen. Grant was lounging on a tipped-back chair, his head resting on a cupboard door. He had a long-necked bottle of beer in his right hand and wore an amused expression.

'If you'd given me a moment to explain, I could have told you – she's not here.'

'What?' Annie screeched. 'Where is she then?'

He shrugged. 'How should I know? I got back from a meeting with this promoter and she'd gone. Left me a little pink Post-it note.' He looked up for a second, then back at Annie. 'Something like "Dad, don't be mad, I've gone out to meet Josh. Be back late. Don't wait up."'

Annie's heart was knocking against her ribs like a steak mallet. Fury coursed through her veins.

'Don't you get it? She's in danger! Who even is this Josh? Have you met him?'

'No, I haven't *met* him. Contrary to what you obviously wish, Annie, this isn't the 1950s. The boy doesn't have to ask the girl's father's permission to start seeing his daughter.'

'How long have they been going out?'

He shrugged, took a swig of beer. 'How should I know? A couple of weeks, maybe? Three?'

'And you didn't think to tell me?'

His face hardened into a sneer. 'No, Annie, I didn't *think to tell you*. Because I knew that this was *exactly* how you'd react.'

Oh, how she wanted to slap him, or punch him, kick the legs of the chair so he tumbled off the right-on dad pedestal he'd erected for himself.

'Well, who is he? Does he go to school with her? How old is he?'

'For God's sake, calm down. Don't come barging into my flat then interrogate me like I've done something wrong. Isla needs

252

her freedom. She's nearly sixteen, Annie. She's a young woman now.'

He tipped the bottle to his lips and took his time finishing it.

She stood there aghast. How could he be so casual? But he wasn't done.

'Look, Josh is fine. I've seen him. He's barely more than a child himself. He's a nice-looking lad – bit of a baby-face, if I'm honest. But Isla likes him and that's good enough for me. What's the problem?'

Fear bloomed inside her like a cold, dank fog spreading over the city, turning familiar streets into dark, forbidding places.

'He's a what?' she asked in a strangled voice.

'I said he's a nice-looking lad. Got this whole floppy fringe thing going on. Very moody, very *Twilight*. But that's just a pose. He's, you know, inoffensive-looking. Not what you'd call a player or a predator or anything like that.'

Grant's description of Josh's fringe set bells clanging like a fire alarm in Annie's head. She yanked out her phone and selected the photo of the male blackmailer she'd grabbed off the *Birmingham Mail*'s website.

She shoved the phone in Grant's face.

'Is that him? Is that Josh?'

He pushed her hand away a little and squinted as he studied the photo.

'Oh Christ! Yes.'

She watched his eyes skittering over the screen as he scanned the article. Then he looked up at her, stricken, his face drained of blood as if someone had opened a tap.

'He's a nutcase, Annie! Look at all this terrible stuff he's done.'

'I know, Grant. That's why I have to find Isla before it's too late.'

'I'm coming with you.'

'No! You need to be here in case she comes back.'

She turned and ran for the door. Behind her, Grant called out.

'Please, Annie. Let me help.'

She spun round, took a breath.

'You've done enough already,' she said.

Then she turned away from him and left, slamming the door behind her.

Chapter 63

They'd agreed to meet on the bench on Black Sabbath Bridge.

Black and white plaques were riveted to the backrest. Pictures of the four guys who were in the band. Geezer, Ozzy, Tony, Bill. Real dad-names. Cool moustaches, though. She knew about them: her own dad had made sure of that. God, he didn't half go on sometimes.

She looked up from her phone. Where was Josh? She hoped he hadn't forgotten. She fingered the sleeve of the vintage biker jacket he had bought her. Real leather. Naomi would have a fit if she knew, what with her being a vegan. Although she still ate KFC after a drunken night out, so what was with that?

It was cold, and Isla shivered, wishing she'd worn a jumper under the jacket instead of her new crochet crop top from Primark. But it matched her eyes and she totally knew Josh would love it.

She checked the time on her phone. He was five minutes late. Where *was* he? She tried not to worry. Checked her Insta. All the girls were so pretty. Maybe he'd dumped her for one of them. The buzz flared up and she had to do some slow breathing.

She switched to Snapchat, and as she was messaging Naomi, she remembered she'd left Find My active. That was all she needed. Mum giving her grief for being out on a school night. She'd need to go into settings and disable it. For tonight, anyway. Then someone tapped her lightly on the shoulder.

'Hey, sorry I'm late. Traffic was murder. Ah, cool, you're wearing the jacket. I love the top, too.'

She looked up, smiling, straight into Josh's face. She stood, kissed him deeply, enjoying the swivelling heads and disapproving glances from a couple of old ladies.

'I'm parked over there,' he said, pointing towards Gas Street. 'Come on.'

Taking her hand, he led her across the road. 'Quick!' he yelped joyfully as a tram bore down on them.

Laughing, they reached the far side and ran round the corner. Josh stopped by a bright yellow hatchback. A BMW something-or-other. It looked new. He rested his hand on the roof.

Isla frowned. 'Wait. This is *your* car?'

'Bought and paid for.'

'It's lush. You're *sure* it's yours? This isn't just for a selfie?'

He pulled out a black plastic fob and pushed the button. The winkers flashed and the door locks clunked open.

'How the hell did you afford this?'

He shrugged. 'Rich parents.'

She realised she didn't really know much about him. But it never seemed to matter when they were together. Shrugging mentally, she climbed in. The inside smelled like her jacket had when Josh had brought it out of the carrier bag.

He started the engine. Made the engine roar. Typical boy. Then they were off.

'Choose some sounds,' he said. 'It's linked up to my phone. Got Spotify.'

Soon, Taylor Swift's beautiful lyrics filled the car.

Isla looked sideways at Josh. 'So, where are we going? Club, pub, pictures?'

He tapped the side of his nose. 'It's a secret.'

Epic. She loved this. Not only had she snuck out, but now they were off in Josh's car – his BMW! – to some secret destination. She imagined her mum losing it. Calling the cops. *My little girl's been seduced by an older boy!*

She and Josh weren't just going out, they were on the run. Like in that old film he'd taken her to at the Everyman Mailbox. *Bonnie and Clyde*. Oh God, this was awesome. And even though he was nineteen and experienced, he'd always been totally respect-ful of her boundaries.

Maybe she should do a quick post. A selfie.

She pulled out her phone. Her message notifications popped up. Tons from Naomi. Even Ronan. Loser. Why couldn't he just leave her alone? Mum had left like ten. Even Dad was getting in on the act. Nope. Not letting the parents ruin things. Not tonight. She put her phone in her lap, screen down.

Josh's voice broke into her thoughts. He sounded kind of irritated.

'Sorry, what did you say?' she asked him.

'I said let's make this all about us. I want you to myself. Let's do a digital detox. No phones for the rest of the night.'

She screwed her face up. 'How old actually are you? Nobody does digital detoxes except boring adults who've probably OD'ed on Facebook.'

'Come on, Isla, hand it over. It'll be fun.'

'No it won't. It'll be lame.'

He held his left hand out, did a *gimme* gesture with his fingers. 'Give it.'

'No.'

'Come on. Look, I'll do mine first.' He chucked his phone onto the back seat.

'Why?'

'Please?' he said, dragging the word out and pouting.

'Fine. But I still think this is lame.'

She handed him her iPhone and he tossed it over his shoulder.

'Give me a kiss,' he said, smiling.

She leaned over. Just as her lips were touching his cheek, he swivelled his head round, leaned towards her and planted a deep one right on her mouth.

She pulled away, startled as an oncoming car hooted at them. 'Look out!'

He pulled the steering wheel over and the car sort of shimmied back onto their side of the road.

'Oh my *God*,' Isla said, her heart fluttering. 'You nutter, you could have killed us!'

Then she giggled out of pure nerves. He was mad!

Josh was laughing, too. Then he nodded to a big illuminated sign up ahead.

'We need petrol.'

Swinging off the road and into the garage, he jumped out and swiped a credit card over the pay-at-pump reader. The nozzle thing clunked as he put it into the petrol tank. He smiled in at her through the window, pulling faces and setting her off again. When the tank was full, he got back inside.

'Hey, can you get us some snacks and drinks from the shop?' He handed her a twenty.

'What do you want?'

He shrugged. 'Anything. No! Chilli Heatwave Doritos. Some Cadbury's Dairy Milk. And a Mars bar. And a Coke. Make it two.'

She rolled her eyes.

'Don't they feed you at your house?'

On her way across the concrete forecourt, trying to avoid inhaling the petrolly stink, she turned to look back at him. He was on his phone. Cheeky boy. He looked up and saw her watching him. She smiled knowingly, and waved.

He gave her a guilty grin and blew her a kiss.

She walked into the shop still smiling. This was literally the wildest night of her life.

Chapter 64

Annie rushed back to her car, almost blinded by terror. They had Isla. Those maniacs had kidnapped her and Annie had no idea where she was. The horrific images from the deepfake video rushed back at her.

She called Isla. It went straight to voicemail. Panicking, she stabbed the end call button. What now? She had to reach her daughter. Then she gasped as salvation presented itself. Isla had put Find My on her phone. Annie could track her.

She tried the app, tapping the icon with a shaking finger, but it was being glitchy and would only confirm that Isla had been at Grant's half an hour ago.

She didn't have time to waste waiting for it to wake up. She put her phone down and pulled away from the kerb. This time she didn't bother sticking to the speed limit as she raced over to Michael's. If a cop did stop her, she'd tell them everything. Her daughter had been kidnapped. They'd have to help her. They'd *have* to.

She felt sick. What if she was too late? What if the baby-faced psychopath had already killed Isla? No. She couldn't let herself believe that. Not even *think* it.

Oh Isla. She was so clever, so articulate. And yet emotionally she was just a mixed-up young girl, so hurt by the divorce she'd had to have therapy. And these evil people had preyed on her without compunction.

Annie promised herself that she would get Isla back unharmed, and then she'd rearrange her life to give her daughter more time. It wasn't her fault her parents couldn't make their marriage work, yet she was the one bearing all the pain.

She pulled up outside Michael's house unaware of how she'd got there. She must have stopped to press the intercom a minute earlier, but even that hadn't registered.

Michael stood in the open doorway, his face creased with worry.

'What's happened?' he asked as she stumbled towards him before collapsing against him and giving in to the tears that had been banking up since she'd left Grant's.

'They've got Isla,' she sobbed. 'Her boyfriend – he calls himself Josh, but it's the male blackmailer from the CCTV picture in the *Mail* – she sneaked out to meet him in town somewhere.'

'What do you want to do?' He held her by the shoulders and stared deeply into her eyes. 'Annie, maybe it's time to involve the police.'

Was he right? Had they actually reached that point? After all, the police had all sorts of ways of locating people from their phones. ANPR cameras, too. But what if 'Josh' found out somehow? He and his accomplice had all kinds of technology at their fingertips. They might easily be monitoring police radio channels. Or even their computer systems. With the net closing in, they might decide to kill Isla and run. That's if the police even believed Annie and Michael. After all, they were wanted for John Varney's murder. It would take too long to convince them otherwise and by then it could be too late.

She shook her head. 'It's too risky.'

'Have you checked Find My? You said she'd installed it.'

Annie sniffed, and blew her nose.

'I did, but it was saying she was still at Grant's.'

'Try it again. Sometimes it's because the phone's in a dead spot for coverage.'

She got her phone out and opened the app. The map of Birmingham appeared and zoomed in. And yes, there it was. Pulsing in the centre of the screen, a blue dot.

'She's back online,' she said. 'Look, she's on Kingsbury Road, at a petrol station.'

'Come on, then, let's go get her. You drive and I'll tell you where they are.'

'What about Aaron?'

'He's fine. His aunt's still here.'

Annie ran back to her car and climbed in behind the wheel. After an agonising wait while the gates crept open, she shot through, took a left turn and tore off down the road.

For a while, Michael's updates were all the same.

'They're still at the Shell garage.'

Annie hurtled along, the car's insane speed rendered surreal by the total lack of engine noise. She weaved through the traffic, even overtaking a queue along the wrong side of the road, narrowly avoiding a collision by swerving round a set of bollards in the centre strip.

Then Michael spoke in a worried tone.

'They're on the move. Still on Kingsbury Road, heading into the city. We're about half a mile behind them. Keep your foot down and we should catch them before they get into the centre.'

Annie accelerated, pulling out round the cars sticking to the speed limit and earning enraged blasts on their horns. A minute or so later, she spotted another car up ahead. She closed to ten yards behind its back bumper.

'I think that's them,' Michael said. 'Hold on, yes. Yes, it's them. Go, Annie!'

She overtook, hauling the wheel over and flooring the accelerator. The Audi surged forward, pushing her back into her seat. Oncoming cars hooted and swerved out of the way.

It was going to be OK. They were going to save Isla.

Chapter 65

Back on the road again, Isla moistened her lips with the strawberry Haribo she was eating and then leaned over to kiss Josh.

He smiled, licked the sweet spit from his mouth. She felt so sexy, so alive. *This* was where she was supposed to be.

Except where actually *were* they supposed to be?

'Hey, boy. When are you going to tell me where we're going?'

He laughed. 'I'm not. I told you, it's a secret.'

'Yeah, but you can tell me now, can't you?'

'Sorry, baby, I wish I could, but that would ruin everything.'

'Can't you even give me a clue?'

He slapped the steering wheel, beeping the horn.

'Jesus! No, I can't, OK? Just shut the fuck up about it.'

She felt it as a physical shock, like he'd slapped her. He'd never even raised his voice before. Tears welled in her eyes.

'What the hell, Josh? Why are you being such a dick about it?'

He frowned. Stuck his bottom lip out.

It looked fake to her. Making a baby face so she wouldn't be angry any more. But Ekaterini said she shouldn't let other people dictate her moods. *Own your anger, Isla. It's yours.*

'Sorry, Isla, I didn't mean it,' he said, turning and offering a guilty smile. Also not real. 'I've got anger issues, that's what my therapist says. Forgive me?'

Anger issues? Really? Sometimes he just sounded like he'd learned a bunch of appropriate things to say. Like the other day when he said he was a trans ally. She wasn't sure he even knew what it meant. She looked down and frowned with irritation. Her top had ridden up over her tummy, showing that annoying little roll that she just couldn't shift. She tugged it down.

'Fine. I forgive you.'

She glanced sideways at him. He was smirking. Like he'd got one over on her. He was actually enjoying this. What was *wrong* with him? The buzz came back with a vengeance. She closed her eyes and tried to breathe her way out of the horrible floaty sensation that always worried her she was going to have a panic attack. If she did, would he even help her? Or would he just laugh and make some totally inappropriate remark?

She pushed the thought away, focused on her breathing.

After a few minutes, she felt better. She opened her eyes. Josh was looking at her. No, he was *studying* her. He quickly looked straight ahead. The buzz hummed loud in her ears and her fingertips started tingling.

'I'm sorry, babes,' he said. 'For just now. If I upset you, I mean. We're cool, right?'

He was saying the right words. The trouble was, when she looked at him, she couldn't see Josh any more. Even his smile looked fake.

'I said we're cool, baby? Yes?' His voice had changed now. Tough-sounding.

Isla eased herself sideways in her seat, as far away from him as the belt would let her. She tuned into the quiet inner voice Ekaterini had told her to listen out for. The one that always told her the truth. And it told her something frightening.

Josh was gone. In his place, a stranger who had learned the words of an apology but not the emotions that ought to go along with it.

Behind them, a horn beeped. She twisted round in her seat. The car was really close, almost on the back bumper. Did they really want to overtake just as a bend was coming up?

Josh glanced up at his rear-view mirror, then swung his head round.

'Why don't you come a bit closer?' he yelled at the other driver. 'I'll stop my car and stick your teeth down your fucking throat!'

Isla shivered. And this time it wasn't from the cold.

Chapter 66

Hammering the horn, Annie overtook the car and swerved to a stop diagonally in front of it, blocking it in. She could hear its tyres screeching through the closed windows as the driver braked sharply to avoid a collision. Other vehicles had to edge round them, their drivers enraged, leaning on their horns. She barely noticed them.

She jumped out, Michael behind her, and ran around to the driver's side, filled with rage and ready to drag the psycho physically out onto the road.

The car's sole occupant, who was even now pulling out her phone, was a woman in her twenties. Dark hair and an expression combining naked terror with boiling rage.

She lowered the window.

'What the hell did you do that for? You could have killed me!'

Ignoring her, Annie yanked the door open. 'Where is she?'

'Get away from me, you bitch! I'll call the police.'

'Good! I'll tell them you kidnapped my daughter. Her phone's in this car.'

The woman's eyes widened until Annie could see white all the way around the irises.

'What the hell are you talking about? You're mad!'

Annie wrenched the rear door open. A blue glow from the footwell caught her eye. She leaned over and closed her fingers around the phone. She took it out and checked the home screen. It was Isla's. They'd been tricked.

As Annie straightened, the woman gave her a searching look. 'Wait a minute, I know you, don't I? They showed your picture on the news.' Her face paled and she shrank back. 'Oh, my God, you're those people who killed that poor bloke.'

Annie and Michael ran for her car as the woman called the police.

Chapter 67

Isla stared out of the window, wondering if she had the courage to just fling the door open and jump out. But Josh – or whoever he was – must've picked up on a vibe, because he sped up, slamming her back against the seat. Then the door buttons all thunked down together.

They were driving down this cracked and weedy road in some sort of crappy old industrial estate. All sad grey concrete buildings covered in tags, and smashed windows.

She tried to tell herself she was perfectly safe, but the buzz was back, worse than ever. She tried to do her breathing exercise, but after two goes she gave up.

'Can I have my phone back so I can call my mum? Just to let her know where I am?'

He didn't reply. She nudged him.

'Hey! Josh! I want my phone back. I need to call my mum.'

'Won't do any good, babe. The battery died while you were in the shop getting the snacks.

'It can't have,' she said, trying to keep her voice steady. 'It had a full charge when I left my dad's flat.'

He shrugged.

'There's no signal out here anyway.'

'How do you know? Have you been here before?'

'No. I mean, yeah. Once. When I was learning to drive.'

'Let me try anyway. Maybe I'll get something.'

He stamped on the brake. She jerked forward, hurting her chest as the seat belt dug in.

He turned round. Fixed her with a really cold stare. When

he spoke, it was in this odd, flat voice, like one of those terrible voiceovers on YouTube ads.

'Isla, I'm going to ask you nicely. Please shut up about your f—' He clamped his jaw for a second, then smiled. 'Your phone. I just told you, didn't I? It's out of charge. So you're going to stop going on about it and I'm not going to lose my temper with you. Do we have a deal?'

She suddenly felt very frightened.

'We're not going to a party, are we?' she said, the buzz jittering along her nerves like electricity.

'I asked you a question, Isla.'

Her tummy flipped over. She swallowed.

'What?'

'I said, do we have a deal?'

Something was wrong with him. His face was all weird. It was horrible to look at.

'Yes,' she said quietly.

He nodded. Turned himself round again. Started driving.

'Good. I have to tell you, Isla, it's been an exhausting couple of months.' He sighed loudly. 'The only fun I've had was beating the shit out of your boyfriend in that stupid club.'

Isla's vision telescoped down to a little circle. Sparks danced around the edge of it. Everything else went black and sort of heavy.

Poor Ronan was right all along. It *was* Josh who'd beaten him up. Only it wasn't, was it? There was no such person as Josh.

Just this stranger sitting next to her.

Chapter 68

There was no other choice. She had to call the police. She'd explain to them about Isla. Tell them about the articles in the *Mail*'s archive. They'd have to believe her.

She snatched up her phone and tapped in the first two digits, then slapped it back down on the table in Michael's kitchen.

No! However desperate she was, calling the police would probably sign Isla's death warrant. By the time they found her – *if* they found her – it would be too late.

The blackmailers had her, and Annie had seen with her own eyes what the man who'd been calling himself Josh was capable of. Her only hope was that they might make some sort of ransom demand. And she'd comply. She'd remortgage the house. Sell it! Call Grant. Get him to hand over whatever cash of hers he'd not squandered.

The phone rang loudly. She jumped. Snatched it up.

Michael rounded the table from where he'd been staring out the window into the darkened garden.

'Isla?' she gasped.

'Hi, Annie. It's Ellie. From the Oaks? I'm calling about Isla,' a woman said. Then her voice changed and all the front-of-house brightness dropped away to be replaced by something cold and humourless. 'We've got her, Annie. And I have some terms if you want to see her in one piece again.'

'Don't you dare hurt her. Don't you *dare*!'

The woman's voice sharpened like a blade. 'Don't tell me what to do, Annie. At the moment, she's fine, more or less. But all that could change. If you want her back, come to the abandoned factory on Wiggins Lane in Sutton Coldfield with fifty grand in cash. Just you. No police.'

'I need to know she's alive. Unhurt,' Annie said, her bottom lip quivering.

'I'm sending you a video. I'm guessing you probably won't be posting this one on Facebook. It's real, by the way.'

Annie took the phone away from her ear and stared at the screen. Twenty seconds passed. The phone pinged. She opened the attachment. Against a dark background in which metal pillars loomed, Isla blinked up at the camera. Annie's heart clenched as she took in her daughter's pale, tear-streaked face. In that moment she would have killed the woman with her bare hands if she could have.

'Please, Mum, you have to bring the money. They...' Isla gulped down a breath, 'they're going to hurt me, Mum. Badly. It's Josh. He's a psycho.'

Off-camera, a male voice shouted, 'That's enough, bitch!'

The image froze.

Horrified, Annie could only stare at Isla's terrified face.

The woman spoke again. 'Sorry about the little bit at the end. He's in one of his unpredictable moods. You've got until ... we'll say midnight. That worked for you last time, didn't it?'

'Midnight? How am I supposed to get that amount of money by then? I don't have it just lying around the house, you know.'

'Not my problem, Annie. You'll have to get creative, won't you?'

'How can I trust you when you already tried to kill Aaron?'

The woman paused. Annie thought she heard her stifle a laugh.

'You *can't*. But Isla dies at midnight unless you bring me the money.'

Chapter 69

Had she passed out? It had gone dark for a second. Isla held her head up and looked around.

They'd brought her to this huge abandoned factory, or warehouse or whatever. Massive iron pillars, rust-stained where water had run down from the holes in the roof. Foul-smelling green stuff all over the floor. Her heart started racing and she felt like she might throw up. She swallowed hard and tried desperately to think about anything except the sick rising in her throat.

And one single thought crashed into her brain.

Mum was right all along.

A tiny whimper escaped her lips. She felt like she was going to cry. Except that would be a totally bad idea. She fought to control herself. *I'm sorry I didn't listen, Mum. I love you. Please find me. Please.*

Graffiti disfigured every surface, right up to the roof. Tags, mainly. *REKO. BURO*, with a smiley face inside the O. *WISO. AGID.* Others too crudely sprayed for her to read.

He'd tied her to a chair. And it wasn't even with rope she could maybe wriggle out of. He'd used those black plastic things you zipped up. What did they call them in the films? Zip ties? Or was that American? Cable ties. That was it. She shook her head. Like it mattered. She tried angling her wrists and cried out from the sharp pain that seared up and down her arms like they were wrapped in red-hot wire.

He kept prowling around her chair. Every time he went behind her, she had to fight the urge to scream. The worst bit was he was singing. Not properly. More like crooning to himself. That old jazz song Dad would wail out when he thought she couldn't hear him. 'My Way'.

He came round to stand in front of her. Put his hands on his hips. Smiled. Her tummy flip-flopped.

'What a turn-up, eh, Isla? Me being twenty-six and not some schoolboy with the hots for Little Miss Mental Health.'

'Please, let me go. You haven't done anything too bad yet. Aaron's not dead. You could still get away without the police finding you.' She knew she sounded terrified. Tried to slow her voice down. 'Look, I don't know who you are, but the longer you keep me here, the higher the risk they'll come looking for me. That means it'll all be over. You'll lose everything.'

'It won't be all over. Not ever. We've got a plan.' He stared at her with those blank, dead eyes. Slowly a smile crept across his features. It terrified her more than if he'd been snarling and shouting. 'You'll love it.'

Isla fought down an urge to scream. She was frightened that if she started, she'd never stop. She snatched a breath, eyeballed him and tried to pretend he was still Josh. She managed to crack a tiny smile, then forced herself to make it a bit more genuine,

'Please just let me go. I'll walk back into Birmingham. It doesn't matter if it takes all night. Or drop me off somewhere. You can still get away before I'd have the chance to get to a phone to call anyone.'

He cocked his head on one side. He was actually considering it. He was going to do it. He was going to let her go. All because she'd stayed calm and not given in to panic. She'd be back with Mum and everything would be all right.

He lunged towards her. She reared back, screaming, almost tipping the chair over. He got down onto one knee like he was about to propose or something, then leaned over and put his mouth to her ear, so close she could actually feel his lips brushing the fine hairs there. His breath was hot against her skin, like a dog's.

'If you don't stop talking,' he murmured, 'I'll cut your ear off and make you eat it.'

He got to his feet. Stared down at her, then, from behind his back, produced a knife with a serrated blade and spun it between his fingers.

Suddenly, shamefully, Isla's bladder let go. The urine was hot against her thigh, then it turned cold. She wept.

He laughed. Looked down at her, spun that wicked blade and laughed.

And she knew, right in that moment, that he was going to kill her.

Chapter 70

Annie's fingers hurt. She looked down.

She was clutching her phone so hard the knuckles on her right hand had whitened. She put it on the table.

'What did she say?' Michael asked, the muscles of his face tight with tension.

Annie blinked. Heard her own voice as if someone else had borrowed it. Everything felt unreal.

'I have to take fifty thousand pounds to an abandoned factory in Sutton Coldfield by midnight or they'll kill Isla.'

It sounded far away, the voice. And so calm, which was odd, wasn't it? Given that she'd just received a death threat from a blackmailer. Was she in shock? A laugh broke free from her lips. Wide-eyed, she clapped her hand over her mouth. Then she collapsed into a chair as her knees gave way.

He quickly filled a glass from the tap.

'Here, drink this.'

She gripped the glass between her hands and brought it to her lips. Managed a couple of sips before setting it down. She looked up at Michael.

'I need to find her, Michael. I need to find Isla.'

He kneeled beside her. Laid a hand on her arm.

'Hey, it's going to be all right. I promise.'

She sniffed and swiped a hand across her nose.

'We have to do what she says. I'll have to find the money. God knows how. It's not as if I can just pop into town and arrange a huge cash withdrawal. Are you even allowed to do that any more? What about money laundering rules? The bank gave me the third degree just for setting up the standing order.'

She could hear her panicky voice and clamped her lips shut, fearful that she might otherwise start screaming and never stop.

'Breathe, Annie. Breathe,' Michael said. 'Look, I've got a thousand or so upstairs. You're welcome to it. Have you got anything valuable in your house?'

'I've got Granny's jewellery. Grant pretty much cleaned me out in the divorce, but I never touched her jewels.'

'Sorry to be crass, but is it worth much?'

Seeing a way out, a way to get, as the blackmailer had so callously put it, 'creative', she nodded excitedly.

'There's diamonds and all sorts. Horrible old-fashioned stuff, if I'm honest, but yes. I took it to an antiques dealer to have it valued once. It's worth tons. We can pawn it!'

Michael frowned.

'You know you won't get the market price? They'll only offer you pennies on the pound.'

'As long as they give me enough, I don't care.'

'We'll try Family Pawnbrokers on Bull Street.' He looked away for a second. Nodded. 'They stay open late.'

Michael drove Annie over to her house, where she emptied her jewellery box into a bag, stuffing in the valuation certificate. Fifteen minutes after that, she was pushing through the door of the pawnbroker's, Michael by her side, setting a brass bell ringing. The negotiation was short, and baffling. Despite proof that the jewellery was worth collectively over seventy-five thousand pounds, the pawnbroker would only offer her thirty.

'But I need fifty!' Annie exclaimed.

The elderly man shrugged. 'Market's not what it was, bab.'

'Please, you have to go higher.'

He sighed. Held his hands wide. 'I could go to thirty-five, but that's it. Me final offer.'

Racked with anxiety, Annie nodded blindly.

Michael unsnapped his watch and laid it beside the jewels on the scratched glass counter.

'That's a Rolex Submariner. Got to be worth twenty at least.'

The pawnbroker picked up the watch and scrutinised it, turning it over in his hand to examine the back.

'Michael, you can't!' Annie exclaimed. 'Lucy gave it to you.'

'It's only a watch. If she knew what I wanted the cash for, she'd tell me to hand it over without a second thought.'

'Oh God, you're sure?'

'Nice piece,' the pawnbroker said. 'Not engraved, which is good. If you don't redeem it, it'll fetch more. Give you twelve for it right now, bab.'

Michael eyeballed him. Said nothing.

The old man grunted. 'All right, then, fifteen. Final offer.'

They drove back to Michael's in convoy. When they got there, Annie transferred all the cash into a black holdall.

She turned to Michael.

'Thank you. This means everything to me.'

He shrugged.

'What choice do we have?'

'We?'

'I'm coming with you.'

'But she said I had to go alone.'

He shook his head.

'It's too dangerous, Annie. These people are psychopaths. You saw what they did to John Varney. I think they'll take the money and then kill you both.'

'But if they see us together, they could do that anyway.'

'Look, we'll go in separate cars. That way if they *are* watching you, they'll see you're alone. I'll take one of the vans from work.'

Annie didn't have the mental shelf-space to see if Michael's plan had any holes in it. All she knew was that her daughter was in mortal danger and Michael wanted to help.

She nodded decisively.

'Thank you. I'll pay you back.'

He smiled tightly. 'Let's worry about the financials after we've rescued Isla, eh?'

Chapter 71

Isla was shivering violently and couldn't stop.

She was trying not to cry by counting the rivets on the rusted iron pillar in front of her. But every time she got above thirty, her eyes began to skitter over the stained and flaking paint and she lost count. All she could think about was the ways the man in front of her might hurt her.

He tossed the hunting knife in the air so it spun, and caught it by the handle on the way down. Did it again. And again.

Isla tried not to imagine what the blade could do to her flesh. As if reading her mind, he advanced on her, the knife pointing towards her chest. She recoiled, flattening herself against the hard back of the chair until the bent steel frame dug into her ribs.

He slowly extended his arm towards her and then lifted the knife so the tip rested just beneath her chin. Breathing shallowly, she tried to hold his gaze and not to cry. Somehow she just knew crying would only make him enjoy it more.

He narrowed his eyes. Raised his chin and looked off to a point behind Isla, somewhere in the dark.

'She'd have a fit if I killed you before your mum gets here. But I could just cut you a bit. She knows how I get sometimes. She'd forgive me.'

He pushed the knife a little. Isla winced as she felt the point dig into the soft flesh under her jaw.

Finding a flash of courage in that moment, she stared up at him, defiantly meeting his gaze. But it was so frightening. There was a cold look behind his eyes, like staring into the windows of a deserted house. If anybody *was* home, no sane person would want to meet them.

She was shaking all over, despite the restraints. And she had a strong urge to pee again. But maybe she could find a way to reach out to him. To connect with him. Surely he wasn't completely devoid of emotion?

She worked hard to force a smile. Softened her gaze.

'Look, I get it. You're not Josh. But when we were dating, that can't all have been fake, can it? At the club? When we were dancing? Didn't you enjoy kissing me? Didn't you feel *anything*?'

He frowned, tipped his head to one side. Withdrew the knife and replaced it in the sheath on his belt. Then stared at her thoughtfully. It was like when a maths teacher asked someone to solve a quadratic equation on the whiteboard. That blank look.

'Did I … *feel* … anything? Did *I* … feel *anything*?' He gazed upwards for a long moment, then dropped his head back and looked at her. 'Well, I felt like hurting you. But my s— I mean my *associate* would have been furious. It wasn't in the plan. Not then, anyway.'

He drew back his hand and slapped her. Hard.

She cried out. Her cheek went tight and hot.

He leaned over her, grabbed her wrists and squeezed them against the metal arms of the chair. He came closer still and gazed directly into her eyes. She caught the sour tang of his sweat and a strange metallic smell as if he wasn't flesh and blood under his clothes at all.

'Killing John was a bit of a spur-of-the-moment thing, you know? He was just,' he shrugged, 'equipment. But what *we* have between us, Isla? I mean, it deserves to be taken seriously.'

She grabbed at this faint flicker of compassion.

'Yes. Exactly. So why don't you cut these cable ties,' she gulped, tried a sexy smile she didn't think landed, 'with that big knife of yours, and let me go?'

She waited, watching the way his eyes moved as he considered her suggestion. Then he nodded. Smiled down at her. Oh, thank God, it was going to be all right. He wasn't mad after all.

He reached behind him and took the knife out again.

Slowly he slid the tip under the cable tie securing her right arm to the chair.

'Like this?' he asked, raising his eyebrows.

'Yes. Just be careful.'

Then he pulled the knife free and hammered the metal hilt down onto her hand with such force she heard the crack as a bone snapped.

As she screamed, he straightened up, sheathed the knife and walked off.

Isla's broken finger was hot and throbbing and the pain was the worst she'd ever felt. Her eyes full of tears of agony, she dropped her head back and stared up at the corrugated-iron ceiling many feet above her head. Dark shapes flittered in and out of the tall iron pillars. The colourful graffiti disappeared into the blackness.

This was it, then. She was going to die here, all alone. Poor Mum would never find her.

No. No. NO! She would *not* go down without a fight. She wriggled and strained against the cable ties until she felt the skin of her left wrist give and hot wetness flood her flexed palm.

She threw her head back and screamed – 'Help!' – until her throat hurt. And then she screamed some more.

Chapter 72

Annie shot along the Aston Expressway.

The traffic was light but there were still plenty of half-asleep drivers hogging the middle lane, dawdling along at sixty-five. She swung right, no indicators, and blasted past them in screaming silence. Their outraged horns blared a diminishing protest as they receded in her mirror.

Somewhere, as if screened by a fire door, she could sense her terror. But it was as if she'd been insulated from it, able to function on a purely physical level, even if her body was wound so tight every muscle, every sinew, every nerve was as taut as the cables on the Symphony Hall suspension bridge.

Because that was how she felt right now. Suspended. Halfway between two lives. The life she'd known with Isla, where they bickered and fought like all mothers and teenage daughters did. And the life that loomed like a cancer diagnosis. One where she'd be wearing black, clutching a white lily, standing at a graveside and sobbing, out of control, as the rest of the gang supported her. Isla's funeral. Real, this time.

The car was surreally quiet as the speedometer nudged ninety. Her heart was racing and her palms were slick with sweat. She took the left off the steering wheel and wiped it on her trousers. Then the right. Gripped the wheel and stared ahead, into the darkness. Her mind was barely functioning. All she could do was drive on muscle memory while disjointed words and phrases whirled through her overstressed brain.

Please don't hurt my baby ... I remember giving birth to you, Isla ... Don't kill her, she did nothing to you ... I've got your money, you monsters, just leave her be ...

The lights of the other vehicles that sporadically illuminated the interior of the car subtly changed colour. Now a pale blue seeped into the mix, flickering and sending a signal into her brain that she knew meant something important, but that right here, right now she couldn't identify.

She glanced at the mirror.

Reality bit hard. Comprehension dawned. And with it, horror. Police.

Electric-blue flashing lights filled the mirror. Even inside the soundproofed car, she could hear the discordant wail of the siren.

Run, Annie! something shrieked inside her head. Briefly her foot dipped on the throttle.

And then reason prevailed. She couldn't outpace a police car. She had no idea what her top speed was, but somehow she doubted it was enough.

Feeling a great weight pushing her down into her seat, she indicated left and pulled over into the middle lane. It was over.

Engine howling, the police car surged past her.

And kept going. Lights strobing. Siren blaring as it shot ahead.

Annie sucked down a huge breath and sighed it out in relief. She floored the throttle.

Chapter 73

Maya supposed she'd always known it. That there was something wrong with Ollie.

It had been there that time he'd come back from killing the dog. When the tight-fisted owners had refused to pay the reward she'd suggested. His face spattered with blood, his clothes streaked with it, he'd thrown himself down in an armchair. A glazed expression, eyes unfocused, lazy smile on his face. Breathing deeply but slowly.

And again when the businessman in Bristol had attacked her in the hotel room. It had taken a hard slap to shock Ollie into stopping his murderous attack. They hadn't bothered forcing the mark to pay up. He'd probably need the money to get his ear sewn back on.

And John Varney. He'd never have been a threat. A drug addict and alcoholic, his mind screwed up with PTSD. Who'd believe any tale he tried to tell them?

Maybe after this she'd try to get Ollie some help. A private psychiatrist. A *discreet* private psychiatrist. They could afford it, after all. Someone with a nice office in London, a city where they could disappear.

He was looking at her, his face screwed into an irritated scowl.

'Did you hear what I just said?'

'Sorry. Miles away. Tell me again?'

'I said once she's inside, you shut the doors. I'll do the mum first, and then…' His eyes widened and a smile stole across his face. 'No. I've got a *much* better idea. Guess what it is?'

She sighed. Was this how their life together was going to be from now on? Ollie coming apart and her having to guess in which direction the bits were going to fly?

'I can't.'

His smile faltered. 'I said guess. It's important to me that you at least try.'

Maya shrugged. This was tedious, and such a waste of time.

'Do the girl first, make the mum watch?'

'Too obvious. No, I was thinking, what if I cut the mum's hamstrings? Then I've got her immobilised, the girl's wetting her pants and I can take all the time I need with them both.'

'As long as you don't take all night about it, I don't really care what you do. But like I said, we want the cash and we want them gone, hidden, and then a clean getaway, yes? My plan still stands.'

He took his knife out and started spinning it on the table. The point came to rest facing her. He stared at it for a while, then up at her.

'Fine,' he said. 'I need to get set up. Come with?'

She followed him into a corner of the vast space lit by a scrappy array of battered lamps Ollie had scavenged from somewhere. A generator he'd got working chuntered quietly, emitting pungent exhaust fumes. She stood, arms folded, as he shook out huge rattling sheets of heavy-duty polythene then duct-taped them to the walls and pillars that demarcated what he proudly told her was his 'kill room'.

He dragged in a broken-down metal-legged table he'd found somewhere. Opened a black nylon holdall and started unloading its contents, placing each implement on the tabletop.

When he'd finished, he turned to her. Held his hands out.

'Well, what do you think?'

She looked down at the items on the table. Maybe they had gone past the point where a private psychiatrist would be of much use.

'Lovely. Where are you going to put the bodies?'

'You're going to love this. Come over here.'

At the edge of the kill room was a metal hatch in the floor, maybe a metre to a side. Rusted hinges on the side closest to the wall. A U-shaped handle on the opposite side.

Ollie grabbed the handle and yanked the hatch upwards as if was made of cardboard and not, as she now saw, thick sheet steel. He moved it past the vertical and let it fall against the wall with a hollow clang that echoed all the way through the factory.

Then he took out his phone and turned on the torch. Standing well back, he pointed it downwards.

Maya peered over the edge. The hole was maybe ten feet deep. The bottom was littered with needles, scraps of blackened tin foil, crushed soft-drink cans, the stubbed-out ends of joints, broken glass. Like whichever junkies had been using the factory had decided what the place really needed was a spring clean.

'It's an inspection pit,' Ollie crowed. 'Or, I don't know, an oil sump, or a space so some machine could work properly. The point is, it's perfect. I just drop them down, chuck some rubbish over the top, not that I really need to, and then shut them in. Nobody'll ever find them.'

Despite herself, Maya was impressed. It *was* perfect. Ollie could have his fun, nobody within a couple of miles in any direction to hear the noise. Then, when he was finished, down they'd go, just like he said.

She wasn't quite so confident that the bodies would never be found. But even if they were, it would be far too late.

She and Ollie would have vanished. New IDs, new looks, new country.

New lives.

Chapter 74

She stood on the access road, shaking.

Not just from the cold, although it was a bitter night and a bone-chilling wind was slicing sideways across the countryside. Her padded jacket wasn't up to the task and felt as though it were made of paper.

Mainly, it was fear. Fear that she'd be too late. Fear that the criminals had already killed Isla and she was walking into a trap. Fear that all that lay waiting for her inside this forbidding brick and metal monolith was her daughter's body.

The crescent moon cast a grey glow over the access road that stretched between her and the factory. As she drew nearer, her boot soles crunching on broken glass, the feeling of dread intensified to the point where she found walking difficult.

Christ, this was worse than she'd imagined.

Tears rose to her eyes and her throat tightened. Would they ever be together again? Bantering – even bickering would be OK – over pancakes or cereal. Orange juice and coffee. Blueberry muffins as a Saturday treat. Girls' nights in watching crap TV with popcorn and hot chocolate.

The handles of the nylon holdall were digging into the soft flesh of her fingers. She switched it from her right hand to her left. On stiff legs that were sending a loud message that all things considered they'd rather run away, she approached the graffiti-covered building until it loomed high above her, blocking out the moon.

She must have been mad, refusing to involve the police. What the hell was she going to do?

And in that moment, the answer came charging to the fore. Anger replaced fear.

'I'm going to save my daughter,' she muttered between gritted teeth.

On the way inside, she spotted a black shape on the ground. Long, thin, ridged in a spiral pattern. She stooped and picked up the length of steel. It was cold in her palm. Heavy. It felt like it might do some damage.

She swung it experimentally and nearly let go as its weight pulled it through her sweaty palm. She put the holdall down and gripped the rebar with both hands like a baseball bat. That was better. She tried to visualise the male blackmailer's face. Imagined smashing the heavy steel bar down onto it. Breaking his nose, pulping his eyeballs. Splitting his cheeks down to the bone. Could she? She nodded. Oh yes, she really, truly could. The man who'd taken Isla was going to learn what a mother's love looked like.

Holdall in one hand, rebar in the other, she pulled the door wide. The corroded hinges shrieked, making her flinch before she remembered she was expected. This was hardly a surprise attack.

She gasped involuntarily. It was like a cathedral inside. A cathedral dedicated to some deity of decay. The far end was bathed in bright white light. Lamps stood on piles of bricks, or hung from the walls in loops like crude Christmas decorations. A low grumbling like an engine provided low-frequency background music.

No sense in hanging back now. She strode forward, breathing heavily and, from somewhere deep inside her, finding reserves of courage and determination that tamped down her anxiety. She could do this.

The woman met her on the edge of the lit-up space. No trace of friendly Ellie now. The cold-eyed stranger standing before her in a blood-red leather jacket looked like a vampire. Skin pale in the harsh lamplight, lips glossy and red.

Annie dropped the holdall to the concrete floor with a soft

thump and hefted the rebar with both hands. She was shaking with renewed terror at coming face to face with one of Isla's kidnappers. But where was the baby-faced bastard calling himself Josh? She looked around, saw nobody. Maybe the woman had decided she could do this on her own.

Suddenly the bar weighed the same as a fridge and the shaking intensified as she struggled to keep it aloft. She waved it at the woman, hating her more than she'd ever hated anything before.

'Where's my daughter? Tell me, you bitch, or you'll get this in the face.'

The young woman smirked.

'Bit old for wet work, aren't we? Or have we been practising at our Pilates class? I didn't notice any weapons in the photos you posted on Instagram.'

Annie bared her teeth and lunged forward, swinging the rebar. The younger woman flinched and stepped back. Annie felt a surge of strength flowing through her.

'Try me,' she gritted out. 'Just fucking try me.'

Chapter 75

Scuffing footsteps had Annie whirling around, heart crashing against her ribs.

It was as if every nightmare she'd ever had had arrived at once.

Isla, left cheek branded with a red handprint, eyes swollen from crying, stumbled towards her. She tripped. Annie caught her breath and started forward to save her from hitting the ground. But Isla didn't fall. Instead she jerked upright, eyes bulging. And that was when Annie saw the rope looped tightly around her daughter's throat.

Holding the other end of the rope was the man she and Michael had watched savagely stab John Varney to death.

An unholy smile played across his unnaturally youthful features, chilling her to the bone. It was the total opposite of what a smile was supposed to be. All it held was the promise of pain, fear, humiliation and death.

'Hi, Annie. So nice to finally meet you,' he said.

Suddenly Annie felt very, very cold. More afraid than she'd ever been in her life. Because she knew now what she was looking at. A psychopath. The kind of emotionless creature who treated people as things.

In his other hand, the hand not gripping the rope, the man held a knife. She recognised it. The last time she'd seen it, he'd been plunging it into John's body, over and over again, as he laughed maniacally amidst the spurting blood.

'Drop the bar, Annie, before somebody gets hurt,' the woman said. 'And by somebody, basically I mean you.'

Annie wasn't aware of her fingers uncurling from around the

cold length of rebar. The harsh clang as it hit the floor barely registered. All she could think of was Isla.

'Please don't hurt her,' she said. 'I brought the cash.'

'Thank you, Annie. I said you'd manage, didn't I?' Then the woman sneered. 'But sadly, we can't release Isla after all. I'm assuming you know that?'

'Mum, please,' Isla whimpered. 'Don't let him hurt me again.'

She held up her hand. It was blackened, and the index finger hung crookedly.

The man smirked at Annie. She clenched her fists and screamed at him. 'Leave her alone! She's just a child!'

He shortened the rope and brought the knife up to Isla's throat. Annie felt a deep pain in the pit of her stomach. Fear rendered her speechless.

'No. She's mine now. And when I'm done with her, I'm going to do you, too. Then I'm going to sling you both down this inspection pit I found, chuck some crap down on top of you and close the hatch. It really is the perfect plan.' He looked at the woman standing to Annie's left. 'Can we get on with it, please? I am literally bored out of my skull right now.'

Shaking and desperate, Annie glanced over her shoulder. The space was empty apart from the three of them. Where was Michael? He should have been there by now.

'Looking for your boyfriend, are you?' the woman crowed. 'I didn't think he'd have so much sense. I was sure he'd have tried to rush us by now. With something a bit more useful than a bit of iron bar, too.'

Annie shook her head. 'You said to come alone. He wanted to, but I told him to wait at home with Aaron in case you tried to take him, too.'

'Doesn't matter. We'll find another way to deal with Michael and Aaron.'

Annie knew death was close. But maybe they'd be satisfied

with hers alone. If she could just die knowing she'd secured Isla's freedom, it wouldn't all have been in vain.

'Please don't kill Isla. She's only fifteen. If you want a victim, kill me instead.' She held her hands out, palms squeezed together. 'Do what you like with me, but spare her life, I beg you.'

Very calmly, the woman said, 'Can't do that, Annie. You broke the rules. Now you have to pay. It's nothing personal. It's the same for all the families we work with.'

Desolate, Annie hung her head. She was so emotionally wrung out, she no longer had the energy to cry. She'd played. And she'd lost. This was real. And it was over.

They were alone, and about to die.

Chapter 76

Annie flinched as the young man handed the end of the rope to the woman. Then again as he advanced on her, swinging the knife in front of her eyes, swapping it from hand to hand, feinting, jabbing it towards her as he took one step after another.

From somewhere, she dredged up a final spark of courage. Dropped to one knee and grabbed the rebar. With a scream of defiance, she swung the heavy steel bar at his head.

It connected, cracking his skull open like an egg, spraying blood and greyish brain matter everywhere. Isla would be saved. They both would be.

And then reality broke through this fleeting fantasy. The man simply leaned back. The end of the bar whistled harmlessly past his face, then he lunged forward and hit her arm as the rebar dragged it around in front of her. She spun, unable to control the weight of all that metal in motion. The next thing she knew, her wrist was on fire as he stepped in and twisted the bar out of her grip.

He swung it underhand and launched it in a high arc over the floodlights. It clanged off a wall, then landed with a series of echoing clonks somewhere out there in the dark.

He extended his left hand and curled his fingers in and out.

The woman placed the rope in his palm and he jerked it viciously, so Isla cried out and stumbled towards him.

'Come with me, Annie. Now!' he barked.

Shaking, Annie could only comply, walking ahead of him and Isla towards a corner of the factory that, to her horror, she now saw was sheathed in thick plastic sheeting.

He turned to face her. His features, so blandly handsome before, were now transformed into something *other*. As if someone had asked an AI tool to generate a person's face but forgot to specify that they should look alive.

He swept his arm in a wide arc, never letting go of the knife or the rope. His mouth loosened and stretched. After a moment, Annie realised he was smiling. Only now he wasn't pretending any more, it was like a child's painting. A curved line on a neutral face devoid of feeling.

'Come over here, Annie.' He beckoned her. 'Come on, I don't bite.'

Her legs felt as though they might give way, but somehow she managed to close the distance between them. He was pointing at a hatch thrown back against the wall.

'That's going to be your final resting place.' He jerked the rope again. 'Isla, why don't you stand on the edge? Pretend you're going to jump in. It'll be fun.'

'Leave her alone, you psycho!' Annie shrieked, impelled to charge him but held back by the sure and certain knowledge he'd push Isla in if she did.

It was too late, she knew that. Paralysed by her fear, she could only stand and watch as this monster forced her daughter closer and closer to the edge.

Isla shuffled to the lip of the pit's coal-black mouth. He prodded her with the point of the knife. She wobbled, throwing her arms out to maintain her precarious balance. She looked over her shoulder. 'Mum, I'm so sorry...'

And then, in slow motion, as Annie watched helplessly, she toppled forward into the pit.

Annie screamed in shock and disbelief. Then gravity went into reverse.

Isla did not fall into the darkness in front of her. She folded at the waist, and the upper half of her body tipped back. Then she twisted, arms lancing out to the sides, her right leg drawing up and inwards. With a loud shout, she shot her foot out, driving the edge hard into the man's groin, doubling him over.

As Isla kicked the knife into the pit, Annie realised this was their chance. Their only chance. She had to follow her daughter's example.

She had to fight back.

Chapter 77

Annie whirled and elbowed the woman in the face.

Then she ran across the slippery rustling plastic towards the man. He was on his knees, gasping for breath.

Without breaking stride, she kicked him as hard as she could in the ribs, sending him rolling onto his side, groaning. She slithered a step closer, murder in her heart.

'Kill him, Mum!' Isla shrieked, as she wrenched the noose over her head and charged at the woman.

There was no time to think. Annie drew her foot back again and swung it forward, aiming for his head this time. But he rolled away and her boot only struck him a glancing blow to the back of his skull. Desperate, she looked around for a weapon.

He'd stacked some planks by the side of the pit, obviously intending to cover their bodies with them.

As he pulled himself to his feet, using the damp, mould-covered brickwork for support, she pulled a length of wood free and hefted it. As long as the rebar, but half the weight. It felt good in her hands.

She was going to finish him. To kill him, just like Isla had urged her. The man who'd discussed torturing and murdering her little girl was going to pay with his life.

Screaming, she ran at him, already swinging the piece of timber like a club. The plastic bunched and shifted beneath her feet, and she slipped, connecting with his right bicep just as he pushed himself off the wall. The shock travelled all the way up her arm from her wrist, through her elbow and into her shoulder.

'Bitch!' he grunted, tears streaming from his eyes, still clutching his balls with his left hand.

Good, Isla's kick had done some proper damage.

Annie jabbed the end of the club at his face, forcing him to step back smartly to avoid having his nose broken.

Behind her, she could hear Isla and the woman tussling. Isla was shouting out like she did at taekwondo practice, while the woman kept up a stream of vile swearing. Maybe her smart, talented, strong daughter stood a chance.

But now she had problems of her own. The man had retrieved a plank from the pile and was swinging it at her in wide arcs as he limped towards her. He jumped forward like a fencer, smashing the plank down towards her head. With a scream, she tried to parry the blow.

The lengths of timber met above her head with a loud crack. An electric shock shot up her arm, numbing her from wrist to shoulder. She smelled a sharp, sappy tang. Then he was on her, forcing her backwards, snarling. Her left foot caught in a rucked-up fold of plastic. She stumbled.

The woman screamed as Isla shouted triumphantly.

'I got her, Mum!'

She shouldn't have, but Annie reacted instinctively. She glanced to her left.

The world exploded. Bright white light blinded her. Pain so intense she thought she would pass out from it crackled through her brain. 'Oh,' she groaned in a low voice not her own. She dropped to her knees, clutching her cheekbone where the man had just smacked her with the plank. Then black curtains swung shut over her vision.

Seconds later, she heard Isla's voice in the distance. 'No! Mum!'

Something was wrong. The factory was upside down. And bobbing rhythmically. She was looking at the man's back. He was holding her over his head as if she weighed no more than a child, his fingers digging agonisingly deep into the soft flesh between her hip bones and her ribs.

Lit by the site lamps, Isla and the woman were locked in each other's grip, struggling to stay upright on the slippery plastic sheeting, battling for supremacy in a fight to the death.

The ink-black rectangular mouth of the pit grew larger in Annie's inverted vision.

Chapter 78

'Leave them alone!'

The shout echoed around the high-roofed factory.

Annie twisted her head round. Michael was charging across the glass-strewn concrete floor towards them.

'Fuck,' the man muttered, then threw Annie towards the pit.

She screamed. Landed awkwardly against the sloping hatch, banging her head so hard her vision went blurry. She began slipping down and saw the gaping maw of the pit opening still wider to swallow her whole.

Her legs disappeared through the hatch, and for one heart-stopping moment, she felt her torso going the same way. She shot her hands out and grabbed at the edge.

She came to a jolting stop, the sharp lip of the steel surround digging painfully into her armpits. She scrabbled her feet against the smooth sides of the pit, but there was nothing to give her any purchase. She was trapped. Grunting with the effort, she tried to haul herself out, but something had happened to her left arm, and a bolt of agony shot through her elbow like a metal spike.

Stunned and helpless, she clung on as best she could, sweating from the effort of keeping herself from plummeting into the stinking hole.

The man had engaged Michael in a dirty fight, clawing at his face, aiming a knee into his balls, grunting like a wild animal. Isla sent the woman staggering back with a well-aimed kick to her knee. Michael scythed his foot round and took the man's legs out from under him, then lunged down and drove an elbow into his mouth.

The man got to his feet, wiping blood from his split lip and baring red-streaked teeth.

'Well, well. This is going to be interesting.'

Then he launched himself at Michael.

The woman called out to Annie, her arms locked around Isla's waist. Isla bucked and screamed, jerking her head back in an effort to butt her opponent in the face.

'Oh look, Annie. Your knight in shining armour's not looking too happy.'

Isla took advantage of the woman's focus on the two men tussling in the corner. She raised her right knee and backheeled her in the shin, raking her heel down the bone and drawing a piercing screech. Then she twisted free and swung a clawed hand at the woman's face.

'Get out of there, Mum!' she shouted, pointing, her eyes wide and terrified. 'Get out!'

Annie saw why. The man had dealt Michael a blow that sent him sprawling to the ground. Now he was advancing on her, teeth bared, feral rage darkening his eyes. Behind him, gasping for breath, Michael was struggling to his hands and knees.

With every ounce of her strength, Annie strained her arms and, ignoring the pain in her elbow, hauled herself halfway out and onto the solid floor. But her feet were scrabbling uselessly against the smooth inner walls of the pit and she had no way to propel the rest of her to safety.

The man was almost on her. He looked down at her gleefully and raised a booted foot to stamp her into oblivion. Then he howled and clutched the back of his head as Michael landed a ringing blow that sent him spinning in a half-circle. He staggered and turned on Michael. Annie gave a tremendous shout of effort and pulled herself far enough out of the pit that she could drag herself clear.

The man had his hands round Michael's throat, knuckles whitened with the effort of choking him. Michael was flailing around, alternately pulling the man's hands away from his throat and hitting him in the face.

The psycho's mouth was stretched wide in a rictus of maniacal aggression as he pulled his head back and shook it from side to side to avoid the incoming blows.

Michael's face had turned dark red and his eyes were bulging. His mouth was stretched wide in an 'O' as he strove to drag air to his lungs past the chokehold.

Annie yelled out a scream of defiance and hauled herself to her feet. She grabbed a length of wood and, still groggy, charged at the psycho.

'Leave him alone!' she shouted, swinging the plank.

Chapter 79

Isla watched, horrified, as Michael sank to his knees, the man straddling him, hands clamped tight around his throat.

Her mum hit the psycho with a bit of wood, but it just glanced off his back and he half turned and kicked out at her knee.

No! No way was Isla going to let those bastards win. She streaked away from the woman, who was still shrieking obscenities after Isla had followed up her shin-scrape by kicking her in the face.

She had almost reached the man strangling Michael when something 'Josh' had said at the club came back to her like a flash of lightning.

I'm claustrophobic, OK? And to be fair, I'm not a massive fan of the dark either.

Maybe it was a lie. But he had seemed twitchy in the dark, confined space of the underground passageway that led to the dance floor.

She swerved away from him and ran over to the yellow generator that was powering the lights. Squatting in front of it, she searched for the off switch. Surely they'd put it somewhere obvious. There ought to be a big green button for 'ON' and a matching red one for 'OFF'.

She heard the woman's taunting voice.

'Come back here, Isla. I'm not finished with you.'

Panicking, she leaned over the generator and peered down at the side facing the wall. Her fingers skittered over the casing as she searched frantically for the controls.

Behind her, footsteps crunched closer on the gritty floor.

And then her finger found soft, squidgy silicon covering two hard circular buttons. One green. One red.

She pushed the red one hard.

And the lights went out.

The factory was plunged into total darkness. She heard running footsteps.

Out of the pitch black rose a howl of pure terror. It was the man's voice. Josh hadn't been lying back there in the club. He was afraid of the dark.

There was a split second of silence as the shriek petered out. Then a crack, followed by a thud.

She turned the lights back on.

Bathed in the blinding white light, her mum stood like some kind of warrior queen over the man, the length of wood gripped in her fists like a battleaxe. He was unconscious and bleeding from a jagged wound on the back of his head. Michael was on his feet, rubbing his throat.

Mum dropped the wood and rushed over, hugging Isla so tight she had to wriggle out of her grip.

'Careful! Please don't suffocate me when I just saved your ass!'

But she was so happy she could have cried from the joy of it. After all the terror and trauma, it was like waking from a nightmare.

Mum was looking down at her hand.

'What?'

'Your poor finger. I think it's broken.'

Isla held it up and inspected it. Weird. No pain, even though there was something really shonky about that angle. No way were fingers supposed to bend that way. Pretty horrible colour, too. Maybe she was in shock. They'd done it in biology. She hoped it wouldn't wear off until she'd got some paracetamol inside her.

Her mum ripped off the bottom of her T-shirt and started bandaging Isla's hand. Isla yelped as she caught the tip of her finger. Behind her, Michael had found some cable ties like the ones the man had used on Isla. She watched as he lashed the man's hands together behind his back. Then his ankles. Then all four limbs together so he was bent backwards. Good. Bastard wasn't going anywhere like that.

Mum smoothed the bandage around Isla's hand and tied the ripped end into a bow

'Just be careful with it, darling. That will do until we get you to hospital.' She looked around. 'Where is she?'

'I think she ran when I turned the lights off.'

Michael joined them.

'Now we *have* to go to the police,' he said. 'If I work till I'm a hundred, I'm never going to reach a pay grade high enough to deal with any more of this crap.'

Mum's face went serious. But Isla saw something cunning come on behind her eyes like a light.

'We'll call them in a minute,' she said, pulling out her phone. 'But I need to talk to Deanna first.'

Day Six

Chapter 80

Aaron and his aunt Jodie were standing on the doorstep waiting for them, hip to hip, Aaron leaning on his crutch.

As soon as the cars rolled to a stop outside the house, they hurried down the front path and hugged Michael. Then they turned to Annie and Isla. More hugs, slightly awkward, but heartfelt all the same.

Inside, they gathered in the kitchen. Jodie made coffee while the three survivors of the fight at the factory recounted their night-long ordeal, ending with a trip to A&E and interviews at the police station. The teenagers took their drinks up to Aaron's room, leaving the adults clustered at the kitchen table.

Jodie squinted at him over her coffee.

'You look like shit,' she deadpanned.

They all laughed, though for Annie it felt more like relief than proper joyful happiness. Too close to the lingering panic she'd felt ever since the police cars had arrived outside the factory, sirens blaring, blue lights flashing.

'You should see the other guy.'

Jodie favoured her brother with an eyeroll.

Annie felt her nerves settling.

'How about you and Isla, Annie?' Jodie asked. 'Those are some nasty injuries you picked up.'

Annie put the tips of her fingers to the butterfly sutures the A&E nurse had applied to her cheek and forehead. Winced.

'Not too bad. That bastard broke Isla's finger, but other than that, it's cuts and bruises, like me.'

'So what happens now? Did the cops say?'

'Full-scale manhunt,' Michael said. 'Helicopters, ANPR cameras on all the major roads out of the city, canine units, coppers on the streets looking for her. They hadn't found her by the time they let us go, though. It's like she vanished into thin air.'

'They'll catch her, Mike, I know they will,' Jodie said with an encouraging smile.

But would they? Annie had seen two versions of the woman. The sweet, chirpy receptionist at the Oaks and the sadistic psychopath at the factory in that blood-red jacket. Totally different looks. What if she'd adopted a third identity? It didn't take much to fool people. A change in hairstyle went a long way. Annie had tried out an ill-advised crop-and-colour job the previous year, and colleagues of ten years' standing had blanked her on campus.

And even if they'd escaped her last night, Isla and Aaron would never truly be safe until she was behind bars. Something about the way she'd talked about 'the deal' made Annie terrified that it wasn't all over.

Chapter 81

As she fled the city, Maya obeyed every single speed limit, even the ridiculous 20 mph on the residential roads she wound through. No sense in being pulled over by a copper doing routine traffic stops.

She'd prefer to avoid any more hiccups in her escape plan. Like driving to the airport with a dead police officer in the boot.

Birmingham airport lay eight miles west of the city. Anyone in a hurry to leave would take the fastest route. North on the A38, then a twenty-minute sprint clockwise round the M6 and the M42. But maybe that person was worried about ANPR cameras and traffic cops in high-speed pursuit vehicles. Then they'd take an indirect route. Slower, but safer.

She drove into the centre of a small village, saw a signpost and scowled. Catherine-de-Barnes. It sounded like that bloody woman's posher sister.

Sticking to the 30 mph speed limit, she had plenty of time to observe the people wandering in and out of the two shops, the church and the village hall, which was currently advertising a bingo session. She wondered how they could bear it. The dullness. The lack of excitement. Such small, confined lives they must lead.

Her plan was to head north when clear of the village, taking back roads and reaching the airport under the cops' radar.

Her phone vibrated in its cradle. The radio, tuned to BBC WM, muted.

The audio-info system, an expensive option on her sporty little car, piped up. Maya enjoyed the way the woman spoke. Clear, calm, no emotion.

'Incoming voice message from Ollie. Accept?'

'Accept,' she said, slowing for a roundabout with an exit sign-posted for the airport.

His voice was calm, devoid of emotion. Typical Ollie.

'Maya, it's me. Look, I managed to get away and I've got the cash, but I need you to come and pick me up. I'm at New Street station. Meet me by the bull. I'm frightened they're going to catch me, Maya. You have to come now.'

The message ended. The jokey banter between the radio presenters faded up again.

She slapped the steering wheel in frustration. 'Fuck, Ollie! Why do you always screw everything up?'

She ignored the airport exit and headed back into the city. This was the last time she'd rescue her brother.

Chapter 82

DC Singh had asked them to stay away from the railway station, but Annie had insisted.

After being wrongly suspected of John's murder, and having their own near-fatal encounter with the dead-eyed blackmailers, there was no way they weren't going to be in on the finish. Besides, New Street was a public place, Annie had pointed out. They had as much right to be there as anyone else.

'Anyway,' she'd added, 'we're the only ones who've seen her as she really is. You need us there.'

Reluctantly, DC Singh had agreed. And now, Annie and Michael were standing with her, leaning against the glass barrier on the upper level of the station.

Above their heads, vast bone-white blades arched towards each other, meeting at the curving glass roof, which was supported by delicate ribs. Like Pinocchio inside the whale, she thought incongruously.

While the detective spoke on her phone and radio, plain-clothes police got into position. Annie looked down at the bustling concourse beneath them. The bull they'd mentioned in the deepfake audio message was Ozzy, the mechanical mascot of the 2022 Commonwealth Games, now proudly snorting, swivelling his illuminated eyes – white, red and purple – swinging his vast head and roaring. Her nerves spiked. Maybe the gigantic steel, copper and glass bovine was too obvious? Should they have chosen somewhere more discreet? It was too late now.

Trying to ignore the fluttery feeling in her stomach, Annie looked sideways at Michael. He offered a tight smile. Like her, he was feeling the tension.

Then she spotted a woman striding across the concourse to-wards Ozzy. She had the right build, although at this angle her face was obscured by a long fringe. She was looking around her as she walked. *Checking*, Annie's subconscious supplied.

'There!' she hissed at DC Singh.

The detective nodded and raised her walkie-talkie. But before she could give the order, Annie got a better look at the woman. She was now embracing a man who'd just come from the dir-ection of the platforms.

'It's not her! Stop!'

DC Singh shook her head and lowered the walkie-talkie with a sigh of frustration.

'Damn.'

Five minutes passed. Annie kept scanning the concourse, straining to detect the female blackmailer among the swirling crowds. Nothing.

Another ten.

Twenty.

'Where is she?' she hissed at Michael.

'She'll come for him. She has to,' he replied.

The detective turned to Annie.

'You're sure this will work?'

'It has to! She thinks he's got the money. And they're brother and sister. There's some weird thing between them. I know she'll come.'

DC Singh frowned. Checked her watch. 'I'll give it another fifteen minutes, then I'm sorry, but we'll have to stop the opera-tion. This is costing a fortune.'

Desperate now, Annie peered over the balcony, willing the woman to appear. But the undercover cops had melted away and nobody was radioing in. Another ten minutes passed in a gut-clenching fog of anxiety. Two more.

DC Singh's police radio crackled. She tipped her head while eyeballing Annie.

'Go ahead.'

'Squad leader from Charlie Team spotter. Confirmed sighting of target. Female IC1 matching description supplied by witness. Red biker jacket, matching lipstick, long reddish hair. She's about to enter the concourse.'

'Stand by.'

She gave Annie a quick nod. 'This is it.'

The tension ratcheted up in Annie's belly. Her knuckles whitened on the edge of the glass sheet in front of her. She swallowed nervously. Looked around, trying to spot the woman among the swarming travellers.

She clutched Michael's arm as she scanned the concourse.

'It's almost over.'

He smiled back.

'You all right?'

'What do you think?'

Beside them, DC Singh drew in a sharp breath. Annie looked around frantically. There! It was *her*. She hadn't even bothered wearing a new disguise. She looked just like she had at the factory. Slim, glamorous, her auburn hair flowing over the back of that blood-red biker jacket, and that garish lipstick. Only an oversized pair of sunglasses marked a difference.

She strolled between the crowds, a shark carving her path among prey-fish, until she reached Ozzy, where she stood looking all around her, checking her watch.

DC Singh spoke sharply into her radio.

'Alpha, Bravo, Charlie teams, go, go, go!'

Twelve members of the milling crowd detached themselves in a synchronised move that had Annie thinking of those flashmob videos she used to enjoy watching on Facebook. No guns, thank God, but plenty of those long, thin batons they all seemed to use nowadays.

They surrounded the woman like a street gang intent on a mugging. Within seconds, she was on the ground, arms flailing, legs kicking. One boot caught a female officer in the chest, sending her sprawling backwards.

She was screaming in terror. All Annie felt was pleasure. It was over.

Around the confused, scrambling mess of arms and legs, people were already holding their phones aloft, capturing the brawl and posting to social media before it had even finished.

What were they thinking? Did they even care that the woman at the centre of the ruck was an out-and-out psychopath? A blackmailer? A child abuctor? A murderer?

Then she experienced a pang of guilt, even as more officers raced over to finally subdue the struggling woman. Wouldn't she have been doing the exact same thing just a week or so ago? Seeing the world not as it was, but through her phone screen, as 'content' to be uploaded and liked, commented on and reposted.

Below her, the woman was still screaming. 'Let me go! What the *fuck*?'

Annie frowned. It didn't sound like the blackmailer.

A male officer grabbed the woman by the hair, and Annie gasped as he ripped it off in a single piece, revealing pale beige skin. Her sunglasses had come off in the scuffle, too.

'It's not her,' Michael said in a low voice.

It wasn't. Together with DC Singh, they raced down the stairs and joined the crowd surrounding the clearly terrified middle-aged woman now shaking herself free of the restraining grip of half a dozen confused-looking undercover officers. What Annie had taken for her scalp was a flesh-coloured wig liner. DC Singh pushed through holding her police ID above her head.

'Gangway, please. Police.'

Annie followed in her wake.

The woman, white-faced, chin trembling, turned to face them.

'Sh-she made me do it,' she wailed, tears streaming down her reddened cheeks as a female officer slapped handcuffs on her behind her back.

In that instant, Annie knew exactly what she meant. And why she'd complied. Her heart went out to the sobbing woman.

Stony-faced, DC Singh asked for her name.

'Caroline. Brooke. Why?'

'Caroline Brooke, I am arresting you on suspicion of conspiracy to kidnap a child.'

As DC Singh recited the official caution to a clearly bewildered victim of blackmail, Annie could only stand and stare. Conflicting emotions roiled in her breast. Sympathy for a woman coerced into deceiving the police. If it had been her, and Isla's life was threatened? Well, she already knew what she'd do. Anything.

So, yes, sympathy. But anger, too.

They'd been played.

Chapter 83

Feeling her brother's loss like a knife wound to the heart. Maya turned the music up loud in the car.

It was a trap. She'd missed it the first time because she was concentrating on taking the airport exit off the roundabout. But when she'd played the voice message back, she'd heard it at once. *I'm frightened they're going to catch me, Maya.* That was when she'd known. Nothing ever frightened Ollie. He boasted about it. And there was no way he would have survived once Isla killed the lights. So she had driven back into Birmingham and stopped at Caroline Brooke's house with a set of instructions.

Reluctantly, she admitted to herself that she had no other option but to split from Ollie. He'd been getting harder to control – no, let's face it, impossible – for the last few days. If he hadn't been caught at the factory, there'd have been another problem. Another set of parents deciding to fight back. More killings. More police on their trail.

He would have ended up drenched in blood in the middle of Birmingham raving at the police until a sniper put him down like a rabid dog.

Poor Ollie. It wasn't his fault he'd turned out that way. That would be their junkie mum. When she had her dealer round, or one of the men he pimped her out to when she couldn't afford his prices, she'd lock them in the cellar.

Walk down or I'll throw you down, Maya. That's the deal, take it or leave it.

So she'd taken it. Comforting Ollie as best she could in the darkness. Until Mum had OD'ed. Three days they were down there, eating out-of-date ice creams from the freezer, using a corner as a toilet. The police finally let them out after a neighbour complained about the stench from next door.

Mouth twisted, she turned into the long-term parking.

'I'm sorry, Ollie,' she muttered, rubbing at her tattoo. 'I can't help you any more.'

Chapter 84

DC Singh missed the screeching.

In the old days, when they'd still used cassette tapes to record interviews, that teeth-grating, nails-down-a-blackboard, seven-second whine unsettled the suspects.

But as she looked across the table at Oliver Kinton, she couldn't imagine anything short of a nuclear explosion unsettling him. It was like staring down a well. There was nothing behind those surprisingly pretty eyes. Just a void. She pitied his solicitor, a sixtyish man in a well-cut but tired-looking pinstripe suit.

Whatever was going on behind that blank stare, they had enough evidence to bang him up for the rest of his natural. Much of it in the two-inch-thick folder in front of her containing details of his crimes stretching back ten years.

This was more about cost-saving than establishing guilt. DC Singh cleared her throat.

'Interview of suspect Oliver Kinton.'

Date and time confirmed, and other participants introduced, she recited the official caution. Normally she did this with a little smile, as if reassuring the suspect that they weren't in any trouble, not really. Probably all some misunderstanding. Best to just be straight with her and get it all off their chest. And the tragic thing was, half of the toerags they got in here believed it.

Normally.

She stared at him.

'Oliver Kinton, you have been arrested for the murder of John Varney, the abduction and attempted murder of Isla Barnes, and the attempted murders of Annie Barnes, Michael Taylor and Aaron Taylor.' Quite the little charge sheet, she wanted to say, but didn't. 'You do not have to say anything but it may harm your defence if you do not mention when questioned something which you later rely on in court. Anything you do say may be given in evidence. Do you understand?'

He nodded, staring at her. That look. She felt sweat break out inside her shirt.

'Could you say it out loud, please. For the recorder.'

He stared at her. Smiled, slyly. Nodded again.

Fine. She wasn't going to play his game.

'For the DIR, and in the presence of his solicitor, Mr Kinton indicated with a nod that he understood the official caution. So, Oliver, why did you kill John Varney?'

'No comment.'

He'd listened to his lawyer. Normally a pretty smart move, but when you were as mired in evidence of your guilt as Kinton was, stonewalling was a limited-value strategy. She thought she'd remind him of that.

'This isn't the telly, Oliver. You don't just say "no comment" a few times and then me and my colleague get frustrated and suspend the interview. We've got you for another twenty hours under PACE – that's the—'

'I know what it is, bitch. I'm not an idiot.'

Frowning, the solicitor leaned sideways and whispered to his client behind his hand.

DC Singh faked a look of shock. Eyes wide, rearing back on the chair. Inside, she was rejoicing. Well, that hadn't taken long, had it? Time for another little push.

She cleared her throat, a little extra bit of play-acting. Suddenly she felt in total control.

'PACE is the Police and Criminal Evidence Act, Oliver. Actually,' she cocked her head, readying another button-press, 'Oliver sounds a bit formal. Why don't I call you Ollie? That's what your sister calls you, isn't it?'

He glared at her. She smiled back, blandly. Waiting.

'I don't want you to talk about Maya,' he grated finally, his fists clenching tighter.

She was glad of the handcuffs locking him to the table.

'No? Why's that, Ollie? I'm assuming she's the brains of your little outfit. What were you, the muscle? The honeytrap? That about it?'

'DC Singh,' the solicitor interjected in a weary voice, 'perhaps you could restrict yourself to relevant questions, rather than insinuations about my client's alleged role in this so-called "outfit".'

She smiled at him. It was all a game, albeit a deadly one. They both knew their parts.

'Well, technically I *was* asking young Ollie here questions. But sure, let's return to your illustrious criminal career, shall we, Ollie? Why did you pose as an eighteen-year-old boy named Josh and then kidnap Isla Barnes?'

He rubbed the tattoo visible on his upper arm. A circlet of rope with a half-knot.

'No comment.'

'Why did you tell her you were going to torture and murder her?'

'No comment.'

'How would you react, Ollie, if I told you we recovered DNA from the scene of John Varney's murder that is a one hundred per cent match for yours?'

His upper lip curled. 'No. Comment.'

'He was a war veteran. A hero. He was highly decorated. While you and your big sister were scamming old ladies out of their life savings, torturing pets, blackmailing and extorting, he was fighting for his country in Afghanistan. Are you proud of murdering him?'

Ollie banged his shackled wrists down onto the table so that the chains clinked and rattled through the eyebolt.

'Varney was a drug addict and an alcoholic! His wife threw him out. And guess what? He ran over the Taylor kid for money. Not much of a hero then, was he?'

'Who gave him the money? You?'

His eyes resumed their hooded look. He kept rubbing the tattoo.

'No comment.'

DC Singh sighed.

'You're facing life inside, Ollie. You do know that, don't you? There's not a jury in the land that won't convict you twelve to nothing. And with the gravity of your crimes, there's no judge who won't impose a whole-life tariff. You're twenty-six. Do you really want to die in prison?'

'You just told me I'm going to. What I want doesn't seem to matter, does it?'

His fingers were still kneading at the tattoo, but now it looked to her almost tender. A caress. She herself had a couple of pieces. Out of sight, on her back and her left hip. Hers had significance. Most people could give you at least a partial explanation for why they chose their ink. So what did Ollie's signify? A rope. A half-knot. Where was the other half?

She saw it suddenly. A flash of that welcome insight that hard-working coppers who kept their noses clean were occasionally permitted by the universe to access. She decided to save it for the time being.

'If you co-operate with our investigation, your solicitor could offer that in mitigation. I'm interested in how many other families you and your sister have been extorting. How many people you've been blackmailing through your Private Liaisons scam. Help us out with that and it will go well with the judge. I'm sure Mr O'Connell would agree?'

She raised her eyebrows at the solicitor.

'She's right, Oliver,' he murmured.

Ollie nodded. 'So what you're saying is, I give you chapter and verse on these supposed scams we've been running and I get, what, forty years instead of life?'

'Obviously I can't predict what a judge would decide. But it's in your best interests.'

'I see.' He looked down at the tattoo again, rubbed it. Back up at her. 'I don't know anything about other scams.'

'Really? Maybe it was all Maya, then? Do you know where she is, Ollie? Because from what we've been able to establish, she's done a runner. She's left you in the lurch, and quite honestly, it doesn't look like she cares about her little brother any more.'

'Yes she does!' he roared, lunging across the table until his handcuffs jerked him back like a guard dog reaching the end of its chain. Tendons stood out on his neck.

DC Singh stayed where she was. She'd been expecting a move like this from the moment she'd taken her seat in the interview room. It was the reason she'd asked for the one with an eyebolt in the table.

The uniformed officer standing silently in the corner rushed forward, baton drawn, and in a baritone voice she'd heard gracing the police choir commanded Ollie back into his chair.

Once calm was restored, DC Singh offered a look of sympathy. To conjure it, she had to imagine he was a bereaved parent rather than a wild-eyed, violent, sadistic psychopath who'd almost tortured a young girl to death. It was hard. But not impossible.

'I don't think she does care, Ollie. Not about you, at any rate. I think Maya's in the wind. I mean, we'll catch her eventually. But here's the thing.' She leaned towards him, so close she caught a sour whiff of his sweat. 'We both agree she's the clever one out of the two of you. I wouldn't be at all surprised if she decides to do a plea bargain. She sticks you right in the frame and pleads to a lesser crime. Then what? She'll be out in ten, maybe less. She'll only be thirty-eight. That's still young enough to rebuild her life. Get married, start a family. And all the while, you're rotting away inside. How would that make you feel?'

'She would never do that. Never. And I'll never betray her, either.'

She pointed at his tattoo.

'Is that what the tat's all about? Has Maya got a matching one? The other half of the knot. Wait!' She flashed her eyes and smiled. 'Don't tell me they line up to complete the knot? Oh my God, that is so sweet!' She turned to her partner and frowned. 'Actually, maybe it's a bit too sweet, don't you think? I mean,' she looked back at Ollie, 'I know you two are related, but you're not in a *relationship*, are you?'

It was her last attempt to get him so off-balance he'd start talking properly. They'd consulted a forensic psychologist before the interview and she'd talked about how psychopaths could 'decompensate' under pressure. It was just a fancy word for coming apart at the seams, but DC Singh liked it all the same.

Ollie looked at her. He was calm again. Cheeks pink. Facial muscles relaxed. Chest rising and falling gently as he inhaled, exhaled, inhaled, exhaled, as if he were watching a nature documentary and not being accused of having an incestuous relationship with his sister.

'She'll come for me. She always does. And *when* she does, and I'm free, I am going to find you, DC Singh. I am going to find you and I am going to spend some quality time with you and your family. I promise.'

She maintained eye contact. Didn't even blink. But deep inside her, where normal human beings' survival instincts dwelled, the ancient fear of predators flickered into life.

She really, *really* hoped the jury would convict.

Chapter 85

After the excitement and then frustration at New Street, Annie had returned with Michael to his place.

They were watching their kids through the kitchen window. Isla and Aaron were sitting on a wooden bench in the garden, heads bent towards each other, laughing, and for the first time in a long while, Annie could see some of the old Isla beginning to resurface.

Aaron had assumed the role of big brother, which Isla had accepted happily. He'd introduced her to gaming, and she'd taken to it like a natural, despite her broken finger. Annie felt it was a good halfway house between going cold turkey on screens and staying immersed in the toxic world of social media. Although Isla had shown zero inclination to revisit Instagram or even Snapchat, despite having lived her life inside their confines for years.

Annie voiced a question that had been revolving in her brain since the debacle at New Street.

'Do you think she'll come looking for us?'

Michael shook his head.

'How? She's on the run. And Ollie's in custody. If she shows her face in the UK, she'll get picked up on CCTV or spotted in the street.'

She nodded. She'd come to the same conclusion herself. She just wanted to hear Michael say it.

'I got the feeling she was all about minimising risk. The disguises, the grooming, the fact that she hid behind screens and deepfakes.'

'We need to let her go, Annie,' he said softly. 'She took our money, but she didn't take our children.'

Annie's phone rang.

'Hello?'

'Annie, it's Mel Singh. I've got some good news and some bad news. The good news is we've located Ollie and Maya Kinton's flat. Our digital forensics team are working through their systems. They're confident we can identify all the families and individuals they've been targeting. It means we can tell them they're no longer in danger.'

Annie's mood lifted at that. 'And the bad?'

'Ollie refuses to tell us anything about where Maya might be. If they did have an escape plan, either she didn't share it with him or he's going to take the secret to prison with him. I just wondered whether either of them said anything at all to you while you were at that dreadful place. Anything that might have been a clue as to where they intended to go.'

Annie closed her eyes. Shuddered violently as the image of that plastic-swathed kill room flashed into vivid three-dimensional reality.

'I'm sorry, nothing. It was just so . . .' she stumbled over her words, felt her throat thickening, 'horrible. I thought we were all going to die in there.'

'It's fine. I'm sorry for making you relive it.'

'So you really have no idea where she is? Don't you have, you know, alerts you put out to airports and ferries and so on?'

'We do. We've circulated the photo you gave us to every other police force in the UK, all ports, airports and railway stations. Plus the British Transport Police. I've contacted Europol and Interpol as well. She won't get far.'

Chapter 86

Maya dropped the keys down a drain. No point making things easy for them.

Cars she could take or leave, but she'd been mourning the loss of her red biker jacket since giving it to her last-minute stand-in.

Inside the terminal, she removed her baseball cap and ran a hand over her new buzz cut. White-blonde. Nine mils on top fading to seven at the sides and back. She grimaced. If her plan didn't work out, she could always apply to the US Marines.

She passed between two black-garbed airport police to reach the back of the security queue. Matching shaved heads that made her new do look like hippie indulgence. Square jaws, biceps pumped by free weights. *Get a little helping hand from a few 'roids, do you, boys?* Machine guns. Pistols. And apparently as alert as a bear in midwinter. She flashed her green eyes at one of them. He smiled self-consciously before resuming his stony gaze.

She put her cap, bag, belt, boots, watch, phone, tablet and laptop into a grey plastic tray and pushed it along the rollers to bump up against the previous passenger's stuff.

The woman in front of her turned and smiled.

'I always get so nervous. Like, what if the alarms go off and I left a pair of scissors in my handbag?'

Maya smiled back.

'I suppose they'd arrest you as a terrorist, subject you to a full cavity search and then stick you in a cell.'

The woman frowned and turned away.

Then it was Maya's turn.

She stepped into the X-ray machine. Followed the diagram for how to stand, how to hold her arms. Lights flashed red. A buzzer sounded. Well, that was odd.

Breathing easily, she wondered what had triggered the alert. It didn't really matter. She stepped towards a female security guard who was motioning her to one side with a hand-held wand.

At the back of the security hall, more armed cops hovered, cradling their machine guns like babies. One looked her way. She smiled. He looked away.

As she waved the wand over Maya's outstretched arms, down over her torso and legs and back up again, the security woman frowned. Maya knew why. The split lip. The bruises to her face. To her arms.

Can you believe a fifteen-year-old private-school girl did that? she wanted to ask. Didn't. Obviously.

'How d'you get the shiner?' the guard murmured, her forehead furrowed with what Maya assumed was sympathy.

She gulped. Winced. Doing 'anxiety'.

'Boyfriend. I'm leaving him.'

The woman nodded. Offered her a small smile. Like they were best mates all of a bloody sudden.

'Good for you, love. You're all clear. Off you go.'

She waited while her tray trundled down the sloped rollers and collected her possessions. Ahead of her, bars, shops and, best of all, the departure gates.

She was walking away from the bench where she'd rested her tray when a man called out behind her. Loud. Assertive.

'Excuse me! Miss? Wait!'

Pulse quiet, she turned. Placed a hand on her chest. Widened her eyes. Raised her eyebrows, doing 'puzzlement'.

'Me?'

It was a male security guard. Tall. Strong-looking. He was hurrying towards her, frowning. Holding something up. Something black.

Her baseball cap.

'You dropped this.'

She accepted it from his outstretched hand and settled it over her shorn scalp.

'Thank you.'

She rolled her eyes and smiled, doing 'self-mockery'. Then headed for departures.

When her row was called, she sauntered up to the desk and handed her passport over. The lady at the desk glanced at it, then at her bashed-up face. Clearly reached the same conclusion as the security woman. She smiled sympathetically and handed the passport back.

'Have a good flight, Miss Reed.'

Chapter 87

Had it really only been a week since Maya's horrific deepfake had arrived in her inbox? Leaning against Isla on the big squashy sofa facing the TV, Annie sipped her gin and tonic. She couldn't fully take it in: the nightmare was over.

Onscreen, the six attractive young New Yorkers bickered. The pair of them had been binge-watching *Friends*. Isla's idea. It was easy, upbeat, silly, and the worst any trigger-warning writer could come up with would be mild sex references, mild language and frequent references to drinking and smoking. On the whole, Annie felt she could cope. They *both* could cope.

Isla laughed at the onscreen antics, but Annie's mind kept drifting back to the events of the last seven days. And the fact that Maya had escaped justice.

Unlike DC Singh, Annie had no confidence they'd catch the woman. She'd be reinventing herself yet again. New name, new identity, new city, new job. Maybe even new country. She swallowed more gin. New victims. She'd slipped through their fingers.

But at least Annie had Isla back. And more of her than she'd had before. During the many hours they'd sat talking about how it had all happened, and Grant's hands-off approach to parenting, Isla had come to see her father for what he was. In a word, unreliable. OK, in more than one word: unreliable, selfish and, in Isla's memorable phrase, 'a total loser, perving over girls on Tinder who are way too young, even for someone who isn't old like Dad'.

Annie held her arm up and Isla snuggled under it, cuddling into her ribs.

'Mum?'

'Yes, Ly-lah?' she said, using three-year-old Isla's version of her own name before she could say it properly.

'What I said before. You know, about you chucking Dad out.'

'Oh lovey, don't worry about that. You were upset.'

'No, Mum, let me finish.' Annie looked down. Isla was rubbing her broken finger. 'The thing is, I know Melissa wasn't his, you know, the first one. Affair, I mean. I knew about the one from school. Becca Hill's mum. I'm so, so sorry I didn't say anything, but Dad told me not to tell you.'

Annie felt a blush creep over her cheeks. And also anger at Grant that he'd forced his teenage daughter to be an accomplice to his infidelities. No sense in revisiting it now, though. She had Isla back, and not just physically. Since that terrifying night in the factory, things had taken a turn for the better between them.

'Well, that's all in the past, where it belongs, yes? We don't need to talk about it.'

'OK, only, I mean, I hated him for it, but I was frightened he'd leave me as well, you know?'

'Of course I do, lovey. I may be a sad old lady, but I'm still your mum.'

Isla twisted round and looked up into Annie's face.

'You're *not* sad!'

'Well, that's a relief.' A beat. 'So you're saying I *am* old?'

Isla's eyes widened. 'No!'

Annie laughed. 'Ha! Got you!'

Isla snuggled in close again. Said nothing for a few minutes.

'You know how Dad kind of dropped the ball, letting me stay out late with Josh? I mean Ollie? And, like, the other stuff? Hitting Michael and everything?'

Annie's pulse picked up. Was Isla going to say she still wanted to stay with him? It was the legal arrangement, after all.

'Yes,' she said, cautiously.

'Well, the thing is, he gave me two tickets for Glasto. Obviously I'm not going with Josh, but I would still love to go, so ...'

'You want to know if I'll let you go with Naomi?'

'Actually, I was wondering if *you'd* come with me.'

Sudden tears pricked Annie's eyes. Isla was looking up at her, waiting. Hopeful.

She cleared her throat.

'Are you sure, Isla? I mean, I'd love it. But, you know, I'd probably want to be in the tent by midnight.'

Isla pulled a face, all goggly eyes and slack jaw.

'Midnight? Oh no! You're staying up with me until at least three.'

Annie laughed and poked her in the ribs, making her giggle.

'Fine. Yes please.'

Isla squealed with delight and squeezed her tightly round the middle.

'Thanks, Mum. I love you! Oh God, it'll be lush!'

She straightened and unwrapped Annie's arm. Started messaging Naomi.

Annie turned her gaze back to the screen, but she wasn't seeing the TV show. She was seeing her life. How it would be from now on. They'd have fun at Glastonbury. But then what? She was divorced and over forty. Unlike Grant, she couldn't imagine herself swiping in any direction, left, right or otherwise. Her career was stalled until she could straighten things out with Dan Gao.

And worst of all, Isla was growing up, and away from her.

It wouldn't be 'Josh'. But it would be someone else. Another boy. Or a girl.

She'd do her A levels and then she'd be off to uni. And Annie would be alone in the house that had once seemed the perfect size for her family but would now be far too big for her. Like walking around in her own mother's coats as a little girl playing dress-up.

What did she have to look forward to? Endless schmoozing of rich foreign donors, massaging their already swollen egos as they tried to charity-wash their reputations for human rights abuses or corporate misconduct? Lonely takeout suppers or ready meals? Drinking too much wine in her immaculate but empty home?

The doorbell rang.

Isla jumped up. 'Pizza!'

'But I didn't order any,' Annie protested.

'I did. Back in a min.'

Isla reappeared a few seconds later.

'Pizza guy wants a tip.'

Then she slipped out, and Annie heard her scampering tread as she raced up the stairs and into her room.

Annie got to her feet, looking for her purse. Wondering if she even had any cash. She used her phone for everything these days. It was on the side table at the other end of the sofa. She bent to retrieve it.

'Hey, Annie.'

His voice startled her and she whirled round.

He was smiling. After the surprise subsided, she smiled, too.

'Michael? What are you doing here?'

Epilogue

Chapter 88

The soft yellow curtains bellied inwards in the breeze, bringing with them the fragrant scent of ripe mangoes and bananas, frying prawns in garlic, ginger and chilli, and the calls in Khmer of the street vendors and tuk-tuk drivers touting for business.

She stood in front of the bathroom mirror, wiping the last of the bruises away with the cleanser she'd bought at the airport. There wasn't much she could do about the split lip. That was real enough. She'd done it herself. A good sharp smack with a clenched fist. But a quick touch of lipstick and she felt ready to face the world. Or Siem Reap, at least.

Cambodia had no extradition treaty with the UK. And she'd wanted to visit Angkor Wat ever since one of her targets had posted about it on Instagram.

Her hair was long, strawberry blonde with dark tints. Pulled up and pinned into a French pleat to keep her neck cool.

She chose an outfit. A lemon-yellow broderie anglaise sundress with spaghetti straps and a pair of wedge-heeled royal-blue espa-drilles. Added a pair of oversized sunnies with Jackie O frames and a wide-brimmed straw *chapeau* with a lemon-yellow ribbon as a band. Perfect for her new identity. She added a dab of Chanel No. 5 on her neck and wrists. Another duty-free purchase.

Peta Higgins was an actress. Nothing huge on her CV. Not yet. A few movies, mostly independent. Some TV work. Couple of ads. A lot of theatre. She was here researching a new part. An Englishwoman who befriended a survivor of Pol Pot's genocide.

At the door, she glanced around the room. In the corner, spilling from her suitcase, more wigs, sunglasses, false teeth and plain-lensed specs. At the bottom of the bathroom bin, a pair of folded-over green contact lenses nestled among the make-up-stained cleansing wipes and cotton buds.

Outside, and into the humidity of the day. The heat and the soupy air agreed with her. She twirled on the spot, earning a giggle from an old man sporting few teeth in a broadly grinning mouth.

'Pos'card, ma'am?' he asked cheerily in English. 'Three for one dollar only.'

She smiled. Took three. Handed him a ten.

He looked at her, shaking his head. 'No change.'

'I don't need it. Keep it all.'

Leaving him with a bemused smile, she strolled across the street, negotiating her way between bicycles, tuk-tuks, cars, trucks and mopeds laden with complete families, including pets. She held the edge of the brim of her hat when a gust of warm, fried-chicken-scented wind threatened to snatch it from her head.

Reaching the relative safety of the far side, she entered the dim interior of a bar. French cane fans revolved slowly overhead, moving the muggy air around rather than displacing it.

A few punters sat at tables. Older Westerners in gaudy Hawaiian shirts, billowing dresses or enormous pastel shorts. Younger ones in slinky bodycon dresses, T-shirts and yoga pants. The baggy kind with elephant motifs that Maya, in her endless hours following her prey on Instagram, had grown to hate.

She took a stool at the bar, a long plank of thickly varnished reddish wood – mahogany, maybe – and ordered a beer.

'What kind, miss? We have Heineken, Cambodia and Angkor.'

'Cambodia. Please.'

She took a sip of the ice-cold beer. Absent-mindedly rubbing her tattoo, she loaded a webpage on her phone. There was a studio nearby on Night Market Street. Absorbed in the details of the process she wanted, she flinched momentarily as someone grunted and heaved themselves onto the stool right next to her.

She turned her head to see who it was who thought that out of all the seats in the entire bar, they were entitled to that one.

A man. Forty-something. Fat. Perspiring heavily.

'Mind if I join you?' he asked, shifting his bulk on the stool's insufficient seat.

'Looks like you already have,' she said, adopting, on a whim, a posh drama-school accent. One of those actresses always whining on about how having a title wasn't all it was cracked up to be.

He laughed, fetching a handkerchief from the pocket of his shorts and dabbing his forehead.

'Name's Myron Farrington the Third, but that's a real mouthful, so you better just call me Ron. And you are?'

She held out a hand.

'Peta Higgins. Enchanted.'

As they shook, she glanced at his left wrist.

'Nice watch. Patek Philippe?'

He turned the stainless-steel timepiece so it glittered in the light.

'Nautilus Jumbo. Cost me a hundred and twenty grand. I collect.'

She leaned towards him. Just a little. 'How exciting.'

The barman came over, polishing a glass.

'What can I get you, sir?'

Myron looked at the beer resting between Maya's fingers.

'I'll have what the lady's having.'

He glanced at the webpage displayed on Maya's phone: *TATTOO REMOVAL*. Then at the rope and half-knot on her arm. He touched a discoloured, hairless patch of skin on his left bicep.

'I had one removed myself.'

'Your regiment?'

He shook his head. 'My ex-wife. It's gonna hurt plenty, you know.'

She stared at him coldly.

'Good. I want it to.'

Chapter 89

He could smell body odour. A sour reek of vomit that disinfectant hadn't touched. And piss.

But that wasn't what was bothering him. It was the cell itself. It was too small. Much too small. And what was coming was bad. Really bad.

He'd tried to distract himself, but there was nothing. He couldn't even count the tiles like in films. These walls were smooth, like skin. Covered in some weird plasticky paint that you couldn't scrape with your nails or even bite.

No window, either. Not even a slit. Just neon tubes behind thick white plastic. Why not just pad the whole place and have done with it?

He punched his forehead, hard. Why had she done it? He didn't understand.

Maya was supposed to look after him. She was always there to rescue him when things went a bit bad. Like in Bristol. Like with that dog that time. The one he'd had to bury after she told him he couldn't leave it in the family's back garden, all ... displayed and whatever.

So where was she, then? Where was Maya? It had been fun screwing around with that detective. Singh. Ollie could imagine quite a lot of things he could do to her that would wipe that superior smile off her face.

He leaned back against the wall. Stretched his legs out in front of him on the floor. He didn't like the bed. It was too narrow. And the blue plastic mattress was a joke. It smelled funny. Like static electricity.

Slowly he let his head fall back until he could feel his Adam's apple pushing out at the soft skin of his throat.

He drew in a breath, blew it out, kept blowing until his lungs were empty and screaming for oxygen. Counted to thirty, almost blacking out, hearing Mum's voice, or was it Maya's?

Don't do that, Ollie, you're frightening me.

He inhaled again. Heard the voice...

All the way. All the way, Ollie, until you can't hold any more. Just like a big birthday balloon.

...and started shouting, tearing at his tattoo with his nails, which, having been bitten down to the bloody quick, did nothing more than redden his skin.

Outside, behind the intake desk in the custody suite, a thirty-five-year-old sergeant rolled her eyes at her latest recruit, who was staring, wide-eyed, at the panelled CCTV feed on her monitor.

'That's just the overture,' she said wearily. 'The opera's about to start for real.'

She checked the time on the large white-faced clock on the wall opposite. As the red sweep second hand passed 12, she hit the switch that turned off the lights in all the cells.

For a few seconds, the silence was total.

Then the custody suite echoed to the shrill, animalistic screeching of the prisoner in cell nine.

'Maya! Mayaaa! Mayaaa! Mayaaa!!! MAYAAA!'

Chapter 90

High-end cars and SUVs clogged the roads in and around Perranporth like blood corpuscles struggling through narrowed arteries. Among the Teslas, Mercedes and Porsches, a gleaming new four-seater pickup sat on tall, rugged tyres.

The Cornish sun was high in the sky, baking the top layer of the golden sand to a fine white dust. Wraiths of the stuff snaked their way across the beach, which was flat and smooth enough for cricket, several games of which were in noisy but good-natured progress.

Watched by their relaxed, expensively underdressed parents, younger children decked out in brightly coloured beachwear dashed about like puppies let off the lead for the first time. Older kids, in wetsuits, board shorts or bikinis, stood in loose, laughing groups, or lounged on towels, easy in their skins and brimming with self-confidence.

A family had recently arrived. Two adults, two teenage kids. The kids hopped from foot to foot, laughing, as they shed their outer clothing to reveal swimwear already donned. An observer close enough to notice such things would have seen a scar across the bridge of the boy's nose. And a bump at the base of the girl's right index finger.

Off to one side, the woman leaned back on her elbows, offering not entirely serious words of encouragement as the man laboured over a foot pump. An inflatable paddleboard slowly unrolled, transforming from a squashy mint-green and white sausage into a seagoing vessel. He detached it from the air hose and began on a second.

Once both boards were taut and stiff, the boy – young man,

really – handed one to the girl and took one for himself. He said something to her that set her off into peals of laughter. Carrying the boards and long paddles under their arms, they strolled companionably away from the adults towards the glittering water, heads turned towards each other as they chatted.

Annie watched them go, a small, happy smile on her face. She marvelled once again at how close she'd come to losing everything seven months earlier.

Isla and Aaron were closer, through their shared trauma, than many biological siblings. She knew that whatever happened in life, they would be there for each other. And it wasn't just them who'd escaped, either. Mel Singh had called her a few days before the holiday. An update. They'd traced the final family Maya and Ollie had been extorting. Everybody now knew that they were safe again.

To her right, Michael dropped the pump onto the sand and sat beside her, panting slightly.

'You all right?' he asked. 'You looked like you were miles away.'

She nodded. 'I was just thinking about all the other families. It's not just us who are free of Maya and Ollie. They are, too. We're all free to live our lives.'

He nodded, smiled and drew her close. She inhaled. Sun lotion and the clean smell of his sweat.

'Come here.'

Their lips met. And as she kissed him, Annie let herself dream of the future.

Acknowledgements

Andy Maslen

First of all, I want to thank my co-author, Matt Arlidge. As well as being a lovely guy and very funny, even as we were thrashing out the details of Maya and Ollie's heinous crimes, he is a seriously talented writer and a plotting demon. I wish I'd met him years ago.

This fantastic project wouldn't have got anywhere without our glorious editor, Leodora Darlington. Leodora pulls off a trick I've rarely come across in publishing. She's a superb editor with a gift for both bold strokes of character and plot and small details that can make or break a scene or sentence. But she also has a solid gold instinct for what will be popular with readers. I hope you agree.

The whole team at Orion Fiction have been fantastic to work with, especially Sam Eades, its head. Thank you all. Also thanks to my fellow writers on this brilliant five-book co-creation adventure: Steph Broadribb, Julia Crouch, Lisa Hall and Alex Khan.

I don't have an agent, but I would like to thank three people who helped me onto the first rung of the publishing ladder: Darren Hardy, Laura Deacon and Jane Snelgrove.

Writing books can be a lonely occupation, which is why, I suspect, authors love to get together at literary festivals, publishing receptions and book launches to gossip and share tales of triumphs and occasional tribulations. Among the many friends I have made there and elsewhere, I'd like to send a wave and a 'hi' to Alessandra Torre, Audrey Harrison, Hannah Lynn, Kerry Harper, Martin Willis, Mark Edwards, Alex Stone, John Marrs, Caroline

Mitchell, Imogen Clark, Teresa Driscoll, Barbara Copperthwaite, Heleen Kist, Dave Sivers, Holly Craig, Anne Corlett, Tracy Buchanan, Clare Swatman and Ruth Heald. I know I'll have missed people out. To you, I'm sorry. Drink may have been taken.

I'd also like to thank the members of my Facebook group, the Wolfe Pack, who have always been there to support me and offer words of encouragement.

Lastly, I owe a deep debt of gratitude and love to my family. Thank you.

Credits

M.J. Arlidge, Andy Maslen and Orion Fiction would like to thank everyone at Orion who worked on the publication of *Your Child Next* in the UK.

Editorial
Leodora Darlington

Copy editor
Jane Selley

Proof reader
Alex Davis

Audio
Paul Stark
Louise Richardson

Contracts
Dan Herron
Ellie Bowker
Oliver Chacón

Design
Tomás Almeida
Nick Shah
Deborah Francois
Helen Ewing

Editorial Management
Anshuman Yadav
Charlie Panayiotou
Jane Hughes
Bartley Shaw
Lucy Bilton

Finance
Jasdip Nandra
Nick Gibson
Sue Baker
Tom Costello

Marketing
Helena Fouracre
Lindsay Terrell

Production
Ruth Sharvell
Fiona McIntosh

Publicity
Ellen Turner

Operations
Group Sales Operations team

Rights
Rebecca Folland
Tara Hiatt
Ben Fowler
Alice Cottrell
Ruth Blakemore
Marie Henckel

Sales
Catherine Worsley
Dave Murphy
Esther Waters
Victoria Laws
Group Sales teams across
Digital, Field, International
and Non-Trade